The Heart Warrior's Mother

Inspired by a true story

MARILYN COHEN
DE VILLIERS

For the little heart warrior who inspired this novel
and her devoted and loving parents

The Heart Warrior's Mother is based on the true story of a South African heart warrior, a child born with a serious congenital heart defect (CHD). Her identity and that of her family have been changed to protect their privacy. While the medical aspects of the child's story are presented as factually as possible, the storyline is a product of the author's imagination. All characters are fictitious and any resemblance to actual persons, living or dead, is purely coincidental.

Marilyn Cohen de Villiers is a mother of two daughters and grandmother of two pigeon pairs. She lives in Johannesburg, South Africa, where she earns her daily crust as a freelance wordsmith.

Other books by the author:

Silverman Saga

A Beautiful Family
When Time Fails
Deceive and Defend

ISBN (print) 978-0-620-99713-3

ISBN (e-book) 978-0-620-99714-0

Published by: Mapolaje Publishers

Cover design: Francois Engelbrecht

Typesetting: Clare-Rose Julius

Set in 11 point on 15 point Lora

Website: www.marilyncohendevilliers.com

Thanks

This novel would not have been possible with the bravery and support of our heart warrior's incredible mother and father – an amazing couple who dealt with the challenges life threw at them with courage, dignity, love and generosity. They welcomed me into their home and shared their story in the hope of raising awareness of congenital birth defects, particularly congenital heart defects.

My admiration also knows no bounds for all those involved in treating and caring for children with these surprisingly common conditions. You are all warriors.

On a personal note, I am so grateful for all those who acted as my sounding boards, made suggestions, provided technical advice, and gave so freely of their time and energy to help me bring this book to fruition. In particular, thanks to James Mitchell, Sue Purbrick, Elaine Ziman and Francois Engelbrecht who has once again outdone himself in designing a brilliant cover for **The Heart Warrior's Mother**.

Chapter 1

"Have you held your baby yet?"

Kerry-Anne Aarons looked at the nurse and blinked back tears.

"No," she whispered. "They wouldn't let me. They told me I couldn't. They wouldn't even let me touch her unless I wore a big yellow gown, and gloves and a mask. They said I couldn't carry her. They said it was too dangerous."

The nurse, who had introduced herself as Sister Janie, the cardiothoracic ICU Team Leader, looked at Kerry sympathetically through her black-framed glasses, and her pale skin flushed angrily. She shook her blonde head and handed Kerry and Imran blue hospital gowns and masks.

"Sit there," she said, indicating a chair next to the incubator. She placed a white towel on Kerry's lap, then lifted the naked, sleeping baby out of the incubator and placed her in her mother's arms.

"Your baby has a big day tomorrow. She needs you to hold her. You need to hold her." She smiled and walked away.

Kerry wanted to laugh, and cry. She bent over her baby and examined her beautiful, peaceful face; she touched her thick thatch of black hair; she beamed as the tiny fingers curled around her index finger; she tried to ignore the bluish tinge of the baby's lips, the oxygen tube in her little button nose. For the first time since Lily's birth at the Parklane Clinic nine days before, Kerry held her baby in her arms.

⟊ ⟊

There had never been any reason to suspect that there was anything wrong. The pregnancy had come as a surprise to both Kerry and Imran. After all, little Leo had just started walking. They hadn't planned on starting a family so soon. They hadn't planned on starting a family at all. When Leo had announced his impending arrival when she'd finally gone to the doctor to get something for the bout of gastro that just wouldn't go away, her mother, Gillian, had snapped at her: "For heaven's sake Kerry – don't you know anything about birth control?"

She'd wept. She was too young. Imran was too young. She'd thought about termination but the idea of aborting – killing – a living being made her shudder. Despite all her mother's protests that she was being ridiculous and was damaging her health, Kerry had not touched a morsel of meat, or fish, or chicken for the past 10 years. Not since that day when, just 14 years old, she'd changed the TV channel and found herself watching a hell she'd never imagined. Frantically mooing cows being whipped and prodded and poked as they were herded into a murder factory in America or somewhere to be turned into steak and hamburger patties and sausages. As the titles rolled at the end of the documentary, she'd vomited into the toilet, and then cried into Triphina's ample bosom as she'd always done when she was miserable. She'd still been green and queasy when her mother returned from her bridge fundraiser just before her father, Stephen, got home from work.

"You look terrible," her mother had said. "You'd better not go to school tomorrow. I have a meeting in the morning but if you're not better when I get home, I'll have to take you to the doctor."

Telling Imran that she was pregnant with Leo was one of the hardest things she'd ever had to do. She had been even more nervous than when she'd told her parents she was moving in with him. So she'd assumed her usual air of false bravado as she'd assured him that she'd understand perfectly if he wanted nothing to do with it. She was going to keep the baby, she'd said. She'd find a way to manage, she'd said. Even if – she'd shuddered – she had to move back in with her parents for a while until she sorted out her life. She wouldn't be the first single mother, and nor would she be the last, she'd said.

"You have so many plans. I can't let this hold you back," she'd said, proud of how steady her voice had been, how reasonable she'd sounded.

Her rising nausea had nothing to do with morning sickness as Imran had stared at her for hours in the seconds it took him to reach for her hands.

"We're in this together," he'd said, "This isn't your problem. This isn't a problem at all. This is a baby. Our baby. Oh my god, we're having a baby!"

Leo had arrived safely at the Parklane Clinic after an uneventful pregnancy and a traumatic eight months. Apart from a scare about a lung infection shortly after his birth which kept him in the neonatal ICU for a few days, their precious son had thrived. He was a good, easy-going baby and Kerry was surprised at just how much she was enjoying being a mother. It had nearly killed her that dreadful morning when she'd had to return to work. Leo was just two months old. She'd had to take him to her parents' house and leave him in Triphina's arms. Triphina was more than happy to take care of Kerry's son, just as she had Kerry and her brothers so many years before. That hadn't got any easier, but Kerry learned to cope with the guilt, reassuring herself that at least he was safe and Triphina was kind and caring. His beaming smile when she walked in the front door every evening to pick him up on her way home from work more than made up for her constant tiredness. It wasn't ideal but Leo didn't seem to mind. Anyway, what choice had she really had?

"You could stay home and be a proper mother, at least until the child is ready for nursery school," Gillian had sniffed.

"Like you Mom?" she'd almost spat back.

Kerry knew her mother, who'd resigned from her job as a se-cretary to be a 'proper wife' the day after her wedding almost thirty years before, had no idea how much her job at Browns meant to her. The ink on her graduation certificate had barely dried when she applied for it, more out of hope than expectation that she'd be selected from the hundreds of more experienced candidates who were also after an opportunity to work for a company widely hailed as the top unlisted company in its sector. She was even more grateful for the opportunity when she discovered that most of her graduating class had battled for months to find a job, any job, let alone one offering her the chance to expand her horizons, grow her skills, possibly become a business leader someday. Many of her peers – particularly her white friends – had been forced to accept dead-end, often temporary positions like tutoring or au pairing privileged kids in the suburbs or temping for companies while employees were on maternity leave.

And then she'd had to tell Mr Brown, the company's founder and managing director, that she was pregnant. He'd tried, without much success, not to show his disappointment.

"I'm happy for you and Imran, Kerry. But I won't lie – managing without you for four months will be difficult. You've become such an integral part of the company. We'll pay you half your salary while you are on maternity leave – your maternity unemployment benefit should make up the rest. We'll have to get in a temp to fill in while you're away … but rest assured that your job will be waiting for you."

Kerry had smiled and vowed that she'd return to work as soon as she could. As kind and understanding as Mr Brown was, there was no way she was going to let some little upstart temp weasel her way into her dream job and upset her career plans. And she needed her full salary; she and Imran and the baby needed her full salary.

Being a working mum of tiny baby who still wasn't sleeping through the night hadn't been easy. But she'd coped. Imran had coped. They'd coped together. And then, surprise! She was pregnant again. Her mother's assertion that she was stupid, irresponsible, crazy and a few other choice insults had merely fed her impotent anger. She'd been angry – with herself and with

Imran. She'd been upset, and not a little frightened: she wasn't prepared for another baby – surely it was too soon? Leo was barely six months old.

Then her gynaecologist told her that the new baby was a girl, and any doubts she might have had disappeared in a burst of totally unexpected, unadulterated joy. A *pigeon pair – a boy and a girl. How absolutely perfect!* she'd thought and mentally kicked herself for her totally un-PC sexism. She'd gone home and hugged Leo until he squealed to make up for her traitorous thoughts.

But she couldn't help the way she felt. She was thrilled. A little girl would be such fun – and hopefully so much more. Kerry was the only girl in her family, after two brothers; and Imran was one of three sons. Hopefully, this baby girl would delight both families. Perhaps a granddaughter would help to heal some of the hurt and anger and disappointment that had poisoned her and Imran's relationships with their respective sets of parents. Perhaps Imran's beloved mother would finally accept the fact that her youngest son's wife was not going anywhere.

At thirty-five weeks into her second uneventful pregnancy, Kerry started leaking amniotic fluid.

"It's nothing to worry about," the gynaecologist said. "But it's still a little too early for the baby to come. Let's try and hold the pregnancy for as long as possible. Bed rest for you, and I'll prescribe medication to hold off any contractions."

Imran was working really long hours. He had to if he had any hope of turning his little kitchen design and installation company into a thriving business. It was finally starting to build the reputation for the quality work that would be so essential for success. But it meant Kerry would be at home alone, without a car, for most of the day. This wasn't ideal – a heavily pregnant woman with potential pregnancy complications all alone with a toddler, miles from her doctor and the hospital where the new baby would be born. They agreed, reluctantly, that Kerry should move in with her parents in Norwood until the birth. Norwood was also closer to her office, making it easier for Jason, Mr Brown's son and heir, to deliver the documents his father needed Kerry to work on.

"We could use email," Kerry said when Jason arrived in her doorway with a briefcase full of documents.

"We could. But my father is old fashioned. He prefers working on hardcopy, especially for final corrections. He'll never change," Jason responded.

Kerry looked at him speculatively. She hadn't seen him for a few years. As far as she knew, he'd been galivanting around London, 'finding himself' as Mr Brown had put it.

"How was London? Are you back for good now?" she'd asked, surreptitiously trying to pull her gaping dressing gown closed over her ginormous bump. She'd never really taken much notice of Jason when she'd seen him drifting around the office back when she'd first started working for Mr Brown. He'd come across as an arrogant twat, too full of his own importance to notice lowly employees like her.

"Yeah. I got tired of the weather, and the overcrowded buses and tubes, and the warm beer ... I guess I got homesick. But I picked up some really good ideas which I'm trying to persuade my dad to implement. He won't, of course."

"Oh! Were you working in London?"

"Of course. What did you think I was doing?"

Kerry flushed. "I don't know. Your dad made it sound like you were on an extended gap year."

Jason threw back his head and laughed. "He would, I suppose. Actually, I was finishing my MBA and worked at a consultancy for a year. It was a great experience. I wouldn't have missed it for the world. But it's good to be home."

"So your dad can use you as a glorified messenger boy?" Kerry taunted, and her flush deepened when he laughed again.

"Well, my dad says that if I want to work for him, I have to start from the bottom and work my way up. That's what I'm doing. And anyway, Petrus is off sick today so I decided to use the opportunity to see how you're doing. My dad misses you."

"Oh," Kerry said. "Oh – well tell him I miss him too. I'll be back as soon as this is all over." She indicated the bump which was protruding through the opening of her gown despite her efforts to hide it.

"Well, good luck for the birth. I look forward to working with you. Just call when you've finished with these documents – they're really important so Dad doesn't trust anyone else to check them, only you. Petrus will come pick them up."

"Mr Brown just wants to keep an eye on you – to make sure you don't forget him so you'll return to work as soon the baby pops her head out," Imran teased when he walked into the bedroom she was sharing with Leo and found her pouring over the thick pack of a complex legal documents Jason had brought.

"No, he said he'll let me have a week off after she's born. Maybe two if I work hard now."

They laughed together, secure in the knowledge everything would be fine.

While Leo played in the garden under Triphina's watchful eye, Kerry rested as much as she could on her narrow bed, laptop at hand, keeping in touch with Jason and clients – and the recently installed temp – via Skype and WhatsApp and email. Sometimes, Imran would take Leo to Kempton Park, where Mrs Reddy from across the road, would take care of him while Imran went to see prospective customers or supervise the two young Zimbabweans he'd taken on to help him in the little factory he'd set up in the back of Mr Naidoo's empty garage in Wynberg. It was ideal, Imran had said when he'd told Kerry about his plans for I & K Kitchens and Cupboards. It was close enough to their rented house in Kempton Park for him to pop home for lunch if he wasn't too busy, and Mr Naidoo was willing to accept a very reasonable rental while the business was finding its feet.

It was hot. Kerry couldn't believe that the skin on her stomach could stretch as far as it had. She couldn't remember the last time she'd seen her toes unless she was lying down with her feet up. She was grateful to be able keep to her feet up – and that her mother was at least trying to be accommodating, and slightly less obnoxious than usual.

Two weeks into her enforced bedrest, Kerry's water broke. Her daughter was clearly impatient to make her entry into the world and start her life.

Chapter 2

Imran made the 15 km trip from Wynberg to Norwood to fetch Kerry in record time. The ten-minute drive to the Parklane Clinic was uneventful: no contractions (thanks to the medication the gynaecologist had prescribed to hold off labour), no pain, no traffic hold-ups. The sun was shining brightly in the blue February sky, and Kerry had just a vague sense of unease that perhaps this wasn't quite going according to plan. At the Parklane, they hurried directly to the Maternity Ward. They knew the way – it hadn't been all that long since Leo had been born there.

The nursing staff were waiting for them. They prepped Kerry and Imran held her hand as a porter wheeled her to theatre for a caesarean section. It was quick, efficient, calm – and hugely reassuring.

"We couldn't wait for contractions to start – not once your water had already broken," the gynaecologist explained after the anaesthetist had administered the epidural spinal block that would allow Kerry to be awake throughout the birth. As he had been with Leo, Imran huddled behind the screen that had been placed strategically over her chest, to block their view of the gory part of the surgical procedure. He kept his head close to hers: it was comforting for Kerry to have him there.

"And here she is," said the gynaecologist, holding up the bloodied baby who squawked her indignation at being pulled from the familiar sensations of her mother's womb.

"She's perfect." said Dr Sinclair, the paediatrician. "We are just going to take her to the nursery to get her weighed and cleaned up a bit. Mr Patel, you can come along with me and the baby, if you like, while my colleague finishes with your wife."

Imran looked at Kerry, torn between wanting to stay with her, and wanting to be with his daughter.

"Go," said Kerry. "I'll be fine."

Kerry dozed. She woke as they wheeled her from the recovery room back to the Maternity Ward. Imran was waiting.

"What took you so long? I was worried," he said.

"I didn't realise ... I'm fine," she responded. Sensation had not yet returned to her legs. She knew the pain would be intense when the anaesthetic wore off, but she didn't care. She was floating on cloud nine: she had a daughter, a beautiful, perfect baby girl.

"How's the baby? Did you see her? Did you hold her?"

"She's fine," Imran said. "I saw her through the nursery window – they were cleaning her up and she was yelling her head off. She weighs 2.4kg. I left her there to come and see how you're doing."

They smiled at each other.

"So, we're agreed – her name is Lily," Kerry said. She loved lilies. She had carried a single white lily the day she and Imran had tied the knot in the Johannesburg Magistrate's Court.

Imran nodded. "Lily Aarons-Patel. She looks like she is going to be a cheeky little thing. A real little tiger. I could hear her shouting all the way down the corridor from the nursery."

They giggled. They wondered how Leo would react when he met his baby sister. They made plans. Their daughter was going to grow up, a radiant, fresh, beautiful child, like the flower she was named for. Kerry could see her going to school, looking beautiful in pretty pink dresses – or blue jeans and torn tee-shirts if she preferred – running around with her big brother, laughing and playing as only happy, secure, deeply loved children can.

Dr Sinclair entered the ward.

"We're a little concerned about your baby," the paediatrician said. "She seems to be having a little trouble breathing. We think she has a lung infection. I've called in a pulmonologist – a lung specialist – and we're going to admit her to the neonatal Intensive

Care Unit and put her on a seven-day course of antibiotics. After that, she should be good to go." The doctor smiled reassuringly.

Kerry squeezed Imran's hand. "Don't stress," she said. "Remember, Leo also had a lung infection when he was born. He was fine – and Lily is bigger than he was at birth. She's strong. We'll be taking our baby girl home before you know it. You'll see."

Three days after her daughter's birth, Kerry was discharged. She didn't want to go home without her baby. The clinic was so far from Kempton Park but she also didn't want to stay on with her parents in Norwood. She consoled herself that it wouldn't be for long. If she sucked it up and remained in Norwood, she would be able to visit Lily three times a day, every day until she was safely at home with Imran where she belonged. And Leo needed her too. She had to take care of her son. Lily would be fine and she'd be getting the best care possible. There really was nothing to worry about, nothing to be upset about.

◞ ◔ ◕ ◟

Kerry expressed milk into the little container that she and Imran would take to the hospital for Lily. Mother's milk – liquid gold for a baby. The indignity and discomfort of expressing milk was nothing compared to the goodness only she was able to give her daughter even while the tiny infant was recovering in ICU. It would give her the best possible start in life, providing all the nourishment she'd need as well as natural immunity to infection.

She walked as quickly as her still healing caesarean scar would allow into the neonatal ICU with the precious liquid and handed the container to a nurse.

"I'm sorry, Mrs Patel. We're giving Lily formula now."

"It's Aarons, I'm Kerry Aarons," Kerry said. "And what do you mean formula? This is my milk – my baby needs it. I don't want her to have formula!"

"I'm sorry," the nurse said again. "Doctor's orders."

Angry and worried, Kerry called Dr Sinclair.

"I'm sorry, Mrs Patel ... umm, Ms Aarons-Patel. The baby isn't responding as well as we'd hoped to the antibiotics, so we tested your milk to see if that could be the problem. I'm afraid you have an infection. I'll prescribe a course of antibiotics for you, but for now we cannot give your milk to the baby."

"But ... but ... that can't be right. Are you saying it's my milk that's making my baby sick?"

"Possibly. I'll give you something to dry you up, if you like, to prevent engorgement. Otherwise, keep on expressing milk but just throw it away until the infection clears."

The nurse handed her a big yellow gown. And gloves. And a mask. "You have to wear these when you go into the baby's room," she said. "We can't risk further infection."

Kerry's legs could no longer support her. Tears rolled. She was a useless mother. It was her fault her baby was in ICU. She'd given her an infection – she had been born with it. And now her own mother was poisoning her with her milk!

"It's not your fault," Imran said.

Kerry didn't believe him.

Day eight. Kerry limped as quickly as she could after Imran through the ICU to the isolation room at the back where Lily lay in her incubator. At last, they'd be taking their baby girl home to Kempton Park. Kerry had spent that last two days preparing for Lily's homecoming. Leo's old crib had been scrubbed, a new pink blanket had been lovingly tucked in. And Leo had seemed really excited when they'd told him that he'd meet his sister later that day. But perhaps not. Leo was still such a baby himself although he'd happily taken Mrs Reddy's hand and toddled with her across the road when she'd promised him a cookie.

"I'll come and fetch you the moment we get home with your new baby sister," Kerry had reassured him. Leo had beamed at her.

Dr Sinclair was waiting for them. "I'm so sorry," she said. "The pulmonologist and I are concerned that Lily hasn't responded to the antibiotics. We suspect that she has a heart condition – possibly a small hole in her heart that is causing her breathing distress. We've asked a paediatric cardiologist – a heart specialist for babies and children – to take a look at her. He works mainly at Sunninghill Hospital, but he'll be along later today. We can't be sure when he'll come through. I suggest you both go home and rest. I'll let you know what he says."

The bell rang to signal the end of visiting hours, and Kerry and Imran walked slowly to their car. They wondered what time the cardiologist would come. They wondered what he would say. They were quiet during the long drive back to Kempton Park.

Kerry collected Leo from Mrs Reddy's house where he'd been playing with eleven-year-old Mohammed. Should she tell Leo what had happened? Would he even understand? He climbed onto her lap and she suppressed her grimace as he sat on her caesarean scar. She didn't care. She just wanted to hold him close. Mrs Reddy would take care of him again in the evening, when they went back to the hospital for the visiting hour.

"I'm Dr Govender. I'm a paediatric cardiologist," the man said to Kerry and Imran when they walked into Lily's isolation ward as soon as the neonatal ICU opened its doors for visiting at 7 pm.

Kerry noted his khaki cargo pants; his white shirt; shiny black hair; dark complexion.

He seems too young to be a specialist, she thought.

"I've just examined your baby. I've done an echocardiogram – an ultrasound scan of her heart – and I'm afraid she has what we call a congenital heart defect."

"What's that? Like a hole in the heart? Dr Sinclair said she may have a hole in her heart. You can fix it, can't you?" she asked.

Dr Govender shook his head. "It's a bit more complicated than that, I'm afraid. Here, I'll show you."

He took a piece of paper and quickly sketched a diagram on it. Kerry remembered some of what he drew from her high school

Life Sciences class. She wished she'd paid more attention.

"This is a normal heart," Dr Govender said. Kerry forced herself to concentrate, to stop her mind from racing, as the cardiologist spoke about ventricles and atriums and veins and arteries and oxygenated blood from the lungs and deoxygenated blood to the lungs – or was it the other way around?

"So, that's the way a normal heart would work. Now, your little one has a condition known as Tricuspid Atresia with a right ventricular septal defect."

"What's that?" Kerry demanded. It sounded horrific. It sounded dangerous.

"It is quite a common defect. Her heart looks something like this."

He drew another diagram. Kerry noticed that one of the sections of the heart, one of the ventricles, was small, much smaller than the one on the normal heart.

"So what does that mean?" she asked, her voice shrill.

"Your baby isn't getting enough oxygen to her body, which is why she looks a little blue. The problem is that she was born with more or less three heart chambers instead of four. One of the valves, the tricuspid valve, didn't develop and this meant that the right ventricle didn't develop either. And she has a very big hole in the heart, what we call a ventricular septal defect or VSD ..."

Kerry tried to focus. The cardiologist was using more long, unfamiliar, unpronounceable words. He finally stopped talking and looked at her and Imran expectantly.

"Any questions?"

Hundreds, Kerry thought. She didn't know where to start. She didn't understand any of this. She stared at the incomprehensible diagram on the paper.

She asked the only question that mattered: "You can fix it, can't you?"

"No," Dr Govender said.

Kerry's heart stood still. Then he continued: "All we can do is make her heart a bit more efficient. We will have to operate. Her first surgery must be done as soon as possible ..."

"Surgery? She's going to have to have an operation? When?"

"I suggest we transfer her to Sunninghill Hospital tomorrow. We have one of the best paediatric cardiac units in the country there, you know. We'll do the surgery on Tuesday after the cardio-thoracic surgeon has seen her."

"And that will fix it? She'll be okay?"

"For now. But you must understand that this is only a temporary repair that will keep her going until we can do a more permanent procedure. She will require two more open heart surgeries when ..."

Kerry interrupted him: "Open heart surgeries? Three open heart surgeries? You are going to cut my baby's chest open three times? You want to cut her open tomorrow – sorry, on Tuesday? She'll only be nine – no, ten days old! Do you really have to cut her chest open?"

"I'm afraid so, Mrs ... ummm, Mrs Patel. But please be assured, this procedure is not very unusual. As I said, Tricuspid Atresia is a relatively common CHD – congenital heart defect. With surgery, children with this defect can live full, satisfactory lives well into adulthood."

"But she's so tiny – can't we wait until she is a little bigger, and stronger before ..."

Dr Govender's quiet response shattered Kerry's world: "Without immediate surgery, your baby is unlikely to survive a month."

Kerry looked at Imran. His beautiful, chiselled cheekbones stood out bleakly in his ashen face.

Kerry and Imran watched in silence as paramedics loaded the incubator into the ambulance. Inside lay their precious baby with an oxygen tube in her nose, drips poking out of her fragile little neck, monitors on her feet and round ECG electrodes plastered across her tiny chest. They got into their black Toyota Corolla and followed behind for the 25 km trip along the M1 motorway towards the N1 which would take them to Sunninghill Hospital in Sandton. The sun was shining brightly in the blue summer sky. The car's tyres made a soothing, whooshing sound as they sped along.

"What are you thinking?" Kerry asked.

"Nothing," Imran said.

She wasn't thinking of anything either, her brain was in overdrive. Her thoughts were swirling, but there was nothing she could hold on to, nothing that made sense.

They turned onto the N1 and followed the ambulance onto the Rivonia offramp.

"Nearly there," Imran said.

A couple of minutes later, the ambulance pulled into the casualty bay at the hospital. Imran found a parking space in the visitors' parking. They got out, locked the car and walked through the imposing foyer, past the pharmacy and coffee shop, and down a level to the cardiothoracic ICU.

They had arrived. Kerry understood exactly how Alice must have felt when she fell down the rabbit hole.

Unaware of Sister Janie, the cardiothoracic ICU team leader's smiling gaze from across the bustling ward, Kerry cradled her baby for the first time since her birth nine days before. She marvelled at the infant's thick black hair.

Tomorrow they would cut her tiny little chest open. They would make some kind of temporary repair to her tiny heart. They were doing this to keep her alive. It would keep her alive until they could do another surgery. Probably an even more dangerous procedure.

Kerry focused on making her mind go blank. She didn't want to think about what was probably months away. She didn't want to think about what was going to happen tomorrow. Right now, she just wanted to savour the sensation of cradling her baby daughter. Right now, she just wanted to be.

The bright lights, the bustling noise of Sunninghill Hospital's

CT ICU faded as Kerry rocked her baby. Then she looked up at Imran standing behind her, his hand resting lightly on her shoulder.

"Look at her, Imran. Look at our baby girl. Isn't she beautiful? Would you like to hold her now?"

Her husband nodded, his thin face lighting up. He sat in the chair and Kerry handed him their precious, sick, delicate daughter.

Imran bent over the baby and one of her little hands flailed up and touched his chin.

"Hello Lily. Hello Tiger," he smiled.

Chapter 3

A very tall man walked towards them as they sat watching Lily in her incubator. He was smiling.

"Mrs Patel? Mr Patel?"

Kerry was about to correct him – and then gave a mental shrug. Why bother? What difference did it make what name they called her? In the greater scheme of things, her feminist leanings seemed a little petty.

The man held out his hand. His eyes twinkled behind his glasses.

"I'm Dr Patterson. I'm a paediatric cardiothoracic surgeon. I'm going to be operating on your little one tomorrow. I just want to have a quick look at her and I'll answer any questions you may have, okay?"

Kerry watched as he listened to Lily's heart. Tomorrow, she realised, her baby's heart would literally be in those enormous hands. How on earth could he work with something so tiny without hurting it. Hadn't Dr Govender said Lily's heart was the size of a walnut?

Almost as if he'd heard her, the surgeon stepped back from the incubator, held up his hands and grinned. "Believe it or not," he waved his long fingers, "these have worked on many, many babies over the years. I've done a lot of surgeries just like the one we're going to be doing on Lily. That's such a pretty name – perfect for such a pretty baby."

Kerry found herself smiling back at him. He radiated warmth and reassurance.

"I'm sure you have a lot of questions," he said.

"Yes. We're not really sure exactly what you ... what the surgery ... what exactly? She faltered. She had so many questions, she didn't know which one to ask first.

Dr Patterson smiled. "It's all pretty overwhelming, isn't it?"

Kerry nodded and blinked, hard. She didn't want to break down in front of this stranger. She didn't want to look at Imran either, because she knew that if she did, she'd really start to cry.

"I know your cardiologist explained it all to you, but it probably went right over your heads, didn't it?"

Kerry nodded.

"Would you like me to go through it all again?"

Again, she nodded.

"Okay. So you know that Lily has a congenital heart defect called Tricuspid Atresia with a right ventricular septal defect. In simple terms, she does not have a tricuspid valve between her right atrium and ventricle. In addition, her right ventricle has not formed properly; and she has a big hole in her heart. Here, I'll show you."

Armed with a piece of paper and a pen, he quickly drew a diagram of a normal heart and another of Lily's heart and placed the two side by side.

Kerry recognised them. They looked almost identical to Dr Govender's drawings. She and Imran had poured over them for what seemed like hours – but she still wasn't quite sure what it all meant.

Dr Patterson pointed at one of his drawings. "The normal heart has two sides – the left side and the right side, but these two sides work together. Each side has two chambers – a left atrium and a left ventricle; and a right atrium and right ventricle."

Kerry nodded. She knew that.

"Let's look at the left side of the heart first," the surgeon continued. "Actually no, let's rather start at the lungs." He quickly added two round objects to his drawing and connected them to the heart with a few lines. "Right. Those are the lungs. We breathe oxygen into our lungs and this oxygen goes into the tiny blood vessels in the lung. Then, this oxygen-rich blood makes its way along these vessels into the pulmonary vein." He indicated one of the lines on his drawing.

"The pulmonary vein carries the oxygen-rich blood, what we call oxygenated blood, from the lungs and empties it into the left atrium, here." He pointed at a spot on the heart part of the diagram.

"The left atrium contracts and pushes the oxygenated blood through a valve – the mitral valve – into the left ventricle. When the ventricle is full, the mitral valve shuts to prevent the blood flowing back into the atrium. The ventricle then contracts and pushes the blood through the aortic valve into the aorta – this big artery here – and from there, it is carried to all parts of the body. That's how the body gets the oxygen it needs. Do you understand?"

Kerry and Imran nodded.

"Okay, now let's look at the right side of the heart. This is important because this is the root of all Lily's problems. As you can see here, there are two big blood vessels that enter the right atrium of the heart," the surgeon said, pointing at the diagram.

"These blood vessels are the inferior – the lower – and the superior – the upper – vena cava. They carry blood from the body to the heart. This blood has already passed on its oxygen to the body, so we call it deoxygenated blood. Now the right atrium contracts, and the deoxygenated blood flows from the right atrium into the right ventricle, through the tricuspid valve."

Kerry interrupted him. "But Lily doesn't have a tricuspid valve."

Dr Patterson beamed at her. "Quite right. She doesn't. But if she had, the deoxygenated blood in the right atrium would pass through the tricuspid valve into the right ventricle, and from there, through the pulmonic valve into the pulmonary artery and on to the lungs where it would be oxygenated."

"So if Lily doesn't have the tricuspid valve, what is happening to her blood? How is it getting to her lungs to get more oxygen – I mean, to be oxygenated?"

"Ah, now we are getting to the crux of the problem," Dr Patterson said. "Because she doesn't have a tricuspid valve, the blood in her right atrium has to find another route through the heart to the lungs to pick up oxygen. It does this through a defect – a hole – in the septa or wall between the left and right sides of her heart. So now what we have is the oxygenated blood from the left side of her heart and oxygen-poor or deoxygenated blood that's in her right atrium and ventricle all mixing together. It's this mixture of blood – rather than nice, pure oxygenated blood – that is being sent out to her body."

"But that can't be good for her."

"You're quite right. It isn't. What is happening is that her body is having to make do with blood that doesn't contain enough oxygen. That's why her lips and fingers and body have a bluish tinge. She is what we call cyanotic – oxygen-deprived. She is just not getting enough oxygen."

Kerry swallowed. It was starting to make sense and it frightened her.

"So tomorrow – you are going to fix the tricuspid valve and close the hole in her heart so that the blood can't mix and she'll get enough oxygen into the blood that goes to her body. Right?" she asked.

"I'm afraid not. There is no way to fix or replace a tricuspid valve."

Kerry's heart dropped. "Then what are you going to do? How are you going to make her better?"

The surgeon paused, as if considering his response.

"At this point, there is another problem that needs to be attended to first, and that's what we will be doing tomorrow. Because of the defects in Lily's heart, there is too much blood flowing to her lungs. The pressure of this can cause serious damage."

Kerry's heart plummeted. "To her lungs? There's a problem with her lungs as well as her heart?"

"No. Not yet. But if we don't do something now to protect them then yes, her lungs will be damaged."

"What will you do?" Kerry asked. She glanced at Imran. He was staring intently at the diagrams the surgeon had drawn.

"We are going to place a band – sort of like an elastic band – around the pulmonary artery. This will control the blood flow to her lungs."

"And then she'll be okay?"

"Well, she'd be out of immediate danger and that's our main concern right now. But she will need at least two more surgeries when she's a little older. Once she's had all three, she will have the best possible chance of living a pretty good, fairly normal life."

"When will you do the other operations? Why don't you just do it all tomorrow so she won't have to go through all this again." Kerry indicated the ICU and the beeping monitors.

"It's too much to do in one surgery. Her tiny body couldn't cope. For now, our goal is to deal with the greatest risk and get her out of immediate danger. As to when we will do the other surgeries, every child is different. Usually the second surgery will take place when she is about six months old; and then the next one will be done when she is about three or four years old. But let's not get ahead of ourselves just yet. Let's get through tomorrow and then we can talk more." The surgeon smiled at them. "Is that okay?"

Kerry nodded. On the other side of the incubator, Imran nodded too. Sadness radiated from his every pore.

"Doctor," she said. There was one question she had to ask. It had been burning a hole in her brain from the time the cardiologist had told them just how badly damaged her baby's heart was. It was a question she wasn't sure she wanted the answer to – but she had to know.

"Doctor – why ... what's the cause ... was it something I did when I was pregnant?"

"Mrs Patel, you cannot blame yourself." Dr Patterson's eyes radiated compassion. "Congenital heart defects are the most common of all birth defects. It's estimated that about one in 100 babies is born with a CHD, and Tricuspid Atresia is the third most common of these. No one knows what causes it – or any congenital heart defect, for that matter. There is nothing you did to cause it, and nothing you could have done to prevent it. But it has happened, and you are going to need to be strong and brave to deal with it. Your daughter will need you to be strong. Don't waste your strength blaming yourself. It was not your fault. Am I making myself clear?"

Kerry found herself nodding.

"Good, then I'll see you both tomorrow, after the surgery."

When the afternoon visiting hour was over and they had been shooed from the ICU, Kerry and Imran retrieved their car and headed back to Kempton Park.

"There's so much traffic!" Kerry said as they crawled along.

"It'll be better when we get onto the highway," Imran said.

But it wasn't.

"There must have been an accident or something. Turn up the radio – 702 will have traffic reports," he said.

Kerry barely heard the 702 Drive Show host jabbering on about something he and the callers to the radio station probably considered important. She wanted to scream at them. Her baby was lying in the Intensive Care Unit with a huge, life-threatening defect in her heart; she had to have a massive operation tomorrow which could kill her. But if she didn't have it she would die. The cardiologist and the cardiothoracic surgeon had made that abundantly clear. And those people thought that the fact that South Africa's corrupt, illiterate president, Jacob Zuma, might finally be forced to resign was important? They didn't know what important was.

At last – the traffic report. Kerry listened closely but nothing was said about a hold up on the N3 South.

"No accident," Imran confirmed when the report finished. "I suppose this is just normal traffic for this time of day."

"How are we going to do this trip three times a day? It'll take hours – and we still have to pick up Leo and give him his bath and supper and ... what are we going to do?" she wailed. She finally allowed the tears that had been threatening all day to spill over and slide down her cheeks.

Imran reached over and squeezed her hand. "We'll manage. We'll try to plan our trips to and from the hospital around the worst of the traffic. We'll work it out. It'll be okay – you'll see."

They drove on in silence, both trying to process what they had heard, what they had seen.

"Do you think the doctor was right? That I ... that it just happened? How can something as big as this just happen? I mean, I'd heard of babies having holes in their hearts but never anything this bad. Did you know this sort of thing happened?" Kerry asked.

"No, but you heard the doctor. It's not your fault! It's no-one's fault."

"Then why did it happen? Why did it happen to our baby? I must have done something. There can't be no reason. Are we being punished in some way? I'm sure that's what my mother thinks."

"My father would say it's God will," Imran said. "He'd say it's not for us to question God's will. I'm not sure I believe that. But it has happened. And we will deal with it, together. My grandmother always said that we are never given challenges – trials – we cannot handle. So I'm going to believe her. We will be okay. I'll make sure of that. And our little Tiger will be okay too. We have to believe that. You have to believe that!"

Kerry looked at her husband and nodded. He was right. With Imran at her side, she could face anything. He was her rock, her strength. She must have sensed that in him the first time she saw him, and promptly fell in love.

Chapter 4

The sky was just beginning to lighten and Kerry breathed a quiet sight of relief. She could finally give up the pretence of sleeping. And yet – and yet, she wished the dawn wouldn't come. She didn't want today to start. She didn't want to face what lay ahead. She got up, and Imran immediately followed. He hadn't slept a wink either. She'd heard him, his breathing shallow all through the long, dark hours after Sandy had finally gone home.

"You have a big day tomorrow," Sandy had said. "Try to get some sleep."

Kerry had hugged her friend who had come over with her husband Paul and brother Josh, almost as soon as they had arrived home after the long, frustratingly slow drive back from Sunninghill. Kerry had collected Leo, who had smiled at her sleepily, and was fast asleep again virtually before she'd put him down on the bed. And then her three friends walked in, with their hesitant questions and transparent concern and love, reinforced by a determination to keep their minds off the enormity of the day ahead. Kerry was grateful. But it was hard, so hard, not to think about it all. Not just the surgery. What would happen after that? Would Lily really be okay? That's what her mother had asked. What if she wasn't, her mother had asked too. How on earth would she cope with a sick baby, a really, really sick baby? As her mother had pointed out, after bluntly asking whether the surgery was the right thing to do at all – what did she know about taking care of a baby with a faulty heart? Kerry had ended the call.

But the vision of the baby in the cot next to Lily's kept floating into her head. She had closed her eyes to try and block it out and had forced herself to laugh at one of Josh's silly jokes.

Now she couldn't procrastinate any longer. And she couldn't stop the clock from ticking remorselessly on. She swung her legs off the bed and quietly got up. Imran quickly followed. Leo slept on.

"What are you doing?" she asked.

"I don't know ... I was thinking ... this can't do any harm. And we need all the help we can get," Imran said, colour rising in his ashen cheeks.

Kerry nodded. Her husband carefully placed the prayer mat he'd retrieved from the back of their cupboard on the floor and knelt. Imran had laughed when he'd told her that his father had given it to him as a gift after his return from his Haj – his once-in-a-lifetime pilgrimage to Mecca. "He hopes it'll make me a better man, a better Muslim," Imran had said as he'd rolled up what to Kerry had looked like an ornate little red and gold Persian rug.

She watched as Imran prepared for the ritual of the dawn prayer – the Fajr, if she remembered correctly from the description Imran had once given her after she'd nagged and nagged him to explain the five daily prayers rituals devout Muslims submit to every day. He'd never actually done any of them before – at least, not since they'd been living together.

As Imran muttered words Kerry could not understand, she felt as if the band the surgeon said he was going to put around the veins in her baby's heart was already wrapped tightly about her own. She had never felt as helpless, as powerless in her life. She watched Imran raise his arms, bow and then prostrate himself on his prayer mat.

She closed her eyes. She clenched her fists. "Please, please, if you are there, guide the surgeon's hands today. Please, save my baby. Please, protect her. Please, just let her be okay. Please ..." she prayed silently.

She opened her eyes. Imran was still praying, his eyes closed in concentration, his face drawn and pale.

She pulled on a pair of leggings and a 'baby doll' dress in a defiantly bright shade of orange – one of her preggie wardrobe favourites – screwed her hair back in a ponytail, gathered her sleeping baby boy into her arms and held him tightly, quietly adding another silent prayer, this one of thanks that he was strong and healthy ... and then yet another for whatever gods were listening to keep him that way.

The six o'clock news had just started on the car radio when she handed Leo over to Mrs Reddy and kissed him gently on his tousled dark head. "Stay safe, my baby," she murmured.

There was a surprising number of cars on the highway, most heading north towards Sandton but the traffic moved swiftly.

"How you do think it is going to go?" Kerry asked as Imran put his foot down and the car sped along at what Kerry suspected was over the 120km/hr speed limit – but most other cars were also moving at the same pace.

"I don't know. We just have to be strong and hope ... no, believe that it will go well," he said.

"I'm sure Dr Patterson knows what he is doing. I like him," she said.

"Me too."

702 Talk Radio's Breakfast Show host, Bongani Bingwa, was going on and on about Jacob Zuma's long overdue resignation he'd announced last night. Kerry tried to concentrate. It was a really important moment for South Africa, Bongani kept saying. The vote in parliament today to elect a new president for the country would be a formality – although the EFF would probably try to stir up some trouble. They always did. But there was no doubt that by the end of today, South Africa would be in the capable, educated, business-savvy and urbane hands of Cyril Ramaphosa. And that could only be good for the country. At last South Africa was rid of the man who was responsible for almost everything that that had gone wrong in the country – the corruption, the stuttering economy, the potholes and broken traffic lights,

the crumbling water infrastructure, the electricity shortages, everything. *Everything, except Lily's heart*, Kerry thought.

"How long do you think it will take?" she asked.

"What?"

"The operation. How long?"

"Dunno. Couple of hours, maybe."

"Yeah, I suppose."

They rode on in silence, the chatter on the radio serving as ineffective white noise to the cacophony in her head. The 6.30am news headlines came and went; a traffic report reported nothing of interest; Bongani sounded so annoyingly cheerful, Kerry wanted to reach into the radio and strangle him. Didn't he understand that today was the worst day of her life?

They turned into the parking area at Sunninghill Hospital.

They walked briskly down the long corridor towards the cardiothoracic ICU. Through the first set of doors; to the second with a glass panel. They peeped through. They wanted to see their daughter before she was taken to the theatre for her surgery. They wanted to say ... not goodbye. Just look at her, perhaps even hold her for a minute or two before they took her away, before they gave her into the surgeon's big hands. They couldn't see her.

They snuck through the ICU doors, knowing they were not supposed to be there. It wasn't visiting time, but perhaps, just this once ... Lily wasn't there. Their baby girl was already on her way to the theatre, or already even in theatre. What would they do to her when she got there? Was the theatre where they would cut her tiny chest open anything like the theatre at the Parklane where Kerry had had her caesarean section? Was that really only 10 days ago? It seemed like a lifetime.

They hurried down more corridors, around corners – following the signs that said 'Theatre'. Outside the firmly closed doors were some chairs. They sat. It was just after 7am.

They waited. They watched stretchers bearing frightened-looking adults being wheeled into the theatre. They stared in anticipation as the doors banged open from the inside, but the drowsy figure on the emerging stretcher was always too big, far too big to be their tiny, precious bundle.

"I can't stay here any longer. Let's go for some coffee – upstairs in the coffee shop," said Imran.

"But what if she comes out while we're up there?" Kerry objected.

"The ICU sister said it would take quite a long time. She has our cellphone numbers. She said they'd call us when the surgery was over."

Kerry nodded. Her throat was parched. Coffee would be nice. She glanced at her watch. 9am.

They ordered their drinks and sat at one of the tables right at the back of the coffee shop. They hadn't had breakfast, but the thought of eating even one of the tasty little pastries in the glass display cabinet made her stomach churn. They finished their coffee. They waited.

"I can't sit here any longer," Kerry said. "Let's get out of here. Let's go."

They drove to the Woodmead Value Mart. Parked. Walked around. Strolled into a factory store, checked out the jeans in another – she wondered how long it would take before she could fit into her old jeans again – walked into a furniture store. She smiled vaguely at the eager young shop assistant who rush over to help them. They were the only people in the shop, and the poor young man was obviously desperate for a sale. Imran shook his head. The shop assistant walked away. They walked out of the store, back into the bright sunshine. Her caesarean scar hurt. She needed to sit down. They kept walking. Noon.

Kerry's phone rang. Jason Brown. She forced herself to answer.

"How did it go?" her employer's son asked.

"She's still in theatre," Kerry said.

She listened politely while he muttered some words, thanked him politely for calling, ended the call and kept walking.

Imran's phone rang. The hospital. Lily's surgery was over.

They ran to their car, and Imran ignored all the speed limits as they raced back to the hospital.

They rushed into the ICU. Lily wasn't there.

"It will still be a while until she comes back," the sister said.

"How did it go? Do you know?" Kerry asked.

The sister shook her head. "All I know is that she is out of surgery. They'll keep her in recovery until she is stable, and then send her back. Why don't you go and sit in the waiting room? It's more comfortable there."

❧ ☙

Kerry stared at the handsome woman on the other side of the waiting room. It was rude, she knew, but she couldn't help it. The woman's face was compelling. She was reading something. A book. It looked like a bible. She had a strong face. She looked so calm. She didn't look up at them, at anyone who came into the room. She just read her bible. Kerry wondered who she was visiting. Why she was waiting, in the waiting room, like them. It was still some time till visiting hours in ICU.

A nurse came through the door.

"Mr and Mrs Patel? Your baby is back. You can come and see her now."

Kerry sprinted into the ICU. She gasped and clutched the back of a chair. She barely recognised her baby. She looked so tiny, so fragile lying in a little cot with her eyes closed, totally naked with a bloodied wound dressing down the front of her chest. There was a thick tube going into her mouth, held in place by strapping and bandages that all but covered her entire face. There were tubes going into her chest, and ECG leads all over her body. There was a bouquet of syringes attached to a drip feeding into her neck. Her little hands were bandaged and tied to the sides of the cot.

"When do you think she will wake up?" Kerry asked the sister who had introduced herself and told them she would be nursing Lily that day.

"Oh, she won't wake today. She's fully sedated – she'll probably be kept sedated for a few days," the nurse said.

"Then why have you tied her hands?"

"It's a precaution. We don't want to risk her starting to wake and possibly dislodging the ventilator or pulling out one of her drains – the tubes coming out of her chest. One of those is draining excess fluid from around her heart; the other one is from her lungs."

"Was the operation a success?" Imran asked.

"You'll have to ask her surgeon that. He'll be around to check on her later."

They waited. Lily lay still, a broken, bloodied doll. Occasionally, something on the little monitor thing above her cot beeped; the nurse approached, pressed a few buttons and the beeping stopped.

Kerry looked at the baby in the cot to the left of Lily's. She couldn't help it. She had got the fright of her life when she'd noticed him yesterday, when they'd first admitted her baby girl. A baby boy, probably about four months old. His little body was bloated and he had what seemed like dozens of tubes all over his body. Some of the tubes were filled with blood – it was as if his whole circulatory system was outside his body. She wondered what was wrong with him.

They waited. Lily's little chest rose and fell, almost imper- ceptibly.

3pm. The ICU's doors opened and visitors streamed in. No more than two visitors per patient. It looked as if that rule was strictly enforced. Kerry had noticed that all the patients in the unit were babies and little children – although she had spotted an older child in a bed on the far side of the ward.

She recognised the tall woman as she came through the doors. Her colourful robes swished as she walked towards them and took a seat next to the baby boy with all the tubes. She gazed intently at her child, then at the monitors next to his cot, her face a finely-etched ebony mask. She opened her bible and continued reading, glancing up occasionally at her baby. She ignored the bustle and noise of the ICU going on around her. Kerry wondered how she could be so serene with her child in such obvious distress.

4pm. The tall, dignified woman closed her bible, touched her baby's forehead with her long fingers and joined the other visitors – parents, grandparents – streaming back out through the ICU doors. Kerry and Imran left with them. They resumed their position on the comfortable chairs in the waiting room. The woman with the bible was back in her chair, on the other side of the room. They waited.

Dr Patterson strode into the waiting room. He was smiling.

"It went well," he said. "We put the band in place and your little one handled it all like a champ. I've just checked on her and I'm happy with how she is doing."

Kerry offered up a silent prayer of thanks, and grinned inwardly. For an agnostic, she was doing a lot of praying. But it was done. Her baby had come through this life-threatening surgery with flying colours. It was all going to be okay. She felt as if an enormous weight had been lifted from her chest. She realised she was starving. Imran was smiling at her. She smiled back.

"When will she wake up?" Imran asked.

"Not for a few days. Go home. Get some rest. You must be exhausted."

Rest. That sounded good. They both needed it.

As they walked slowly out the hospital doors, they heard their names being called. Sandy and Paul and Josh were there, waiting.

Josh, they knew, had an absolute horror of hospitals. Nothing would induce him to go inside, not even into the foyer which bore a greater resemblance to a hotel than a hospital. But there he was – waiting. To hear the news. To be with them.

"It went well," Imran said before they could ask. "The operation was a success!"

Chapter 5

Kerry's phone rang. Imran had just rolled up his prayer mat and stowed it in the cupboard. Kerry had found herself silently thanking the gods or whatever power there was up there, for watching over her babies. Leo was still fast asleep. Much to her surprise, Kerry had slept well too, despite the terse semi-argument she'd had with her mother. Just as she'd crawled into bed, her phone had rung. She'd snatched it up and grimaced.

"Hi Mom," she'd said.

"Kerry. I've been waiting and waiting for you to call. I tried to convince myself that no news is good news but honestly, I've been so worried."

"I'm sorry Mom, it went fine. The doctors are happy."

"Well, you could have let me know. I know I'm only your mother, but Lily – silly name – what possessed you to give your child such an old-fashioned name – I had an Aunty Lily, horrible woman – anyway she is my granddaughter and I was concerned and I expected you to phone me the minute she came out of surgery. I said to your father that I couldn't believe you'd be so inconsiderate as to leave me waiting and worrying the whole day and half the night and ..."

"Mom, I'm sorry. I said I was sorry. I had a lot on my mind and I just didn't think ..."

"That's your problem, Kerry-Anne. That's always been your problem. You don't think. You never think. You never thought of what it would mean when you married him, did you?"

"Mom, I'm tired. I'm going to bed now – actually, I am in bed ..."

"So you were just going to let me stew all night? You had no

intention of picking up the phone and telling me, your mother –
the child's grandmother ..."

"You could have called me! You should have called me," Kerry
exploded.

"I didn't want to disturb you. I know how you hate it when I
interrupt you when you're busy."

Kerry sighed. "I'm sorry Mom. I should have phoned you. But
now you know. It went well. I'm tired – it's been a really long day.
So I'm going to say goodnight now."

Kerry had ended the call, turned over and had promptly fallen
asleep. Exhaustion probably.

But this morning, this new day – the start of what the
cardiologist and the surgeon had warned would be a long, hard
road ahead – she felt ready to tackle anything. Before leaving for
the hospital to get there for visiting at 10am she would express
some milk. She was glad, so glad, she had decided to ditch the
drying-up tablets Dr Sinclair had given her. She was glad she had
made up her mind to keep her milk supply going, even if she'd
had to pour it all down the drain. But when she had finished the
course of antibiotics, when her mysterious infection was finally
gone, when Lily was able to drink from a bottle, or even a dropper
while she recovered from the surgery, she would be able to give
her baby the milk she would need to make her strong.

"Hello?" Kerry said. She didn't recognise caller's number.
Probably a wrong number. Who else could be calling her at 6.30
on a Wednesday morning?

"Mrs Patel?"

"Yes." She recognised the voice – and her heart turned over.

"Mrs Patel, it's Dr Patterson, Lily's cardiothoracic surgeon."

"Who is it? What's wrong?" Imran demanded.

"It's Dr Patterson," she whispered.

He paled. "Put the phone on speaker," he said.

"Mrs Patel, I'm sorry to have to call you so early, but I need
your consent to take Lily back into theatre. She ..."

"What!" Kerry and Imran exclaimed together.

"Why?" she demanded.

Imran looked stunned. He was clearly too shocked to say anything more. Kerry's hand was shaking so much, she was afraid she'd drop the phone. She put it on the table.

"It seems the band we put in yesterday is a little too tight. We have to adjust it," the surgeon said.

"But you said she was fine. You said everything went well! How did this happen?" Kerry asked. She swallowed the scream bubbling up in her throat. Now was not the time for recriminations, for yelling, for anything other than keeping it together. Now she had to understand what was going on.

"This is unfortunate, but not unusual. If you remember, I told you that it was possible we'd have to adjust the band."

Kerry didn't remember. But there had been so much to take in. So much information to absorb. Maybe he had told them about an adjustment. No big deal – just an adjustment, how serious could that be?

"How do you do it? Adjust the band, I mean? Why does she have to go back into theatre? Can't you just do it in the ICU?" she asked and, as the words left her lips, she realised just how stupid that was. The band was inside Lily – right by or inside her heart. The only way to get to it, to adjust it would be to ...

"You are going to have to open her up again, aren't you?" she whispered.

"I'm afraid so," Dr Patterson confirmed. "We are going to take her back to theatre now. That's why I need your consent."

"But we signed a consent form yesterday."

"I know. But this is a new procedure."

"Well, we were coming through to the hospital this morning. We can sign a new form then."

Kerry's mind was whirling, forming a mental list of everything they would have to do in order to get on the highway to rush to the hospital before the traffic got too heavy: she had to get dressed, change Leo and take him to his grandmother or Mrs Reddy – probably Mrs Reddy, she was closer and Leo loved playing with Mohammed. She also had to wash the dishes she'd been too tired to wash up last night, but maybe they could wait ...

"I'm afraid we can't wait. I need your verbal consent now. There's an opening in the theatre list and we need to take her in immediately," the surgeon said.

Kerry's legs could no longer hold her. She sat down heavily.

"Is it the same procedure as yesterday?" she asked.

"Pretty much."

"So she'll be put under anaesthetic again, for hours and hours? She's so little," Kerry paused, and wiped her eyes. "But we don't have a choice, do we?"

"I'm afraid not," Dr Patterson's voice was gentle.

"Okay, go head. Save our baby girl."

At last, they were on the road, heading north to Sunninghill. The early rush hour traffic had long since eased. Imran had pointed out that there was no need to hurry to the hospital: Lily wouldn't be out of surgery for hours. And then she'd be sent to Recovery and that would take a few more hours. It would probably only around lunch time – or even later – before they'd be able to see her.

"And they'll phone us as soon as the surgery is over," he said.

Kerry had curbed her impatience. It made sense to rather wait at home, get things done, and then travel through ... but it was so hard when her every instinct was screaming at her to be there, be at least closer to her baby than 40 km away, while they were cutting her open again. She bit her lip.

Déjà vu. They walked into the hospital and took the stairs down to the cardiothoracic ICU – this time going directly to the waiting room to kick their heels until a nurse came to fetch them when Lily was back in her cot, ventilator in place, hooked up to all the monitors and drains and drips ...

The dignified woman was there, reading her bible. She glanced up at them as they came into the room, nodded almost imperceptibly, and turned back to her bible. They waited.

Kerry's phone rang.

"So how did it go?" Jason Brown asked.

"She's still in theatre," Kerry said, wondering how he knew about today's surgery. She hadn't told him. They hadn't told anyone. Not yet. Not till it was over. They didn't want anyone fussing; they didn't want the platitudes and empty assurances that everything would be okay. It had been exhausting having to deal with all that yesterday.

"What? She's in theatre? Still?" his shock was palpable.

"No – they had to take her back to theatre today. To make an adjustment."

"Oh. Oh sorry. I didn't know."

"Yes, well ..." Kerry's voice trailed away.

"Umm. Well, let me know how it goes," he said.

"Sure. Bye."

Kerry ended the call.

"Mr Brown," she said to Imran. It wasn't exactly a lie.

"I think I'd better let my parents know," Imran said.

"Okay, if that's what you want. I can't deal with my mother right now."

They waited.

At last, they could go into the ICU. Kerry examined her daughter's little face intently: she looked exactly as she had the day before. Peaceful. Everything was exactly the same ... or was it?

"It went well. She's doing well. Now we just have to let her grow and get stronger," Dr Patterson said.

Two days later, Kerry walked into the ICU with all the other parents. From the doorway, she could see Lily lying motionless in her cot, the tubes and monitors and everything in place. And then she drew in a deep breath and moved quickly to her daughter's bedside. Something was different.

"We've started weaning her off the sedation," the nurse smiled.

"But she's still on the ventilator. She's still intubated."

"Hopefully, it won't be for much longer. She's doing really nicely."

Kerry took her place on the right side of the cot. Imran sat on the left. They kept their eyes glued to Lily's face. They watched, and waited.

And then, Lily's eyelids fluttered.

"Look!" Imran whispered. "She's waking up!"

Her eyelids fluttered again. And opened. Kerry looked into her baby's big brown eyes. Her daughter looked back at her, and then her eyes closed again.

Tears slid down Kerry's cheeks. Joy flooded through her.

"Hello Tiger," Imran whispered, his voice choked. "Welcome back little one."

Day 28. Kerry walked into the ICU and stopped so suddenly that Imran almost tripped over her. The cot on the left of Lily's was empty. The baby boy with all the tubes and his circulation outside of his body was not there.

"Where's the baby from that cot?" she asked Lily's nurse as she handed her a container with her expressed milk.

"He didn't make it," the nurse said.

Kerry gripped the rail around Lily's cot. She felt ... she didn't know how she felt. She felt sad, so sad for the tall, dignified woman who had waited patiently, day after day at her baby's bedside and in the ICU waiting room, as her baby boy fought his battle to live. Kerry didn't even know her name. She hadn't known the baby's name either. Or what had been wrong with him. ICU protocol seemed to be to not ask any questions about the other patients, to not get too close to any of the other parents, to not become involved.

And now she understood why. She had seen cots filled and cots emptied in the almost three weeks Lily had been there. But she hadn't wanted to think too much about where those children, babies many of them, had gone when they were no longer in the ICU.

She wished she hadn't asked about the baby from the next cot. Because now it had been confirmed: some babies didn't make it. Some of them died. And some went home – but were they better, or was their discharge just a hiatus until their next admission?

She wondered how the tall woman, who had never allowed her strong face to register even a flicker of emotion or her true thoughts, had coped with the death of her child.

She wondered how she would cope if her baby lost her battle to live.

She crossed her fingers and hoped she would never find out. She would do everything in her power to ensure her baby lived. Everything.

But what kind of life would Lily have? That was the question Gillian insisted on asking. Kerry tried to shut her mother's nagging doubts out of her mind. She swore to herself that Lily would have the best life she possibly could. No matter what.

Two weeks later, Lily Aarons-Patel aged one month and twelve days, went home with her delighted parents to meet her excited older brother.

Chapter 6

As they drove past the notorious Tembisa Hostel with its plethora of broken windows, the knot in Kerry's stomach tightened. It wasn't the ever-present pall of danger that hung over the squat, three-storey building that troubled her. She barely noticed the hostel anymore. In the almost three years she'd been living in Kempton Park, the hostel had become nothing more than a vague, nagging blight on the environment, no more or less noteworthy than the littered, dusty, treeless streets of the township that had been a designated a Black group area in the days of Apartheid. The township was less than a kilometre from her home, but it was only when there were reports of another armed robbery, another break-in, another car hijacking in the area that she noticed it and reminded herself to keep the front and back doors locked. And to be extra careful when going out. Everyone suspected that the culprits of the latest attack lived in the hostel, home to who knew how many desperate men, women and, some said, even children. No one was ever arrested for these crimes. No one expected any arrests to be made. The perpetrators would just disappear, probably into the bowels of the hostel – and the police dared not follow. So Kerry and Imran would join their neighbours in tut-tutting and bemoaning the level of crime in their area; and staring suspiciously at anyone who didn't look as if he (never she) belonged as he walked past their houses. There'd be regular calls for "something to be done"; and threats of vigilante action … and then life would go on, perhaps with a temporarily increased awareness and wariness of the next stranger begging at their gate.

"Nearly home," Imran said as the hostel disappeared behind them. In just three or four minutes they would draw up at their little house. She would carry Lily into her home, and place gently into her cot in the main bedroom.

And then, for the first time since her birth, Kerry would have to take care of her baby, her heart baby, on her own. Her stomach turned over.

"What if I can't manage?" she muttered to Imran, fear threatening to choke her "What if she gets sick and I don't know what to do? What if I get her medicines muddled? There are so many of them. What if ..."

"We'll be fine. You can do it. Look how well you have done since she was discharged from Sunninghill," he reassured her.

"But that was at my mom's house. Triphina was there to help me if something went wrong. Here, I'll be all alone, with Leo. You'll be at work and you'll have the car. What if something happens while you're at work?"

"Nothing has happened to Lily since she left hospital, and there's no reason to think anything will happen to her now. She is doing really well, you said so yourself."

Kerry nodded. Imran was right. Lily was doing well, all things considered. Her sats – which indicated the amount of oxygen in her blood – were still low. Dr Govender had explained that a normal baby's sats would be between 90 and 100 percent – usually closer to 100 percent. But Lily's were between 80 and 90 percent.

"Isn't that bad?" Kerry had asked.

"Her body will adjust to this level of saturation. What would be considered low for any other child, or adult, will be normal for her. As long as her sats remain above 80, she will be fine," he said.

Lily was even breastfeeding now, which was helping to increase Kerry's milk supply – and that could only be good. But she was so tiny. She still hadn't regained her birth weight.

Dr Sinclair, her paediatrician, had explained that heart babies like Lily would never be chubby. Almost all their energy was needed just to breathe and keep their little hearts beating. Even nursing on her mother's breast or drinking from a bottle was exhausting for her, so feeding her took far longer than it had with Leo. With frequent, short feeds the order of the day, Kerry was exhausted. Triphina – and even her mom when she was home – had been a huge help: even just taking care of Leo who, after all, was still just a baby himself had meant Kerry was able to snatch some welcome sleep whenever Lily didn't need her.

Kerry consoled herself that her perpetual state of exhaustion was worth it. Lily was getting stronger every day. Kerry was sure she'd soon be able to support her head; she wasn't nearly as floppy as she had been just a few days before. Anyway, Kerry reckoned, her mother was right: she couldn't expect her or Triphina to take on the burden and responsibility of caring for Lily, or Leo. Her mother had a life of her own as she frequently reminded her; and her health wasn't what it used to be either, as she reminded her too. And Triphina had other work to do. She, Kerry, was young and strong: it was time for her to step up and be the mother she was going to have to be.

"I've said it before and I'll say it again," Gillian had said as she'd watched Kerry pack up Lily's medicines while Imran waited in the lounge, making stilted conversation with her father who was pretending to watch a gardening show on the television. Stephen Aarons hated gardening.

Gillian continued her daily homily: "You have to deal with whatever life throws at you. You chose your path – now you must walk it."

Kerry was infuriated. "You sound as if you think what's happened to Lily is a punishment for marrying Imran!"

"Oh, don't be ridiculous," her mother said, her lips puckering as if she was sucking on a lemon. "Of course I'm not *blaming* you. But if you hadn't been so ..." Kerry stopped listening. Clearly, her mother would never forgive her for marrying Imran. Only threats from her brothers and the surprising insistence of her father had got Gillian Aarons to the Magistrate's Court for their wedding, where she'd barely smothered her sneer at Kerry's scanty bouquet and glowered at Imran throughout the short service. But at least she'd come. Imran's parents, and his brothers, had stayed away. They still didn't acknowledge her existence although Imran said his mother loved it when he took Leo to visit. At least *her* mother was reasonably civil – cold, but civil – to Imran.

Imran stopped the car in front of their house. Kerry drew in a deep breath and got out.

"Welcome home, Tiger," she said as she carried Lily through the front door. And smiled. Now even she was starting to use Imran's pet name for their daughter. Leo, having heard his father call his baby sister Tiger, had tried out the name too. But he'd soon reverted to La-la, which was far easier for a not-yet two-year-old to pronounce.

"Do you mind if I ask you something?"

The gynaecologist smiled. "Of course you may, Kerry-Anne. You can get dressed now. Everything seems to be just fine. Your uterus is almost back to normal, your caesarean scar has healed nicely. Do you want to know about contraception? You are breastfeeding, but that's no guarantee against conception and I shouldn't think you'd want another baby just yet."

Kerry suppressed a shudder. Lily was nearly eight weeks old. It was hard for any mother to cope with an eight-week-old baby, let alone one with a serious congenital heart defect whose health, whose very future, was so uncertain. She hadn't given contraception a thought.

"No, I mean yes, I mean no, that's not what I wanted to talk to you about, although I suppose I should. What I really wanted to ask you about is Lily."

The gynaecologist looked at her in surprise. "Lily? I don't know if I can tell you any more about her condition than what her cardiologist and paediatrician have already told you."

"No. I mean ... what I want to know is ... why was there no warning ... why wasn't I told ... I mean, surely something should have shown up in the ultrasound scans I had before she was born.

Shouldn't the scans have shown that there was something wrong with her heart? That she didn't have a proper tricuspid valve? That her one ventricle hadn't formed properly? Aren't there tests that could have been done?"

There. Finally, she had got up the courage to ask the other question that had been plaguing her since the day the cardiologist had told her about the problem with her baby's heart.

The gynaecologist nodded thoughtfully. Kerry fought to hide the anger that threatened to spill over.

"Kerry-Anne," she said gently, "while there are some very sophisticated scans and tests that can detect CHD in an unborn child, these are not done routinely for healthy young mothers who have no history of CHD in their families, or any other indications or risk factors for CHD."

"Yes, but ... so the scans I had wouldn't have shown anything?"

"That's correct."

"And you couldn't hear anything wrong when you listened to her heart?"

"All we could hear was her heart beating nicely and strongly. There was nothing to indicate that there was anything untoward. I'm so sorry."

"If ... if it had been ... I mean, if you had been able to see that something was wrong, couldn't something have been done?"

"As I said, Coronary Heart Defects like the one Lily has can be detected with special tests from about 20 weeks. But even then, there is nothing that can be done to repair the defect until after the baby is born."

"So why do the tests then? What's the point?"

"I suppose it's to give parents a choice."

"A choice?"

The gynaecologist paused again. "Well, yes. The parents can decide how they want to proceed; they may not want to continue with the pregnancy, they may want ..."

"You mean have an abortion? At 20 weeks?" Kerry was horrified.

"Well, some may choose to terminate the pregnancy, I suppose. But the tests would also enable them to prepare themselves for what is to come and allow for treatment to be instituted almost immediately following birth, instead of waiting for a diagnosis which could take days – sometimes even weeks, or not at all until it is too late."

Kerry's anger evaporated. There was nothing that could have been done. And she was glad, so glad she hadn't known. What would have been the point? There was no way she would have terminated her pregnancy. She wasn't religious, but ... no, it would never have been an option. It hadn't been with Leo and it certainly wouldn't have been with Lily. But because she hadn't known, or even suspected, that there was anything wrong with the baby girl growing so 'normally' in her uterus, she had been able to enjoy the exciting anticipation of her pregnancy, without a care in the world.

She would never, ever regret having given birth to Lily – heart defect and all. Yes, she was exhausting and demanding; yes, she required constant monitoring; and yes, she faced some huge hurdles along her road to what the cardiologist said could be a 'relatively normal' adulthood.

But Lily – Tiger Lily – as tiny and frail as she was, had already shown that she was a fighter, a feisty little heart warrior ready to take on every challenge thrust at her. And as her mother, Kerry had to do whatever it took for her daughter to live the happiest and most fulfilling life possible. There was no other option.

Chapter 7

"But she can't have it. That's the bad infection, isn't it?"

Kerry stared at the pulmonologist accusingly. How was this possible? They had been so careful. She'd been so careful. The doctors, the nurses, everyone had warned her how easily a heart baby could succumb to an upper respiratory tract infection. Even a little cold could make her really sick and require her to be hospitalised. So Kerry had told Sandy, her best friend, that while she'd love to see her, it was just too dangerous. Jade too had wanted to pop over, just to peek at the new baby. Kerry had heard the hurt in her voice when she'd turned her down too. Even Jason Brown had wanted to come over, using the pretext he'd some questions about the business to discuss with her now that his father was intent on retiring. Instead, he'd sent – or rather Browns had sent – an enormous bouquet of flowers for her, an even larger teddy bear for Lily, and a tip-truck for Leo. Her mother and father had also been refused access, despite Gillian's protestations that Kerry and Lily had, after all, lived with them after her discharge from hospital. As far as she was aware, Imran's parents hadn't wanted to come – or perhaps they had and Imran had turned them down too.

But it had been no use. Despite all their precautions. Despite everything, it had happened.

She listened, writhing in guilt as Dr Sibanda told her that her baby was really, really sick. And not just any old sickness – Lily had somehow caught the infection everyone had said she must not get. Kerry bit back tears of frustration, anger and despair. Had she become too complacent. Was it all her fault?

Should she have taken Lily to hospital sooner? She hadn't wanted to seem like a paranoid mother ... but who was she kidding? She *was* a paranoid mother. Any mother of a heart baby would be. And if people thought she was paranoid, well, she really shouldn't care. She should have done something as soon as she noticed that Lily's breathing had changed. She had become so attuned to her daughter's breathing that she'd heard the change, so slight, almost imperceptible, before the other symptoms emerged. She'd thought she might have been imagining it. She'd thought – she hadn't known what to think.

"I think there's something wrong with Lily," she'd said to Imran. He'd got up and looked at his baby intently. "Are you sure?"

"Listen to her breathing. It's ... I don't know ... sort of heavier than usual. And look at her face, around her nose and mouth. She's really blue, don't you think?"

"She's always blue," he said. "But if you think there's something wrong, then let's take her to the hospital."

"I don't know. Perhaps we should just watch her for a while."

So they watched. And waited. Lily snuffled, struggling to breathe through her clogged-up nose. She was also getting very warm – was she developing a fever? And then she coughed and coughed – a horrible, wet cough that sent a chill down Kerry's spine.

"Let's go," she said.

"We'll take her to that new Zamokhule Hospital in Tembisa. It's the closest," Imran said, trying unsuccessfully to hide his anxiety.

"No. Let's go to Sunninghill. They know her there."

With Leo safely ensconced at Mrs Reddy's across the road, they bundled Lily into the car and once again hit the long road to Sunninghill Hospital. When they'd driven Lily away from there, just one month before, Kerry hadn't dreamed they'd be returning so soon.

"I'm sure the car could probably find its own way there, by now," Imran joked as he turned onto the highway.

Kerry smiled. She didn't feel like smiling, but she appreciated her husband's efforts to lighten her mood despite his own concern.

❧ ❦

The doctor at Sunninghill Hospital's casualty department listened to Lily's chest with a frown.

"Given her history, you did the right thing, bringing her in," he said. "She's pretty congested, she clearly has a virus. I think it will be best if we admit her to the paediatric ward where we can keep an eye on her and ensure she doesn't dehydrate. She may also need a little oxygen, just to help her out until the virus works its way out of her body."

"Don't you think she should be admitted to the ICU?" Kerry asked, watching her two-month-old daughter's body shudder from the force of another barking coughing spell. "Oh no! Now she's vomiting!"

"It's just because of the coughing, poor little thing. She has a bad infection. We'll take some bloods so we can see exactly what's going on – and ensure she gets the right treatment. Just to be on the safe side, I've called Dr Sibanda. He's a pulmonologist – a lung specialist. He'll have a look at her and if he thinks it's necessary, he'll admit her to the ICU."

Kerry and Imran followed their baby to the paediatric ward. Despite the cute pictures of popular characters – Winnie the Pooh and Tigger and Eehore – the ward felt dull and gloomy. And hot. Lily was assigned a cot in a room with five other babies. A young nurse, armed with what seemed like a book of documents that had to be filled out – all part of the standard admission process, she explained – pulled blue curtains around Lily's cot and proceeded to ask a million questions about Lily's medical history. She checked Lily's vital signs: temperature (elevated), blood pressure (normal) and sats (low – way too low). They had gone through the same procedure in the casualty department, less than one hour before. Didn't hospital departments speak to each other, Kerry wondered, trying to hide her irritation and anxiety.

The nurse also stuck lots of electrodes onto Lily's heaving little chest and ankles, for an ECG. Lily squealed in protest, and then barked a long series of coughs that turned her blue-hued skin a shade darker. Kerry held her breath, waiting for Lily to vomit. She didn't.

"They must have her medical history on record. Why do we have to go through it all again?" Kerry whispered to Imran.

"Like the nurse said, it's all part of their process," he whispered back.

"Well, it's crazy."

It was a process they would get to know so well, too well.

They waited, watching their baby shudder through each awful coughing spasm. A ward nurse came over, watched as Kerry lifted the baby and patted her back, smiled and scurried off, presumably to attend to whoever was crying in one of the other rooms.

They waited. Another nurse came and checked Lily's drip. She smiled reassuringly at them and moved on to check on the child in the next cot.

"It's so stuffy in here. I'm going outside for some air," Imran said.

Kerry nodded. She waited. Imran returned.

"I think I need some air too," she said.

Outside, it was a warm late summer day. The sky was clear, with just a few white clouds. No threatening storm today. Kerry's feet, on autopilot, carried her back to the paediatric ward. If anything, the ward seemed even more stuffy than before. Imran was waiting. She waited with him.

Dr Sibanda arrived, bustling with productive efficiency.

"She has a bad infection, but she seems to be holding her own," the pulmonologist declared. "We should get the results back from the lab soon, and then we'll know exactly what we are dealing with."

"Shouldn't she be in the ICU?" Kerry demanded. In ICU, Lily would have her own dedicated nurse, who would watch her constantly, be there to ensure she didn't choke if the coughing caused her to vomit again. In ICU she'd be hooked up to monitors that would send out an immediate alarm should her condition change for the worse.

"If she deteriorates, we may have to move her. But right now, she's better off here – it's quieter, less stressful – and they aren't as strict about visiting hours so you can stay with her if you want," Dr Sibanda said.

Kerry forced herself to smile back.

⌒⌒

The next morning, Kerry and Imran sat next to Lily's cot in the paediatric ward. She was awake, and her big brown eyes were wide open. She was watching them with what was fast becoming her trademark expression – a slight frown of curious concentration.

"I think she's looking better," Imran said optimistically. A nurse told them she thought Lily had had a 'reasonable night', but she would have to check the night staff's notes to be sure.

"She's a fighter, our baby. I'm sure we'll be able to take her home soon. Leo misses her," Kerry said.

They waited, and watched. Lily coughed. Kerry lifted her and held her in her arms. She patted her back. The coughing subsided and Kerry put her down.

Dr Sibanda arrived.

"We have the results of Lily's blood tests," he said. "It seems she has RSV – the respiratory syncytial virus."

Kerry made no effort to hide her shock. Just yesterday, while they'd debated whether or not to bring Lily to the hospital, poor Imran had spent ages on the phone trying to get clarity from a call centre agent at their medical insurance company about why it had refused to pay for the first of Lily's anti-RSV injections, the one she'd had in the ICU a few days before she'd been discharged after her surgeries.

They had bumped into the cardiologist, Dr Govender, during a morning visit to the ICU, one of the rare occasions when his visit to Lily had coincided with theirs. Kerry had watched closely as he'd listened to Lily's heart and checked her charts. He'd agreed with their considered opinion that their baby daughter was making excellent progress. Kerry had been surprised to see flecks of grey in his dark hair – he certainly wasn't as young as she had originally thought all those weeks ago at the Parklane Clinic. Experience and knowledge, that's exactly what she wanted from the doctors to whom she was prepared to entrust her baby.

"Your little one is doing very nicely," Dr Govender had said. "I think we'll be able to discharge her soon."

Kerry's heart had soared, but before she could respond, the doctor continued: "However, before you take her home, I think we need to start her on a course of Synagis."

"What's that?" she'd asked

"It's to prevent her from getting RSV."

"What's RSV?" Kerry and Imran had chorused.

"RSV – Respiratory syncytial virus. It causes lung and upper respiratory tract infections. It's very common and for most of us, it's harmless, causing mild, cold-like symptoms. In fact, most children have had an RSV infection by the time they are two years old. There is no treatment for it, and it usually goes away on its own. However, for babies like your little one, RSV can be very serious. It can cause pneumonia or bronchiolitis. That's a type of bronchitis that affects the very small airways in the lungs. Sometimes, if the infection is really bad, a very young patient may need to be put on a ventilator. That's why we need to do everything we can to prevent your baby from getting it".

"How do we do that? With that Syn ... that medicine you mentioned," Kerry asked, thoroughly frightened.

"Synagis. Yes. But you must do other things as well which are also extremely important. You must maintain strict hygiene around her. For example, you must wash your hands with warm water and soap regularly, especially before you handle her. Keep her way from anyone with a cold. If you get a cold, wear a surgical mask. Don't allow anyone to smoke inside your house, or anywhere near her. All that will help. But Synagis is essential."

"Is it a vaccination?" Lily had already had one vaccination – against tuberculosis.

"You can't vaccinate against RSV in the same way you can against measles or chicken pox. But she needs a course of four

Synagis injections – we usually give one per month over four months, before the start of what we call 'flu season' in winter every year. That's what helps to prevent vulnerable young people like your little one, from getting the disease."

So before she had been discharged from the ICU, Lily had received her first shot of Synagis – the one the medical insurance company was now refusing to pay for. Her second was scheduled for next week.

"But she had the Synagis injection. How could she still get RSV?" Kerry glared at the pulmonologist.

"Unfortunately, one dose is not enough," Dr Sibanda said. "She must have all four to get enough of the infection-fighting antibodies she needs to avoid getting the infection."

"That's crazy. But now that she has RSV, does that mean she can't get it again? Once we get through this, will she be immune?"

"No. RSV is not like the measles and Synagis is not a vaccine. Unfortunately, getting RSV once does not make you immune. Your baby can get it again so she must still have the remaining injections. And next year, she must get the full course of injections again."

"The medical aid won't pay for it," Imran blurted. Kerry had been horrified when Imran had told her that the pharmacist had told him that a single dose of Synagis could cost between R12,000 and R22,000. She estimated that the cost of just the first year's four doses would be the equivalent of putting down a large deposit on a very, very nice house of their own; it would enable them to buy a good, small second car; or even pay for all Lily's – and Leo's – tuition at a very fancy private pre-primary school. They didn't have the money for any of those things. But Imran had agreed with her – they would find it somewhere, if the medical aid company didn't relent. There was no price too high for their precious daughter's health.

Dr Sibanda shook his head in disgust. "Medical Aids," he snorted. "Look, I'll write a letter of motivation to try and persuade them to pay."

Kerry, however, didn't care. Right now, all she wanted was for Lily to recover, so they could take her home.

Dr Sinclair, the paediatrician, came with Dr Govender to check on Lily. Kerry was happy to see her. She stood with her while Dr Govender listened to Lily's heart again; he rubbed some gel on her little scarred chest and put a dollop on the little wand-thing which he passed over her chest. He looked intently at the monitor on the echocardiogram heart ultrasound machine. He frowned.

Kerry held her breath. There couldn't be anything wrong ... could there?

"Hmmm," he said. His frown deepened and he passed the wand over Lily's chest again.

Kerry couldn't stop herself: "What is it?"

"It looks like your little one has developed cardiomyopathy."

Kerry gulped. She didn't want to ask anything more. She didn't want to hear any bad news. She fought the urge to grab Lily out of her cot and run.

"What's cardiomy ... what's that?" The words forced themselves out through her clenched teeth before she could swallow them.

"Her heart has enlarged. It is bigger than it should be."

"Why?"

"I'm not sure. Cardiomyopathy is unusual in a child with Tricuspid Atresia."

Cardiomyopathy – the word reverberated in Kerry's head. It sounded frightening.

"Is it dangerous?"

"Possibly," said Dr Sinclair.

"Not necessarily," Dr Govender said.

Kerry looked from one doctor to the other, confused.

"Why ... how did she get this cardio-thingy?" she demanded.

"It's probably a result of the infection," Dr Govender said. "Her heart should return to its normal size once she recovers."

"And if it doesn't?"

The doctor hesitated. "We'll cross that bridge when we come to it."

"And in the meantime?"

"We'll increase her medications, and then we'll keep an eye on it, Dr Sinclair and I. You shouldn't worry too much about it – it's probably just a temporary situation."

One week after her admission to Sunninghill Hospital with the RSV infection, Kerry and Imran took their baby home again. She was still coughing a little. But the doctors had all agreed that it was better for her to be at home where her mother could administer the only treatment she still required – lots of fluids, some oxygen occasionally to relieve the burden on her now enlarged heart, and regular nebulising. Keeping her in a busy hospital ward where all kinds of bugs were lurking, preparing to pounce on immune compromised babies like Lily, was far from ideal.

Kerry wished she shared their faith in her nursing abilities. What did she know about taking care of a sick baby, let alone one as sick as Lily? She was terrified. What if Lily started coughing so badly she couldn't breathe? What if she turned blue? What if the coughing got worse – how would she know when she was panicking unnecessarily, and when she really should get her to the hospital as quickly as possible? What if ... what if ...

Imran phoned the oxygen rental company. He called the medical aid. The medical aid would pay for an oxygen concentrator for their home. For three months. After that?

"She probably won't need oxygen after that," Imran said reassuringly.

Kerry prayed he was correct. She still wasn't sure that there was a god, but she prayed. She was praying a lot. She prayed that

Lily's heart would return to its normal size; she prayed that she would recover fully from the RSV infection and would get the remaining Synagis injections to ensure she didn't get the bug again; she prayed that she would continue to get stronger and undergo her second open heart surgery on schedule in four months' time. And she prayed that her baby girl would come through that with flying colours. She prayed.

Chapter 8

Kerry bit her lip and battled to suppress the giggle that threatened to defeat her efforts to keep her face composed. She tightened her hold on her squirming daughter as Lily screamed and fought, trying desperately to shake off the gas mask the anaesthetist was trying to hold over her nose and mouth.

"That's some little tiger you've got there," the awestruck anaesthetist said.

With Imran hovering at her shoulder, Kerry had carried Lily from the paediatric ward into the theatre, and the anaesthetist had explained that she could continue to hold her while he placed the mask over Lily's face for the few seconds it would take for her to fall asleep.

But it had been several long minutes, and five-and-a-half-month-old Lily was making her indignation at the treatment being meted out to her clear in no uncertain terms.

Suddenly the crying stopped and the baby went limp. A nurse took her from Kerry and placed her gently on the table.

"You can go now, Mrs Patel, Mr Patel. This won't take long. We'll have her back in the ICU before you know it," Dr Govender said.

Kerry and Imran walked the familiar corridors to the hospital restaurant. They ordered coffee, sat at their usual table at the back of the coffee shop and tried to focus on the cardiologist's reassurances.

"Catheterisation is a routine procedure," the cardiologist had assured them.

They knew that. It was just something that had to be done

to check the pressure in their baby's lungs. They were simply going to insert a probe of some sort into her groin, and somehow that would be able to tell if the pressure in her lungs was normal. High pressure in the lungs was an indication of pulmonary hypertension – a very dangerous condition. But it was unlikely Lily had PH – she was a heart warrior, not a PH baby. Kerry had seen a lot of posts about PH children and babies on Instagram. She had been in contact with a few of their mothers. None of their PH babies had heart defects like Lily. The cath procedure was just because Dr Govender was being extra cautious, that's all. It was part of the protocol for her upcoming second open heart surgery. It was routine, just routine ...

But it wasn't routine. Not for Kerry, nor Imran. Things could go wrong. Things went wrong all the time with routine procedures. Anything involving an anaesthetic carried a risk. That's why they made you sign indemnity forms, even for routine procedures. There had to be some risk – why else was Lily going to be admitted to ICU afterwards, and not taken back to the paediatric ward where they had prepped her for the procedure?

"The anaesthetist is right. Lily is a real little fighter," Imran said, oblivious to the fact that his coffee was getting colder and colder on the table next to his drumming fingers.

"A warrior – a heart warrior. A little tiger," Kerry agreed. She was proud of her daughter's fighting spirit – but sometimes, it was exhausting. Her routine check-ups at the paediatrician and cardiologist were always a battle of wills as Lily objected, loudly, to having ECG leads placed on her chest; she yelled when the pulse oxymeter was attached to her foot to measure her sats; and shrieked even louder when gel was applied to her chest for her echogram.

But then she'd light up the room with a beaming smile, her brown eyes sparkling, and let loose a booming chortle that would have everyone else in the vicinity laughing too, and Kerry's heart would melt.

But somehow, she never laughed for her grandparents. Perhaps it was because she hardly knew them. After Dr Sinclair has said it was probably a good idea to live as normal a life as possible and allow visitors into their home, Gillian and Stephen seldom came. Gillian said they lived too far away to just pop in and anyway, they never knew when Lily would be well enough for visitors, or when she'd be awake. Yet Lily shared her beaming smile and guffaws quite readily with Sandy and Paul when they came over, even though that wasn't very often. She'd also seemed to take to Jason Brown when he arrived unexpectedly one day baring more gifts for both children and news that his father had finally handed over the reins of the business to him.

"Are you sure I can't persuade you to come back to work, even on a part-time basis?" Jason had asked. His eyes – a beautiful shade of greeny blue, Kerry noticed – were twinkling and laughing at her.

Kerry had smiled and declined. She didn't have time for a job, even for a few hours a week. Perhaps later, when Lily was better, or at least a bit stronger.

It seemed Lily reserved her affection for strangers. Perhaps she intuitively picked up on the antagonism between her mother and grandmother. But she had afforded her grandfather a semi-smile, and Stephen's eyes had filled.

"I'm sure everything will be okay," Imran said, yet again.

Kerry nodded. Silence hung between them for what seemed like hours.

"Did you notice," Imran said a few minutes later, "Dr Govender seems to be worried about her weight. He keeps going on about it."

Kerry frowned, irritated that Imran had raised the subject now when there was so much else to worry about. But he had, and the guilt, the all too familiar guilt, welled up again, threatening to overwhelm her. She didn't know what to do. She was worried, so worried about Lily's weight. Dr Sinclair had also mentioned it. It wasn't as if she was oblivious to the fact that the scale remained stubbornly stuck on five kilograms every morning when she weighed Lily. She was trying everything she could think of to help her baby grow. And it wasn't as if Lily didn't eat. She was still being breastfed; and she also loved to hold her bottle and drink her top-up formula – usually finishing it all. And now she had started eating solids – gem squash, butternut, rice and her favourites: porridge and Marie biscuits. It should be making a difference. If anything, she should be getting quite fat the way she yelled for everything she saw Leo eating, even if she was still far too young for a toasted cheese sandwich. All this had to make a difference. It just had to.

But every time she changed Lily, and especially when she was having her bath, Kerry was confronted by the indisputable evidence that her baby was almost as tiny as a newborn. The tops of her little legs had none of that lovely chubbiness that Leo's had had. She was still wearing her birth-to-three-month clothing. But perhaps she was worrying for nothing. It wasn't as if she hadn't gained any weight at all. She had almost doubled her birth weight. And she was only five months old. And she'd been through so much. No baby should have to go through all that. And she was catching up on her milestones – even Sandy had commented on that just last week. Lily was holding her head beautifully; she loved tummy time; she could sit quite nicely if she was well propped up.

"Get a grip, get a grip," Kerry told herself. "It will be okay. It will all be okay."

"Lily is a fighter," she reassured Imran, and herself. "She will be just fine, you'll see."

Kerry's phone rang: Lily was back in the ICU. They jumped up, ignored the coffee that slopped out of their cups onto the table and hurried downstairs to the familiar doors of the cardiothoracic ICU where they had spent so many hours waiting for them to open at visiting time. This time they rang the bell and a nurse let them in.

Lily smiled at them groggily before closing her eyes again. Kerry heaved a sigh of relief.

Dr Govender arrived and gave Lily a cursory once over.

"She came through the cath very well," he said.

The weight that had been attached to Kerry's shoulders, and heart, for the past few days in the build-up to today's routine procedure disappeared. She mentally kicked herself for worrying unnecessarily. Dr Govender had been right – it had been routine. She had been worrying for nothing.

"However," the doctor continued, and the weight came crashing down again. "The pressure in your little one's lungs is a little high."

Kerry gripped the metal side of Lily's cot to keep her legs from crumpling. She looked at Imran. He was as white as a ghost.

"What? How ... why?" Kerry croaked.

"We don't need to worry too much about it now. But it would not be advisable to proceed with her second open heart surgery. Not until the pressure comes down a bit."

"Why not? What've her lungs got to do with her heart?"

"Because she has too much pressure in her lungs, there could be unnecessary complications if we go ahead with such a delicate operation. The pressure could force too much blood up into her brain, causing the brain to swell and at the same time depriving the rest of her body of much needed oxygenated blood."

"But she's supposed to have the surgery when she's six months old," Kerry objected. She was surprised at how steady her voice sounded – she was glad the doctor couldn't see how her legs were shaking. She'd been psyching herself up for Lily's next open-heart surgery since the day her daughter had opened her eyes after the first surgery. She had prepared for it. She was prepared for it. She felt like an Olympic athlete who had twisted an ankle during the opening ceremony.

"What will happen if she doesn't have the surgery now – if we have to wait? Won't that be even more dangerous?"

"Actually, your baby is holding her own quite nicely at the

moment, even though her cardiomyopathy – her heart enlargement – has not reversed yet. Strange that. Very strange. Anyway," Dr Govender continued hurriedly, "the bottom line is that there's no need to rush to proceed to the next surgery. Let's rather let her get a little stronger. You said she has started eating solids – that's good. Very good. If she eats nicely and all goes well, there's no reason why she shouldn't manage quite well with her heart as it is for a little longer."

Kerry nodded uncertainly. It sounded reasonable. Lily was doing well. Perhaps waiting a while would enable her not only to catch up on her milestones, but to consolidate them. She'd be so much stronger when she was cut open again that she'd come through it with flying colours.

Dr Govender interrupted her reassuring internal monologue.

"I also think it's a good idea to continue giving her some home oxygen – not all the time, of course. Her sats are satisfactory, but we need to watch them because they are on the borderline. She will manage fine if they don't drop below 80, and a little oxygen now and then will give her a boost."

"I spoke to the medical aid about keeping the oxygen concentrator – we had it for three months after her RSV infection, but they said she didn't qualify to have it any longer," Imran said.

The conversation with the medical aid's call centre agent over an extension for the oxygen concentrator had been long and heated and futile.

"Let's just leave it," Imran had said afterwards. "I'm so tired of fighting and fighting with them. I don't know how they think they know better than Lily's doctors what she needs, but they've agreed to pay for the RSV treatment so let's not push it. We could buy our own oxygen concentrator. Then if she ever needs it again, we'll have it for her."

Kerry had hoped they wouldn't need it. An oxygen concentrator was so expensive, and they really couldn't afford it. Especially now that her unemployment benefits had run out after her resignation from Browns. She'd told Jason that it just wasn't fair to him or the company to keep her job open. She couldn't expect him to wait when she had no idea when – if – she'd be able to get back to work. And the temp seemed to be doing well.

"I understand Kerry," he'd said. "But if you change your mind – if things improve … perhaps once Lily is on the mend … well, whenever you feel ready. You call me. There'll always be a job for you at Browns."

Kerry had ended the call – and sobbed. She knew she'd never go back. There was no going back to the life she'd had. Lily was her life now.

"Okay," Kerry sighed. "Let's find out about buying a concentrator."

What choice did they have? Anyway, it would be a comfort to know that it would be there, just in case.

"Should we take the oxygen?" Imran asked.

Kerry shook her head. She'd been thinking about it, ever since Jade had phoned her a few days before and suggested they all go to Warmbaths, where they had booked a chalet, for the weekend.

"You need a break, you really do," Jade had said. "And I'd like to get away for a relaxing weekend before the baby comes – and before I get too big to fit into a cozzie."

Kerry laughed. Jade's baby was due in February. It would be amazing – wonderful and amazing – if Jade's baby and Lily were to share a birthday. But before that, Lily would still have to have that second operation, the one that had been postponed. The Glenn Shunt procedure, Dr Govender had said it was called. It sounded complicated and dangerous and so many things could go wrong and … enough! Right now, Lily was well. She was doing fine. She was eating nicely. She was not sick. Her sleeping was improving – she wasn't sleeping through the night yet, but a lot of nine-month-old babies didn't sleep through the night yet either. And Leo, poor little Leo – he would love Warmbaths, and being able to swim and play with his dad all day.

She needed the break, Leo needed the break – and she and

Imran certainly needed time away, out of the house where they could just relax and be like any other couple.

"Okay," she'd told Jade, "Warmbaths sounds wonderful."

Now Imran was looking doubtfully at the pile of stuff that would have to be loaded into the car – suitcases and swimming towels and nappies, lots and lots of nappies for Lily and Leo, and food and meat, and charcoal for the braai, and hats and sunscreen and a big beach umbrella and folding chairs. "I don't think we have room for the concentrator too," he said.

"I don't think we'll need it. I haven't had to use it for weeks. She'll be fine," Kerry said happily. She could barely wait to get on the road, out of the little house; to have two-and-a-half days of adult company; to be able to giggle with a friend and talk about nothing; to swim a little; to just sit in the sun all day ... to just sit.

"Here, don't forget this, otherwise we'll have to come all the way back to fetch it," she said, handing Imran the insulated box into which she'd carefully placed all Lily's medications and two frozen dry ice blocks. That should keep them cool until they reached the holiday resort and could put them into the fridge in their chalet. Fortunately Warmbaths wasn't too far away – only about one hour north of Pretoria, less than two hours from Kempton Park, and a little more than an hour from Sunninghill Hospital. Close enough to go for a lovely, stress-free, weekend break.

The car ate up the kilometres as they sped along the N1 highway, through two toll gates. They followed the signposts directing them to Bela-Bela. The government might have given the popular resort town a new name, but the resort's name, emblazoned on the high white wall as they turned into the town, still stated 'Warmbaths', and in smaller letters: 'A Forever Resort'. The resort had been there forever – certainly for as long as Kerry could remember.

Watching Leo splashing about in the children's paddling pool with a host of children of varying shades – from deep chocolate to pale pinky-white, Kerry couldn't help but think how much Imran's parents had had to miss out on when they had been growing up. Unlike her parents, Imran's had not been permitted to set a foot inside the resort back then. It had been reserved for whites only. Things had changed though. When her parents had taken her and her brothers to Warmbaths, there had always been a sprinkling of children of darker hue, although her mother had tried to discourage her from playing with them. If she remembered correctly, it had been called Warmbaths Aventura back then.

She'd always loved it, especially the huge, outdoor pool which was heated by the bubbling mineral spring that gave Warmbaths – and Bela-Bela ('the pot that boils' in the local Tswana language) – its name. The pool was shaped like a flower, the centre of which was a high, rock-clad structure over the hot pool that was fed directly from the spring. Surrounding this were the petals – cooler open-air pools fed directly from the hot spring pool via gushing fountains.

There was nothing nicer than just wallowing in the pleasantly warm water of the outside pools, or swimming a few laps if she got up the energy, and stopping to let the cool water of the fountains pour over her head, refreshing her. Then she'd head back into the hotter, inner pool, where she could just lie back and relax. Some people found the inner pool too warm, but it was Lily's favourite.

Kerry moved her legs gently in the warm water. Alongside her, Jade lay back, holding Lily on her chest. The women chatted quietly. Lily didn't move.

"I think she's sleeping," Jade whispered.

"Why are you whispering?" Kerry whispered back.

"I don't want to wake her."

"She probably found our conversation really boring," Kerry giggled.

They chatted on quietly, while Lily slept. Imran and Jade's husband, Dean, arrived with Leo scampering along behind. They joined them in the warm water.

"Ily, Ily, me … ook meee!" Leo yelled, kicking his little feet as hard as he could.

"Shh, Lily's sleeping," Imran said.

Kerry got up reluctantly. "Sorry Jade, Dean. I think I should take her back to the chalet. She's had enough sun and swimming for one day," she said, cradling her wet, precious daughter. "We'll have to do this again – after your baby's born and Lily has recovered from her second surgery."

After the wonderful Warmbaths break, Kerry felt ready to tackle anything, even Lily's strenuous objection to her next routine cardiac check-up.

Dr Govender listened to her chest, examined her ECG; and scrutinised the echocardiogram scan of her heart. Kerry tried to read his expression, without success.

She was sure he'd be delighted at the progress her daughter had made. She certainly was.

"How is she doing?" he asked.

Kerry couldn't wait to tell him. "As you can see, she's sitting now. She started sitting on her own when she was seven months, but she was very wobbly. But look how nicely she is sitting now," she said proudly.

Dr Govender nodded and beamed. "That's very good."

"And she loves swimming. We've got a little plastic pool which we put in the yard – she really enjoys that. You should have seen how much she enjoyed the pools at Warmbaths too. She still isn't rolling or crawling but she's catching up. She's still so little ..."

"Yes, that's what I wanted to speak to you about. Is she eating well?"

"Oh yes! She loves her food. I'm still breastfeeding her and she loves her bottle as well. But she also loves her solids. She eats more than her brother, and he turned two three months ago, in July."

Kerry waited for the cardiologist to praise Lily, who was sitting bolt upright on the examination table with her legs stuck out in front of her like little matchsticks. She was listening intently, almost as if she understood every word.

He frowned. "She's not growing as well or as quickly as she should be," he said. "She has barely doubled her birth weight and she should have done that months ago. This is because of her condition – she needs more calories than the average child, and it is difficult for her to eat enough to keep up."

He must have seen the expression on her face because he hastened to add: "It's not your fault, Mrs Patel – it's no-one's fault. Failure to thrive is a difficult condition to manage, especially in CHD babies."

Kerry felt as if she had been sandbagged. Her cute, funny, clever, demanding baby who despite everything that had been thrown at her – her serious congenital heart defect, complicated and delicate open-heart surgery, a serious RSV lung infection, cardiomyopathy which was not reversing – now had another awful diagnosis to add to the list. Failure to thrive.

Chapter 9

Perhaps it was the diagnosis of 'Failure to Thrive', but suddenly Kerry found herself acutely aware that Lily was not doing as well as she had been. Or perhaps she hadn't been doing well at all. Perhaps she had just been seeing what she wanted to see, what she hoped and prayed was there. Or perhaps she had just been too harried, too tired to notice. She tried so hard to be sensible and level-headed, but once or twice she couldn't help it and the tears flowed.

"Mama? Mama?" little Leo said, taking her hand and staring at her face intently. "Mama crying?" His lip trembled and tears welled up in his dark eyes too.

"No, I've just got something in my eye," Kerry reassured her beautiful, sensitive little boy.

The next time she hadn't been able to check the tears, she'd shut herself in the bathroom, let it all out, and then hurried back to the madness that was her home before Leo noticed her distress; before she had to take care of Lily again – sit her up, lie her down, give her some water, or a Marie biscuit, prepare her bottle, or her food, change her nappy, bath her, feed her, prepare her medicines, give her some oxygen ... All the stuff any other mother of a helpless baby had to do, she told herself sternly. Of course, she also had to take care of Leo, poor little Leo who always had to wait until his mother could squeeze him in between this task for his sister or that for his father. And the next day, and the one after that, she would do it all again.

But other mothers also had to take care of a husband and two children under the age of three – and they managed, didn't they?

Was she a bad mother that instead of noticing that her baby was struggling, was failing to thrive, she counted the minutes until her ears, straining above the crying and chaos, would hear her husband's car stopping outside?

"Here, you take them," she'd tell Imran as he came through the front door, before collapsing in a heap on the couch.

But now she noticed. She noticed that Lily's breathing was getting more laboured by the day. She noticed that Lily was eating a little less; that she wanted to lie down more and sit up less; that she was slightly more blue, and needed an oxygen boost slightly more often.

"I don't think we can put off the second surgery for much longer," Dr Govender said when Kerry told him about her concerns. "It's already been postponed for longer than I would have liked. I was hoping that her cardiomyopathy would have reversed by now but as you can see, her heart now fills about 60% of her chest cavity." He indicated the scan of Lily's chest on the monitor in his examination room.

"She is also considerably smaller than we'd like but she clearly isn't going to get stronger without the surgery. At this stage, any further delay might just be counterproductive. However, before we make any final decisions, we'll have to check her lung pressure again."

"Another catheterisation?"

"Yes. As soon as possible. I'll make arrangements for you to come in early next week."

"What if the pressure hasn't come down?" Kerry asked.

"We'll cross that bridge when we come to it," the cardiologist said.

So at five o'clock that Friday morning, Kerry and Imran dropped a sleeping Leo off at Mrs Reddy's house across the road and once again headed north on the highway to Sunninghill Hospital.

At six o'clock, they checked Lily into the paediatric ward, patiently answered all the usual admission questions, watched the nurse measure her blood pressure and, as always whenever a nurse who didn't know Lily checked her saturation levels, stared in wide-eyed alarm at the oxymeter.

"This has to be wrong. I think I'd better check again. Her saturation is very low, very low," the nurse said.

Kerry's heart sank. Lily's sats were below 80. "There's no need to check. It's not a mistake," she reassured the nurse, wishing with all her heart that it was.

They waited. When the porter came to take Lily to the cath theatre, they went too. They put on blue theatre gowns and masks and Kerry sat in the chair next to the operating table, holding her daughter. The anaesthetist put the mask over Lily's face. Lily shrieked and fought – and then fell asleep. They left the theatre.

It was déjà vu, all over again – including the result.

"I'm afraid the pressure in her lungs is still too high for us to do the Glenn Shunt procedure," Dr Govender said when he came to the ICU later to check on her.

Kerry felt the blood drain from her brain. Her tongue wouldn't move. She opened her mouth, closed it, cleared the elephant from her throat and whispered: "So now what?"

Imran, as always, said nothing. He just watched, pale and grim.

"I'm going to adjust her meds. Hopefully that will help. We'll do another cath in a couple of weeks and take it from there."

"And what if the pressure doesn't go down? She can't carry on like this – her sats are dropping all the time."

"If things don't improve – and I'm hopeful that they will. But if they don't, there is another option. Instead of doing the Glenn Shunt procedure, we could do Blalock-Taussig shunts, or BT shunts. This would be only a temporary measure until she is well enough to have the Glenn Shunt – so it would mean another major surgery. I'd much prefer it if she didn't have to have an additional surgery."

Me too, Kerry thought.

"However, I'm hopeful the new medication regime will help get her pressures down enough for us to go straight to the Glenn Shunt. Take her home, give her oxygen whenever you think she needs it, and try to ensure she doesn't get an infection, any infection, at all; and we'll check her again in two weeks."

"It's not fair, it's just not fair. Our poor little Lily, poor Lily," Imran blurted when they reached the car. Kerry reached over and squeezed his hand.

"She'll be okay, you'll see. She always is. She'll fight through this as well."

Imran nodded.

"Would you like me to drive?" Kerry asked.

Imran shook his head and wiped his eyes. "No, it's okay. Just give me a couple of minutes."

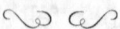

Two weeks later, they returned to the hospital for Lily's next, all-important catheterisation. This time, Kerry and Imran didn't bother with the pretence that this was just another routine procedure. They waited outside the theatre for Dr Govender to emerge. When he did, he didn't have to say a word: his face said it all – the new medication hadn't worked. The pressure in her lungs was still too high for the Glen Shunt procedure.

"However, we can't delay any longer. She is not getting enough oxygen and the longer we wait, the greater the risk of irreversible damage, including brain damage," Dr Govender said.

Kerry and Imran nodded. They knew that. They'd known that for months.

"The paediatric cardiothoracic surgeon will be along later to see you and explain exactly how the BT procedure works," the cardiologist continued.

"Oh good. I like Dr Patterson," Kerry said. She was looking forward to seeing him. He made her feel so safe.

"No, Dr Patterson is on leave until after the Christmas holidays. I've asked Dr Modau to take care of your little one. He's Dr Patterson's colleague – he's also very good."

Dr Modau came into the ICU to examine Lily. He was nothing like Dr Patterson: short, young, dark with close-cropped dark hair, quietly spoken, huge glasses.

Like Dr Patterson, he drew pictures to explain what he'd be

doing when he opened their baby's chest again.

"The reason we can't do the Glen Shunt is because today's cath showed that Lily has pulmonary hypertension and this is an absolute contraindication for the procedure as the blood has to flow without the force of the heart pumping, which is not possible with PH. Do you understand?"

Kerry nodded. Imran squeezed her hand, hard. She flinched.

"So we'll do a Blalock-Taussig or BT shunt. Don't be concerned," Dr Modau said, pushing his glasses back up his nose. "This procedure's been around for almost seventy years and it has saved the lives of many hundreds, even thousands, of babies with conditions like Tricuspid Atresia and other defects that result in a compromised left ventricle. Like the Glenn Shunt, the BT shunt helps to improve the flow of blood to the lungs. Unlike the Glenn, it's a closed heart procedure. We use a plastic tube to make a little detour of her heart blood vessels in a way that that will allow enough blood to go directly to her lungs, rather than into her heart, so that she can pick up more oxygen."

Kerry liked fact that they wouldn't actually be cutting into Lily heart. But there had to be a catch – why were the doctors reluctant to do it?

As if he'd heard her, Dr Modau continued: "The problem with the BT procedure is that it is only a temporary stop-gap – it will only work for a few months, and then the shunt will have to be replaced. There are also some potentially serious side effects. Blockages can form in the shunt, so Lily will have to take anticoagulants. There is also a risk of the tube becoming infected. Sometimes, there's excessive blood flow to the lungs which can result in a blood vessel being damaged and decreased flow of blood to the brain and the body."

"But there must be risks with the Glenn Shunt procedure too," Kerry said, desperate to convince herself that this BT surgery was not so much worse.

"Of course," Dr Modau said. "In the first place, the Glenn Shunt is an open-heart procedure – and there's always a risk attached to that. We put the patient on to a heart lung bypass machine while we connect the superior vena cava – that's the blood vessel that returns deoxygenated blood from the head and upper body to the lungs – so while we connect the superior vena cava to the right pulmonary artery. In this way, this blood can go directly to the lungs for oxygenation without going through the heart. Thus, the flow of blood to the lungs is increased, while the work the heart has to do is decreased. The Glenn Shunt is also a more permanent solution than the BT shunt."

"Are you saying that once Tiger – I mean Lily – has had a Glenn Shunt, it won't have to be repeated?" Kerry asked.

"It's unlikely."

"So if she could have the Glenn shunt surgery now, rather than the BT shunt, she wouldn't have to have another major surgery?"

"Well, she will still need to have a Fontan procedure to direct the deoxygenated blood from the lower part of her body directly to her lungs, but that will only be done when she is older and stronger. We usually do it when a child is three or four years old. However, you are correct. If she could have the Glenn Shunt now, that would probably be the only major surgery she should need until the Fontan procedure. With the BT shunt, she will have to have more surgery either to replace the shunt or to undergo the Glenn procedure, in four to six months."

"Is there no chance of her having the Glenn Shunt now? Are you sure?" Kerry asked anxiously. She really didn't want her baby to have to have more surgeries than was absolutely necessary.

Dr Modau shook his head. "Based on the readings from today's catheterisation, no. Take her home for the weekend, and when you bring her back on Monday and we take her to theatre, we'll check the pressure in her lungs again. You never know – things could change over the next two days," he said.

From the expression on his face, Kerry got the impression that he thought it highly unlikely.

As the surgeon walked away, Kerry stared at Imran. He was grinning.

"Doesn't he remind you of Steve Urkel from Family Matters?"

Kerry burst out laughing.

"We'd better be careful not to call him that to his face," he added, and Kerry laughed even harder. It wasn't that funny, but it felt so good to laugh. It had been such a long time since she'd laughed. She wanted to hug her husband – he'd always known how to make her laugh. It reminded her of why she'd fallen in love with him. But lately they never laughed together. Sometimes he seemed like a stranger. Sometimes, she felt so alone.

"Thank you," she mouthed at him over the top of Lily's cot.

"What for?"

"Just for being you."

He flushed. Kerry smiled. With so much on her mind lately, she'd almost forgotten how cute he used to be – how cute he still was, beard and all.

Chapter 10

How do you explain to a 10-month-old baby who is hungry and thirsty that she can't have anything – no porridge, no milk, no rice with a little chicken, no crisps, no ice cream, not even some water – because she is about to undergo a major four-to-five-hour operation? And how do you, as a mother, reconcile the fact that the surgery, the very dangerous and delicate surgery, could kill your child with the alternative – that without the surgery your child *will* die, maybe not today or tomorrow, but 'soon'?

Kerry had wrestled with these thoughts all night. They continued to plague her as she dressed for comfort in her de facto surgery day uniform – summer dress and leggings – pulled her hair up into a ponytail and moved like an automaton through the 'getting-ready-to-take-Lily-to-hospital' routine. She tried not to think of the what's, if's and maybe's as she sat on a plastic chair in the paediatric ward, rocking Lily in her arms.

"Shh, shh, shh," she whispered to the sobbing baby. "It won't be long now."

"Should I take her for a walk?" Imran asked. Kerry handed her over, and Imran walked up and down the corridor with the squirming baby in his arms.

"It's not helping," he said.

Kerry changed Lily's nappy, hoping that would make her more comfortable. Lily, however, was having none of it. She shrieked. It was hot and stuffy in the paediatric ward and she was sweaty and thirsty. The blood pressure monitor that covered her entire lower leg from knee to ankle was not helping matters. She pulled her pink dummy out of her mouth and cried. She was hungry. She couldn't understand why her mommy hadn't given her a bottle when she'd woken at 2 am. She'd cried and cried, but all she'd got was a cuddle. Then just as the sun began to lighten the eastern sky, she'd been strapped into her car seat and driven back to Sunninghill Hospital. They'd been instructed to have her there by 6 am at the latest. As soon as Kerry carried her through the foyer, along silent corridors and into the paediatric ward, Lily's whimpers metamorphosed into full-throated screams.

"She's starting to hate this place," Kerry had explained to the young nurse who was taking them through the laborious admissions process.

"Not to worry," the nurse said cheerfully. "She'll soon settle."

Kerry and Imran looked at each other and smiled. *She doesn't know Lily,* Kerry thought, half in admiration at her daughter's fighting obstinacy, half in impotent frustration at not being able to comfort her distressed, frightened baby.

Kerry was frightened too. She and Imran had spent the weekend picking over every aspect of Lily's situation. They'd dissected and analysed every word Dr Govender and Dr Modau had told them. Dr Sinclair had sent over some additional information she thought they might find helpful and reassuring. They'd googled 'Blalock-Taussig shunt' and 'Glenn Shunt', searching in vain for new academic articles, articles they hadn't read so often they virtually knew them by heart. They needed articles that would give them guaranteed reassurance that everything was going to be okay. They didn't find any. They'd played with Lily and held her so tightly, she'd squealed and tried to push them away. And they'd prayed – at least, Imran had, going through his now routine five daily prayers which seemed to have taken on an unprecedented depth of urgency in the past few months.

"They mean so much more now," he'd explained. He'd always said that he'd gone through the prayer rituals by rote when he was a teenager, hiding his disbelief and irritation from his father's critical eye. He'd stopped the day he'd no longer been obliged to live under his father's roof. But now he'd started again – and Kerry couldn't blame him. His older brother, Muhammed, had persuaded him to meet with Imam Omar, a young spiritual leader heading up an intimate mosque operating from a house on the edge of Tembisa. The Imam was really helping him deal with everything, he said. In some ways, Kerry wished she could get the same comfort from her faith, but she couldn't. She'd never had faith; her Jewish upbringing had been more ritualistic than spiritual – lighting candles on Friday night before going out to movies.

While Imran prostrated himself on his prayer mat and chanted incomprehensibly, Kerry found herself murmuring an unformed, silent liturgy of incoherent repetition: "please, please, please, please ..." to whichever unseen power was listening when she prepared Lily's bottle; when she changed her nappy; when she wiped her hands. She thanked all the nameless gods when she saw Lily giggle at something Leo said or did; or when she cuddled her soft Barney toy dragon; and as she slept – her little mouth slightly agape and tinged with a dark shadow of blue.

Last night, after Lily had fallen asleep in her little camp cot in their bedroom, Kerry and Imran had stood and watched over her, unable to sleep themselves – and knowing they should because they knew tomorrow (now today) was going to be a long, long day.

It was only 7am. It felt like 7pm. The ward sister didn't know exactly when Lily would be taken to theatre. "It shouldn't be too long," she said. Lily's sobs subsided and she started to drift off. Kerry exhaled a sigh of relief and stiffened in anxious irritation as a nurse bustled in, armed with a baby bath half filled with warm water.

"We have to wash her in antiseptic soap to prepare her for surgery," she explained. Lily shrieked.

After the bath, Kerry rocked and soothed her until she drifted off again. She placed her gently on the cot and held her breath. Lily slept.

A nurse rustled past, stopped and turned back. "We have to keep the cot sides raised," she said. She rattled the metal bars into place. Lily shrieked and shrieked.

A dumpy doctor with floppy brown hair stopped at the cot. The anaesthetist. She asked a few questions: when last had Lily had something to eat and drink (too long ago); had she ever had an adverse reaction to an anaesthetic (no); how many anaesthetics had she had (two for open heart surgery and two for catheterisations); did they have any questions (yes, can you guarantee you will return my child to me, alive)?

Kerry shook her head. No questions.

"Well, see you in theatre soon," she said cheerfully, brushing her hair back out of her eyes.

They waited.

"It's so hot in here, I'm going outside for some air. Call me if they come for her," Imran said.

He returned a short while later and took over the vigil at their exhausted baby's side. Kerry's feet navigated to the hospital's front entrance. The sky was a bright, deep blue. There was a slight breeze. It was going to be another scorching day, but right now, it was still pleasantly fresh. Her feet returned her to the overheated, stuffy ward. She took up her post next to Lily's cot.

They waited. Lily whimpered but didn't wake. The ward felt like a furnace.

A porter arrived. Kerry blinked at him. "Shh," she whispered. "She's sleeping."

He took hold of the cot and started to push it towards the door. Lily woke with a shriek which quickly transformed into heart wrenching sobs.

"Wait!" Kerry insisted. The porter stopped. Kerry clambered over the rails of the cot and sat, cross-legged on the mattress. She gathered her baby into her arms. The porter shrugged and resumed pushing the cot. Imran walked alongside. Kerry bent her head over her baby and murmured soothing nothings.

"People are looking at you," Imran whispered.

"I don't care," she responded, rocking to and fro, to and fro.

Lily's distressed wails were dissipating into intermittent gulps and sobs. "I really don't care."

"Clever Mom," said a theatre sister approvingly as Kerry clambered back out of the cot. She handed her a theatre gown and mask. "You hold on to your little one until the anaesthetist has put her under."

True to form, Lily had no intention of succumbing to the anaesthetic procedure without a very noisy fight. Once again, Kerry felt a frisson of pride at the sight and sound of her daughter's spirited refusal to accept what the gowned, masked grown-ups were doing to her. She might be a tiny scrap of humanity, weighing in at less than most babies half her age, but she had the figuratively big heart of a true warrior. It was just a pity that her literal extra-large heart was a hinderance, not a help, to her survival.

As they had done almost 10 months before, Kerry and Imran prowled the shops of the bustling Woodmead shopping precinct, now garnished with garish Christmas trees, silvery faux snow, cherubs and reindeer. Sweating Santas exuding forced bonhomie to the jaunty strains of Boney M. They found a table in the air-conditioned coolth of a little coffee shop and ordered lunch. Kerry didn't think she'd be able to eat, but when the Chef's Special arrived – a salad of crisp lettuce, tomato, cucumber, sprouts, fried haloumi instead of chicken, and fried croutons smothered in a creamy dressing – she wolfed it down. They ate in silence. Occasionally they spoke, about this and that. Mostly they rehashed the same arguments they'd analysed incessantly: had they made the right decision, agreeing to do the BT shunt now, instead of hanging on for a month or two when perhaps, maybe, possibly, they might have been able to do the Glenn procedure? They hadn't really had a choice – had they? They had already waited almost too long for today's surgery – hadn't they? It would not have been in Lily's best interest to wait – would it? What if they had made a dreadful, fatal mistake? What if the doctors were wrong? What if …

Kerry wondered how long it would take Lily to recover; together she and Imran speculated about a potential date for her next and final surgery. They wondered whether there would be another thunderstorm later, and if it would bring hail.

"At least there won't be any traffic when we drive home," Imran said.

Kerry nodded. In the past couple of weeks, Johannesburg's highways and byways had transformed from terminally clogged traffic arterials into free-flowing, uncongested rivers of potholed macadam now that most businesses had closed for the festive season. The city's burgeoning population had left in droves – the poor to their customary family homes in the rural areas; political and economic refugees to their home countries in the north; the richer to holiday accommodation at the coast; and the wealthy to exotic locations overseas – or Cape Town. Those remaining swarmed into thc city's many malls and marts, in search of the perfect gift or unneeded bargain on which to dissipate their Christmas bonus.

"The hospital seems pretty quiet too. You'd almost think people don't get sick at Christmas time," she said.

"I hope that means more attention for Lily."

"She'll be in ICU for a while. She'll have her own nurse. I wonder who it will be?"

They paid for their meal and returned to the heat outside. They walked on.

Imran's phone rang. Lily was out of theatre. They rushed to the car and raced back to the hospital – and slumped down on two plastic chairs in the cardiothoracic ICU waiting room where they had spent so many hours in the past.

"We should have remembered that it would be a while before she's back in ICU and we'll be able to see her," Kerry said.

"I don't know about you, but I'm having trouble remembering my own name today," Imran said.

They waited. Kerry looked across the empty room. The last time they had waited for admittance to the ICU after Lily's first open heart surgery, the chair on the far side had been occupied by that tall, dignified woman with her bible and her inscrutable, handsome face. Kerry wondered, fleetingly, how she was getting on ... how she had managed ... if she had managed to survive the death of her baby. She mentally shook her head.

Happy thoughts, Kerry. Think only positive, happy thoughts, she admonished herself.

Imran's phone rang. They could go and see Lily now.

Imran clasped her hand as they walked quickly down the long corridor, turned the corner and continued on through the first set of doors. They came to the second door with the glass panel. They pushed it open, walked into the ICU and stopped. They looked around. They couldn't see their daughter.

"There she is," said a nurse, indicating the cot directly opposite the door.

They stared. Kerry swallowed. Beside her, Imran paled.

Chapter 11

"Okay, Kerry," she said to herself. "You can do this. Just walk over there and see exactly what is going on. It can't be as bad as it looks from here."

She forced her legs to carry her across the ICU to Lily's cot. She could sense Imran walking next to her. She kept her eyes fixed on the cot. She stopped and grasped the cold metal cot side. She took a deep breath. She looked. She made a mental list of what her eyes were seeing.

Machines, lots of machines, blinking and beeping.

A nurse fiddling with one of the machines.

A naked baby girl.

A shock of thick black hair. Lily had thick black hair.

A round little face barely visible beneath thick white tapes holding a fat tube in place in her mouth. That meant the baby had been intubated and was breathing with the aid of a ventilator.

Bruised-looking eyes, closed.

"I'm ... I'm going outside for some air," Imran said.

Kerry nodded vaguely and continued her itemised examination.

Limp arms. Little hands tied to the cot's sides.

A large, bloodstained dressing stretching from vulnerable little throat to belly button.

A blood machine circulating the baby's blood outside her body, just like the baby son of that dignified woman with the bible. That baby had died.

Stitches. Lots of black stitches. Everywhere.

Kerry looked up. Her eyes took in Imran through the glass panel on the ICU door. His eyes were closed. His face was twisted in silent agony. She returned her gaze to the baby.

Catheter draining urine from the bladder.

Drips, feeding medication into the baby's neck.

Drains, lots of drains, blood-filled drains. Coming out of her tummy and her chest. Draining fluid from somewhere.

So much blood. Why so much blood?

"How is she?" Kerry heard a voice whisper. Had she spoken? Her throat was parched. Her tongue was thick.

"She's just come out of theatre. She's holding her own," the nurse said.

Kerry nodded. She returned to her examination of the almost lifeless body. It looked like a prop from a horror movie – a damaged doll, disfigured and tortured by a sadistic Chucky-child.

A thought squeezed into her frozen consciousness. That was her baby lying there. Her Lily. She turned and strode across the ICU. She pushed open the glass panel door. She walked towards her husband. She began to shake uncontrollably.

"My baby! My baby!" she screamed.

Imran caught her as she fell. Tears were streaming down his face.

Sandy, Jade, Paul, Eliot and Josh – Josh who never entered a hospital – came down the corridor towards the ICU. They watched in horrified silence as Kerry and Imran rocked together in a slow shuffle of anguish, Kerry wailing incoherently, inconsolably.

"What is it? What's happened," Eliot asked as his younger sister's wails shuddered into hiccupping sobs.

"Lily – is she ...," Sandy's voice faded. Josh stood stiffy, silently, poised to take off back down the corridor if Kerry started howling again. Paul and Jade looked intently at an invisible mark on the wall above Kerry's head.

"It's okay. It's just that she's ... it was such a shock seeing her like that. It's just ... it's awful. It's horrible. There's all these tubes and blood and the respirator and ... and she looks, she looks ..." Kerry couldn't continue.

Imran pulled her close again. "She looks terrible. I ... I couldn't bear to see her like that. You have no idea ..."

They all stood there in the corridor, in a huddle of friendship and love ... and terror.

"Let's get out of here," Imran said after a while.

Josh gratefully led the subdued little troop upstairs, through the foyer and out into the still bright sunshine. They sat on the hospital's front steps.

"Yo – you're still a noisy cry baby, aren't you," Eliot teased. "You should have seen her when she was a kid. We just had to look at her sideways, Neville and me, and she'd start howling."

Kerry giggled. It wasn't true, of course. Eliot and Neville had been pretty kind to her when they were growing up, all things considered. When they hadn't been ignoring her.

"Yeah, and I remember that time when Imran ..." Sandy chimed in, quickly taking up the task of trying to distract her friends, trying to make them laugh a little, before they'd have to go back and face the sight that no parent should ever have to see.

Kerry was grateful for their efforts. She hated the fact that she'd allowed her emotions to get the better of her in public; it was awful that all her friends, let alone her brother, had seen her in such a state. She'd worked so hard at presenting a façade of calm control to outsiders – doctors, nurses, friends, family ... even Imran. Because Imran had so much to worry about. Kerry could see. He never let spoke about just how worried he was about Lily, about their ever-mounting medical bills, about how difficult it was to get new contracts, about how much he was hurting. But Kerry knew. She understood because she felt the same. She wished he'd talk to her. She wished ... But she knew she'd get through this. They'd get through this. What choice did they have?

"Don't you dare tell Mom about my little performance in there," she hissed at Eliot. "Promise me you won't tell – it was just the shock. It won't happen again."

"Okay," he said, rather doubtfully. "But hell, you scared me Kerry. I thought ... when we came down that corridor and heard you screaming and crying like that, I honestly thought it was over."

"Me too," Paul said.

"If I hadn't been behind him, I swear Josh would have run away," Sandy giggled. "He always was a baby."

"Ha, you're a good one to talk. You wouldn't have even walked into the hospital if I hadn't gone first," he assured his sister.

They bickered gently; they teased each other; they cracked weak jokes and laughed. And then Kerry and Imran couldn't put it off any longer. They had to go back to the ICU, to their daughter, and face what they had to face.

Lily hadn't moved. The machines were still beeping. Her blood was still circulating outside her body where, the nurse explained, it was being cleaned and oxygenated before being sent back into her body. The drips, the catheter, the blood-filled drains, the respirator – it was all as it had been. Kerry and Imran sat down on either side of the cot. They watched their daughter's little chest rise and fall, rise and fall. She was alive – and they were grateful.

"It's good news," Dr Modau said, when he arrived to examine his young patient. "We checked her lung pressure in theatre this morning as I said we would, and the pressure had reduced sufficiently for us to do the Glenn Shunt."

Kerry stared at him, trying to make sense of what he was saying.

"So, you didn't do the BT shunt?" she finally managed to stammer.

"That's right, we didn't have to," the surgeon smiled.

"And she won't have to have another open-heart surgery? Well, not until she's three or four?"

"Probably not. And with the procedure today, we have actually gone a little further towards preparing her for the next surgery. Basically, we shaved back the septum between her two atria so that now she effectively has only one atrium and one ventricle. With the Glenn Shunt in place as well, that will be all she'll need for the next few years. Then, once she has had the Fontan procedure – that's the next big surgery – no deoxygenated blood will reach her heart at all. It will all go directly to her lungs. That's why she doesn't need two atria and two ventricles. At the moment, the deoxygenated blood from her lower limbs is still getting to her heart and mixing with the oxygenated blood there. But we are making good progress. Lily tolerated the surgery well. She's a strong little girl. She's a real little fighter."

The massive rock that had been sitting on Kerry's chest for the past few days shifted. Slightly. But thrilled as she was about the fact that the doctors had decided to move directly to the Glenn Shunt and not risk the interim BT Shunt, Kerry wasn't about to celebrate just yet. Lily still had a mountain to climb before she'd be out of the woods. However, mixed metaphors aside, she felt a whole lot better.

That night, Kerry slept more soundly than she had in weeks.

Chapter 12

The first thing Kerry heard that morning as she entered the ICU was a sound she'd recognise anywhere: Lily crying. Her heart soared. If her daughter had her voice back, it meant the ventilator tubes had been taken out of her throat. Hopefully for good. It had been such a battle to 'wean' her off it. They'd tried a few times, but they'd had to reconnect her to the machine as she'd quickly turned blue.

"Don't worry too much," the nurse who had been assigned to take care of Lily that day tried to console her after yet another attempt had failed. Because of the festive season, many of the hospital's permanent staff were away, with temporary agency nurses filling in. Kerry had never seen this nurse before.

"They tend to get a little lazy about breathing on their own when they've been on a ventilator. She'll come off the ventilator when she's good and ready."

"And if she doesn't? What then?" Kerry had almost asked, but hadn't, because she didn't want to know the answer.

Now she hurried over to Lily's cot. The baby was lying on her side, in a foetal position and yes, the ventilator was gone. The frightening blood circulation machine, and the blood transfusion drips, and the drains, and the catheter had also been removed. And her little hands were free, no longer tied to the cot sides as there were no more tubes for her to pull out.

The crying had stopped. Perhaps it hadn't been Lily after all. Perhaps it had just been Kerry's wishful imagination. It could have been any one of the more than a dozen babies in the cardiothoracic ICU.

Kerry sat down next to the cot and examined her daughter's face – what she could see of it under the plasters holding the tubes from high-flow oxygen machine in place in her poor little bruised and battered nose. Kerry checked the machine. It was delivering 12 litres of oxygen per second.

She waited. And watched. On the other side of the cot, Imran did the same. The nurse – another that Kerry didn't recognise – bustled about, checking the beeping machines, doing this and that. She smiled reassuringly at Kerry.

"Your little girl is a fighter," she said.

Kerry nodded and smiled automatically. She knew that.

"I'm sure she'll start to wake up soon, and with the new ointment we're applying, the little pressure sore should start to heal nicely too. I really wouldn't worry ..."

"What did you say?" Kerry demanded.

"I said she should start to wake up soon," the nurse replied, clearly taken aback at the vehemence of Kerry's tone.

"No, you said Lily has a pressure sore. What pressure sore? She doesn't have a pressure sore! You must be confusing her with another patient."

"I'm sorry. I thought you knew. It was one of the first things I noticed when I came on duty and checked her chart – that's when I saw that new ointment had been ordered. It was sent up from the pharmacy this morning and I applied it when I changed her nappy."

"I want to see it," Kerry said.

The nurse nodded. She removed Lily's nappy, turned her slightly and pointed to a small, circular, black mark on her lower back, just above her coccyx.

"How did that happen? I thought she was supposed to be turned regularly, and rubbed, so that she wouldn't get a pressure sore." Kerry battled to keep her voice steady. She was furious. As if her baby didn't have enough to contend with, as if she wasn't in enough pain ... now this.

"I don't know," the nurse said. "I've never nursed her before but it should be in her chart."

Together, Kerry and the nurse poured over the large chart at the foot of Lily's cot – one page for every day since her admission to the ICU following her surgery. Each page recorded every detail of Lily's condition and treatment: her blood pressure, sats, fluid intake and output, medications. There were scrawled comments and instructions from the doctors, neater entries from the nurses ... and on every page, there was a reference, sometimes two or more, to a pressure sore.

"It looks like she's had the pressure sore for a while," the nurse said.

"Well she didn't have it before she went to theatre. I know. I changed her," Kerry said. "Could she have got it during the operation? Is that possible?"

The nurse shrugged. "I don't know. I suppose it might be. Anyway, we're doing all we can to ensure it heals quickly. It might also help if you get her a pressure sore cushion. They have a little hole in them to take pressure off the sore – you can probably get one at the pharmacy."

"I'll go look for one," Imran said.

Kerry tried to smile her thanks at him but she couldn't. She was too angry and upset – angry that someone, somehow had allowed Lily to develop a pressure sore; furious that she had not been told about it for days; and aching inside because once again, she had not been able to prevent her baby from suffering even more pain – and this time from something that should have been entirely preventable.

Kerry's heart leaped. Lily's eyes had flickered. Briefly. She hadn't imagined it. There! It happened again. And then Lily's eyes opened.

"Hello Tiger," Kerry whispered. "Welcome back."

Lily's big brown eyes closed again. Imran returned from the pharmacy empty-handed. They didn't have a pressure sore pillow for a baby. They'd suggested he try a bigger pharmacy, or a company that sold medical equipment. But that didn't matter now. Lily had opened her eyes. Imran smiled at her and she smiled back. One of the first nurses who had cared for Lily after her admission to the ICU had explained that she would be weaned off the sedation medications really slowly. Every day, Kerry had noticed that the long list of medications that had been kept next to her bed was not as long as it had been. And now she was finally starting to wake up. That was good.

She stroked Lily's little chest, taking care not to touch the big wound dressing which, thankfully, had been changed and was no longer blood stained. Her baby was burning with fever.

"It's not unusual for a baby to run a bit of a temperature after surgery. We're giving her medication for it, so it should hopefully break soon. The good news is that she's been able to take some formula orally. She's doing really well," the nurse said.

"When can I hold her?"

"Soon," the nurse replied.

Kerry shrugged. It was always the same. At every visit – in the morning, and again in the evening – she'd ask Lily's latest nurse about her progress. And the nurse would always say something reassuring about how well she was doing ... but Kerry could see that although Lily was making progress, it was slow, very slow. Her eyes would stay open for longer; sometimes she'd cry. But she still had a fever. She still wasn't conscious, not really. She was barely drinking anything from her bottle.

On Christmas day, almost two weeks after her open-heart surgery, that all changed. Lily's eyes opened and stayed open. And she looked around. She focused on Kerry's face.

"Mama," she said.

If Jewish-born Kerry and Muslim-born Imran had celebrated the Christian festival of Christmas, this would have been the best Christmas present they could have hoped for.

"Why have you propped Lily up so much?" Kerry asked the new nurse who was doing the New Year's Day night shift.

"We're hoping this will help to control her reflux. She's been throwing up after eating."

"She's always vomited a little after a feed," Kerry informed her.

"Unfortunately, she is throwing up quite a lot. We are worried that she's not keeping down as much as she needs. It's not just her milk, also sometimes her food."

"Maybe it will help to burp her before you put her down."

The nurse smiled condescendingly. "We're doing that. But keeping her as upright as possible should also help."

But it didn't. Her reflux medication was increased.

Kerry noticed that the oxygen flow from the high-pressure machine had been reduced again, but not enough. Not enough to get her onto ordinary cannulas. When they tried, her sats dropped alarmingly.

"It can take a while for these babies to get used to being off the ventilator – it kinda makes them a little lazy as the ventilator does all the hard breathing work for them," another nurse reassured her.

Kerry tried not to worry. It was only a little more than two weeks since the open-heart surgery. They had to give Lily more time. She just needed a little longer. Like Nala's baby sister.

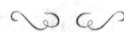

Leo had looked suspiciously at the little girl who was sitting on one of the chairs in the ICU waiting room, kicking her legs back and forth.

"Hello," Kerry had said. "Are you waiting for your mommy?"

"Yes," said the child. "She's gone to see my little sister. My mommy told me she's getting better."

"That's wonderful. What's your name?"

"Nala – like in the Lion King," said the child.

"What a pretty name. This is Leo. Would you like to play with him while we go and visit his little sister?"

"Okay. I'm nearly five so I can look after him."

Kerry smiled at the bubbly, confident little girl. "Leo is two-and-a-half, and I'm sure you can."

The first time Kerry and Imran had taken Leo with them on one of their hospital visits, they'd worried about having to leave him alone in the ICU waiting room while they went into the unit itself to see Lily. But what choice did they have? They couldn't keep farming him out to whoever would or could take him, twice a day, every day, for weeks on end. Other ICU parents were also forced to leave young siblings alone in there. It was quite safe. The waiting room was almost inside the ICU itself, behind the first set of locked doors.

When visiting hour ended, Kerry returned to the waiting room to collect Leo who was sitting on the floor with Nala. Kerry thanked the little girl for taking such good care of her son.

"She's had to grow up very quickly," said the child's mother, a beautiful Somali-looking woman.

They all do, Kerry thought. All children with special needs siblings have to grow up long before they should. Look at little Leo, not even three and he was used to sitting alone in hospital waiting rooms, falling asleep on the waiting room chairs, being shunted between neighbours and family members, having promised outings cancelled because the sibling was in hospital again, or wasn't well enough to go out and couldn't be left with anyone else.

She swallowed the familiar surge of guilt that threatened to choke her and touched the silky curls that framed the little girl's dark, elfin face.

"She seems very comfortable, waiting here," Kerry said.

"She should be. We've been coming here virtually every day for almost three months."

"Three months! All that time in ICU?"

"Yes. It's been a long battle."

"And you've been coming every day?"

"Well yes, most days."

The woman looked at her husband and raised an eyebrow, as if asking him something. He nodded. The woman continued: "But there was a time – a couple of months ago – when we didn't come for a week. A whole week."

Kerry wanted so badly to ask why, but she didn't want to pry. ICU etiquette.

"Our baby was bad, really bad, and she was getting worse," the woman said. "The doctors said she wasn't going to make it. They gave me permission to stay with her all the time. They said I should stay with her, spend as much time with her as I could. While I could. But I didn't. I stayed away."

Kerry looked at Imran who was clearly as shocked as she was. How could a mother stay away from her sick child? How could she choose to stay away? How could she bear it?

"I felt so helpless. I couldn't just sit there and watch my baby struggling to live, battling not to die as the doctors said she would."

Kerry nodded uncertainly. She couldn't imagine what that would be like. She hoped she'd never have to find out

"What happened?" Imran asked.

"Well, we stayed away and we prayed. We prayed and prayed. For a whole week. And every day, I was waiting for the call from the hospital to say it was over. And I prayed that the call would never come. It was the hardest thing we'd ever done, my husband and I. But it was something we had to do."

"Did she ... I mean, has she ... will she ..." Kerry couldn't frame the question she desperately wanted to ask.

"She's much better. So much better. We stayed away, and when we returned, she started to improve. Hopefully we'll be able to take her home soon. Come Nala, it's time to go. Say goodbye to your little friend."

The little girl hugged Leo. "Bye Leo," she said.

"Mrs Patel, Mr Patel good morning. I'm glad I ran into you. I was going to call you," Dr Govender, the cardiologist, said just as Kerry and Imran tore themselves away from their wailing daughter, girding themselves to walk off briskly without looking back, at the end of the visiting hour. They knew they'd hear her distress all the way down the corridor. They'd debated taking it in turns – one to stay with Lily while the other left. Then only one of them would have to hear the heartbreaking cries as their baby tried to keep her remaining parent from deserting her as well.

"Good morning doctor. I was going to call you too."

Kerry was worried. Lily was still on the high-flow oxygen machine and the nurse had said she was still vomiting after every feed. And her pressure sore didn't seem to be getting better even though they'd called in a plastic surgeon who'd simply prescribed yet another type of ointment. In fact, she didn't seem to be making any real progress at all and the nurse couldn't explain what was going on.

"Unfortunately, we seem to have experienced another little set back," Dr Govender said. "It's not too serious, but it must be attended to as soon as possible. Let's talk in here." He indicated the now empty ICU waiting room.

Kerry desperately wanted to stand straight and strong while the cardiologist explained exactly what this latest 'little setback' was, but her legs would no longer support her. She sank down onto the nearest chair. Imran gripped her shoulder.

"We aren't happy with her breathing. It seems to be deteriorating. We thought she might have got another infection, although her fever has subsided. We did some blood tests, just to be sure."

Kerry wanted to cry. Not another infection! Lily wasn't strong enough after her surgery to fight off yet another infection.

"However, the tests show that there is no infection."

"So what's the problem?" Kerry asked, not sure whether to feel relieved that Lily didn't have an infection or concerned that it was something even more serious.

"We took an x-ray of your little one's chest earlier this morning and it seems her left lung has collapsed."

Chapter 13

Lily's lung had collapsed!

"When? How did that happen? Why?" Kerry asked, fighting to keep her voice steady. Imran's fingers were digging painfully into her shoulder but she welcomed the discomfort. It stopped her from screaming her anguish.

"Fortunately, it's not her whole lung – just the lower lobe," Dr Govender said. "As for why it happened, I'm afraid I can't answer that. Her diaphragm is not working as it should and this could be preventing her lung from expanding fully. There is also the problem, of course, that her heart is still very enlarged, and that is also putting pressure on her lung."

"What can we do about it?"

"The cardiomyopathy – the enlarged heart? She is on medication for that and we're still hopeful that it will reverse."

"Is it reversing? Is her heart starting to return to normal?" she asked hopefully.

"Unfortunately not. If anything, her heart seems to have enlarged a little more since her surgery."

Kerry winced as Imran's fingers dug deeper into her shoulder. She squeezed his hand, and the painful grip turned into a comforting pressure.

"But right now, however, our concern is the collapsed lung," Dr Govender continued.

He quickly drew a diagram and explained how the diaphragm, a dome-shaped muscle that separates the chest from the abdomen, played a major role in breathing.

"When the diaphragm contracts and flattens, there is more

space in the chest for the lungs to inflate. If it doesn't contract, the lungs can't inflate. Because the left side of the diaphragm is not working in sync with the right side and isn't flattening as it should, the lower lobe of her left lung cannot inflate."

"Why isn't her diaphragm working properly?" Kerry demanded.

"It's probably the result of damage to the phrenic nerve that controls the diaphragm. Unfortunately, this can sometimes occur during cardiothoracic surgery."

Kerry swallowed the fury that rose in her throat. "Are you saying her diaphragm got damaged during her heart surgery?"

"It's possible. We can't be sure. But what we need to do right now is to focus on what has to be done now."

"Fix it, of course. You can fix it, can't you?" Kerry asked.

"Well yes. Of course. We'll have to do a little procedure. It's pretty straight forward. What we'll do is make an incision on the side of her chest, and then reposition or reshape the diaphragm so that there will be more space in her chest for the lung to cxpand."

"Another surgery?" Kerry's heart sank. "Will she have to go back to theatre and have another anaesthetic and have her chest cut open again?"

"I'm afraid so, yes. But this time we won't have to crack open her chest again. We will cut between her ribs on her left side, more or less under her armpit. It's not a complex procedure. It's called a diaphragm plication. We are hopeful that it will help her lung to re-inflate – and, it could also help to address the problem she is having with the vomiting."

Dr Govender smiled reassuringly at Kerry and Imran. Kerry didn't feel reassured at all.

"And if she doesn't have this … this diaphragm plication surgery? What then? Couldn't her lung come right without it?" she asked.

She didn't know what to think. This was all such a shock. Her baby had been admitted to hospital for surgery to fix her heart, and now the doctor was saying they wanted to operate on her diaphragm because the heart surgery may have damaged her diaphragm and caused her lung to collapse. She needed time to digest this new information. She wanted to think about it.

"It's possible that the lung could re-inflate on its own," Dr Govender said in that all-too-familiar tone doctors used when they were saying something they clearly didn't believe. "But we need to consider the fact that it's been three weeks since the Glenn Shunt procedure, and she still isn't breathing well. She should have been off the high-flow oxygen by now. And her reflux – the vomiting – is also a concern. As I said, this too could be directly related to the problem with her diaphragm."

Kerry looked at Imran for reassurance. He looked as unhappy as she felt.

"When would you want to do this ... this plication procedure?" she asked.

"As soon as possible. Tomorrow."

Lily was fascinated with her toes. She lay on her back on her heart-shaped pillow that was protecting her pressure sore (Kerry had eventually found it at one of the big retail chain pharmacies). She was slightly propped up on a pillow and pulled at her feet, trying to get them into her mouth. She didn't seem to be at all uncomfortable, despite all the new battle scars covering her battered little body, the latest wounds all covered in white surgical dressings. There was the big white dressing still covering the long scar down the front of her chest; a collection of smaller dressings on the right side of her chest from drains that had thankfully been removed; and the latest wound, a twenty centimetre long red slash that ran like an ironic smile from her thin little chest under her arm and around to her back.

Kerry had been shocked the first time she'd seen the plication wound. The cardiologist, the pulmonologist, the surgeon, Dr Sinclair, her paediatrician, the nurses – even Dr Patterson who had done Lily's first open-heart surgery when she was just ten days old and who Kerry had bumped into in the corridor outside the ICU on the day of Lily's plication – had all assured her that it was a quick and simple procedure. This had given her the false impression that the plication cut was going to be small. Lesson learned: never surmise anything. Ask.

So she asked why, when Lily was put down to sleep, the nurses were careful not to place her onto her left side. Instead they propped her up on her back or placed her on her right side.

"It's got nothing to do with her wounds, Mrs Patel. It's to try and keep as much pressure off the left side of her chest as possible, to give her lung the best chance of inflating," the nurse explained.

"She's looking much better, isn't she?" Kerry asked, desperate for reassurance.

"She's coming along nicely," the nurse responded, as the nurses always did.

"How is her breathing doing? Is her lung starting to re-inflate?"

"I'm not sure, you'll have to ask the doctor that. However, I noticed that we've been able to reduce her oxygen pressure." The nurse checked the large chart at the end of Lily's cot. "Yes. She was on twelve litres, and today she's on ten, and she's holding her own. Her sats are steady, so that's all good. And she's eating nicely too. She loves her Purity."

Kerry smiled. Lily had always enjoyed the bottled baby food. It was good to know she was eating well again. She looked at the machine that measured Lily's saturation levels. The digital reading was seventy-five. Satisfactory – for a baby in Lily's condition; extremely dangerous and worryingly low for a 'normal' baby. With sats continuously below eight-five, or even ninety, the low oxygen levels could put a normal baby at risk for brain damage or slow development. Lily, however, had never had "normal" sats, and her brain seemed to be developing just fine.

"Mama," she said, giving Kerry a tiny smile. She half raised her arms as if asking her mother to pick her up.

"Can I hold her?" Kerry asked, as she did on every visit to the ICU. It had been so long since she'd been allowed to hold Lily in her arms. She didn't bother to wait for the nurse's answer, knowing that the response would be a routine reassurance that she would be allowed to hold her baby 'soon'.

"Of course," said the nurse.

Kerry sat down on the chair next to Lily's cot and looked down at her baby who looked back up at her with her big brown eyes.

"Aren't you going to hold her?" the nurse asked.

"What? I can hold her? I can hold her now?"

"That's what I said," the nurse smiled.

With her heart hammering, Kerry gently lifted Lily out of the cot. She couldn't believe the day had finally come. She held the precious, fragile, tiny scrap of humanity on her lap and gazed in awe at her beautiful little face. Her heart soared. Lily was getting better. She could see the improvement. It was a miracle. Despite the Glenn Shunt surgery, the fevers that followed, the collapsed lung, the pressure sore that had deteriorated into a raw, red mess edged in black, the plication procedure – despite everything – Tiger Lily was fighting back and she was going to recover.

But Kerry also knew she had to be realistic. She knew it wouldn't happen overnight. First, they had to wean Lily off the high-flow oxygen onto ordinary nasal cannulas – and then get her out of ICU. The next step would be to get her off oxygen support altogether.

"Baby steps. Baby steps," Kerry admonished herself.

Kerry noticed little Nala, held high in her father's arms in the small crowd of parents waiting for the doors of the ICU to be opened for visiting. Nala saw them and waved.

"Hello! Where's Leo?" she shouted.

"At his grandmother," Kerry answered. She nodded at the little girl's beaming mother.

The Somali woman made her way through the throng to Kerry's side.

"I'm so excited, I just have to tell you," she said. "We're taking our daughter home today. After ninety-seven days, we can take her home."

"That's fantastic. I'm so happy for you," Kerry said.

"This is the last time we are coming to the hospital so I won't be able to say goodbye to Leo," little Nala said sadly.

Kerry tousled her dark hair. "I'll tell Leo you said goodbye, okay? I'm sure you will love playing with your little sister at home."

The doors to the ICU opened and the parents swarmed through towards their children's cots. Kerry glanced over at the Somali child's cot. There were curtains around it. Her heart sank. Surely nothing had gone wrong?

Then the curtains parted and a miniature Nala – about two or three years old – walked unsteadily towards the ICU doors, holding tightly to her parents' hands. The mother stopped briefly and waved at Kerry. She pointed at Lily, crossed her fingers and mouthed: "Your turn soon."

A few days later, Lily was transferred from the ICU to the high care unit.

Her lung had still not inflated, but she was managing to breathe comfortably with ordinary nasal cannulas, the lowest level of oxygen support.

"Baby steps," Kerry reminded herself.

Forty days after her Glenn Shunt procedure, Lily was discharged from Sunninghill Hospital.

Kerry was overjoyed, and terrified.

"This is the script for your little one's medications," Dr Govender said after he had completed his examination. "You will see that I have added ... same time every day ... do not skip ..."

Dr Govender's voice was drowned out by the roaring in Kerry's head. She stared in horror at the script and swallowed her nausea. She wanted to thrust the magical formula that was designed to keep her baby alive back at the doctor and run. The full page was filled with the doctor's spiderish writing – and there was a closely written second page too.

Before her admission for the Glenn Shunt, Lily had had three chronic medications which she took twice a day. Now there were ... Kerry ran her eyes down the list and counted: now there were twelve.

In a daze, she followed Imran from the ward, Lily sleepy but cheerful in her arms while Imran carried the portable oxygen cylinder. Kerry barely noticed the sympathetic stares that followed their progress across the hospital foyer into the hospital pharmacy to collect a month's supply of the medications before heading to her parents' house in Norwood where she and Lily and Leo would stay for a while. She needed Triphina's help, and her mother's of course, while she adjusted to taking care of Lily. Alone.

She handed the script to the pharmacist and waited, and waited.

"Calm down," she told herself. "It can't be as bad or as complicated as it looks."

It was worse.

"Sorry I took so long," the pharmacist said, carrying what looked like half the pharmacy's stock in a big container to the counter. "It was quite a complex script and your doctor has given some specific instructions about administration. I've put the instructions on the containers but let me go through it all with you. Okay?"

Not okay. Kerry listened and tried to absorb the pharmacist's instructions: some of the medications had to be crushed and mixed with water; some had to be refrigerated; some had different dosages for the different times of day; some had to be given once daily, some twice daily, others four times a day. How would she ever get her head around it all? There was no time for baby steps now; this required a giant leap into the unknown.

She wasn't a nurse. She had no formal medical training at all. How was she supposed to take care of a baby with serious cardiomyopathy and a collapsed lung? And a gaping, oozing, bright red pressure sore that was now considerably larger than the black spot it had been when Kerry had seen it for the first time.

She had to clean it at every nappy change with antiseptic before applying special ointment and a fresh dressing. Dr Sinclair's stern warning, which echoed that of the wound clinic sister, rang in her head: if she didn't clean the pressure sore properly, it would get infected – and that would send her baby right back into the ICU.

And how was she going to manage the oxygen? Lily needed oxygen all the time. For twenty-four-hours a day. At a pressure of one litre per second. Before, when she'd only needed the oxygen for occasional support, they'd set the electric oxygen concentrator to half-a-litre per second. They would have to take the portable oxygen cylinder with them wherever they went. And she would have to be sure it never ran empty in case there was a power failure, or load shedding. Without electricity, the big oxygen concentrator would be useless ... and if the portable cylinder was empty, Lily could die and it would be her fault.

She tried to comfort herself with Dr Govender's reassurance that Lily would only need oxygen support until her lung re-inflated properly. She probably wouldn't need continuous oxygen for more than three months, probably less, he'd said.

"And what if her lung doesn't re-inflate?" she'd wanted to ask but had swallowed the question. Three months. She just had to hang in there for three months. That wasn't too bad. Three months would go by in a flash. For three months, she'd manage.

Chapter 14

Lily shrieked. Fat tears streamed down her flushed little face.

"Mama, mama, mama," she wept. "No! Mama nooo,"

"Stop! Stop it. You're hurting her," Kerry wanted to shout, but instead she clenched her hands and asked mildly: "Can't you be a little more gentle?"

"No," said Agnes, as she pressed the saline-soaked white gauze into the weeping, open pressure sore on Lily's bony buttocks again and wiped. Lily's shrieks grew louder.

"This is the only way that wound is ever going to heal. It must be very, very clean. Do you want it to get infected? It will make her very sick if it gets infected. If it gets bad, she may even have to have skin grafts. Do you want that?"

Kerry bit her lip and shook her head. What she wanted was to run away. Like Imran had done. He'd gone off to work and left her to deal with a miserable sick baby and a frightened three-year-old who was wailing almost as loudly as his baby sister. Except there was no work. I & K Kitchens and Cupboards hadn't won a new contract in months.

"Now it's your turn." Agnes was relentless. "Put the saline on the gauze. Now wipe."

Kerry's stomach turned over.

"Wipe! Press harder – there could be horrible germs in there. You must get them out," Agnes instructed.

Kerry clenched her teeth and tried to shut out Lily's anguished protests as she pressed down on the wound and wiped.

"Good. Now take some of this gel and put it on the wound. Make sure you cover all of it, around the edges too," Agnes said.

Kerry's trembling hands were sweating in the plastic gloves. She dabbed a tiny drop of the antiseptic gel over the open wound and patted it in as gently as she could.

Lily screamed in agony as the antiseptic burned into her raw flesh. Tears tickled down Kerry's face; her jaw ached.

"I can't do this," she whispered.

"Yes you can," Agnes said. "Just do it – and put a little more of the gel on the wound. Good. Now cover it with the sterile dressing. Okay – all done. Now put her nappy on."

Kerry sucked in a relieved gulp as Lily's sobs subsided. Leo rushed over and wrapped his arms around her legs as she cradled Lily in her arms and crooned: "It's finished, baby. It's all over now. Shh, shh, shh. It's finished."

But she knew it wasn't over. She knew she would have to put Lily through the agony of having her pressure sore cleaned and dressed again the next time she wet her diaper, and again after that until the dreadful sore was healed.

She'd been so grateful when her father, who must have realised how overwhelmed she was at having to care for Lily on her own, had suggested contacting Agnes, the kind, gentle qualified nurse who had taken care of her frail grandmother in her final months.

"Please ask her to come. Ask her if she'll stay for a few days – a week – to help me, please. Tell her I need her," Kerry had begged.

But Agnes couldn't come for long. Only one morning. It would have to do.

She arrived at precisely nine o'clock the day after Lily's first birthday.

"Should we give her a little party," Imran had asked a few days before.

From the look on his face, Kerry knew what he was thinking. So was she. They were both horribly aware that this could be the only chance they'd ever have to give Lily a birthday party. That it was a miracle – or whatever the agnostic equivalent of a miracle was – that Lily had even reached this milestone.

But Kerry shook her head. Lily wasn't well enough. She'd be overwhelmed by suddenly having a whole lot of people she barely knew – including her grandparents – fussing over her. And who knew what germs they'd pass on to her along with their gifts. That was if the grandparents even came. None of them had ever set foot inside their little Kempton Park home. Neither had any of their uncles.

"Let's rather donate the money we'd have spent on the party to a charity," she'd suggested. Imran had nodded and smiled, so sadly it almost broke Kerry's heart.

Kerry tried to make Lily's birthday special. Not trusting her baking skills, she bought some beautifully decorated cupcakes from the bakery in Kempton Park. Lily beamed as Kerry held up a cupcake with a tower of garish purple icing. The single purple birthday candle flickered in the breeze blowing in through the open window.

"Blow," she instructed Lily who was cradled in her father's arms on the couch.

"Bring it closer, she can't blow the candle out from there," he said.

"She can't blow yet – she's too little. And I don't want to take an open flame any closer to her oxygen – it's dangerous!"

"Me, me, meeee," Leo said and blew so hard, some of the icing splattered onto Kerry's blouse.

Laughing, they launched into "Happy birthday dear Lily, happy birthday to you," loudly and increasingly out-of-tune as Kerry and Imran's voices began to falter. Tears streamed down Kerry's face. Imran sniffed and wiped his eyes.

"For me, me, for meee?" Leo demanded, gazing longingly at the plate of cupcakes.

"Of course," Kerry said. "And here, Lily. This is yours."

She held the purple cupcake out to Lily, who took it and raised it to her mouth. Kerry held her breath – and then sighed as Lily dropped it onto the floor.

Kerry retrieved it, broke off a small piece and held it out to the baby. "Here you go, Lily. It's your birthday cake. It's yummy. Try a piece."

Lily clamped her mouth shut and turned her face away.

Kerry had hugged Agnes who looked like an angel of mercy in her crisp nurse's uniform with her close-cropped greying, peppercorn hair and cataract-misted eyes behind red-framed spectacles. Her relief couldn't have been greater had Florence Nightingale herself materialised in the lounge where Lily lay sleeping on her soft bed of blankets on the floor.

"I hate leaving her alone in the bedroom all the time," Kerry explained. "At least here, I can keep an eye on her and when she wakes, she has company and can watch TV with Leo."

At the sound of his name, Leo looked up from the blocks he was diligently building into a tall tower, smiled shyly at Agnes, and resumed his game.

"Do you have to turn her?" Agnes asked.

"Yes. She can't roll by herself yet. She can't sit either – well she could; she was sitting before her surgery in December but now, with the pressure sore, it's too painful. So she has to lie down ... although I prop her up a little, to try and take some of the pressure off her lung. It's difficult."

Agnes nodded. "You seem to be doing the right things. Your father said you were having trouble with all her medicine. Do you want me to help you go through them while Lily is still asleep?"

Kerry wanted to kiss her. It took ages to mix and measure and shake and crush this or that tablet, and then try and coax Lily to swallow the various concoctions. And just when she had finally got the last dose of medicine into her, it was time to start mixing and measuring again. And then Lily would wake in pain from the discomfort of a wet nappy burning her pressure sore and Kerry would have to attend to that – and lose track of where she was in the medicine preparations. There had to be an easier way.

But before Kerry could take Agnes through to the kitchen where the bottles of capsules and tables and syrups and powders were spread across the kitchen counter – those that weren't cluttering up the fridge – Lily opened her eyes, saw the stranger in a nurse's uniform and wailed.

Kerry bent over her daughter and checked her nappy, praying that it was dry and clean. It wasn't.

"I have to change her," she told Agnes sadly.

"And her wound dressing," Agnes said.

Kerry swallowed the dread that was rising in her throat, threatening to choke her. It hopefully wouldn't be as bad now that Agnes was here. Agnes would show her how to deal with the pressure sore without Lily shrieking as if she was being murdered. The screaming was so bad at times that Kerry wouldn't have been surprised to find the police or a social worker from the Department of Social Services on the doorstep one day, coming to investigate a complaint of alleged child abuse.

But there was nothing she could do. She had to traumatise her baby – both her children, and herself, she acknowledged wryly – in order help Lily heal. It wasn't fair.

"I'm worried about Lily," Kerry told Imran when he got home from work a week after Agnes' visit. Agnes had shown her how to sort and prepare all fifteen doses of medication Lily would receive throughout the day only once, in the morning.

"It's probably best to get up a bit early to prepare it all, so you can do it without being interrupted by Lily or Leo," Agnes had suggested.

Kerry was so grateful for this advice. Now, all she had to do when it was time for Lily's medication was select the right syringe and give it to her – which was easier said than done. Lily would fight as hard as she could to prevent the syringe going anywhere near her mouth. Kerry was afraid of just squirting it down her throat in case she choked. It was a battle to get Lily to put anything in her mouth. Sometimes it was hard to believe that this was the same baby who, only a few months before – before her surgery – would wolf down everything from rice and noodles to chicken, cookies, and even toasted sandwiches and mild curry (Imran's mother sometimes sent some home with Leo) – despite not yet having a tooth. Now she'd only drink her formula from a bottle.

"She's been so miserable all day. I think she is starting to run a fever. Do you think she could be teething?" she asked Imran hopefully – but she was sure that wasn't the case. Leo had managed to cut all his teeth without any major upsets.

She put her hand on the baby's forehead: it felt warm, and clammy. Her stomach churned. She prayed that Lily wasn't getting a chest infection.

Dr Govender and Dr Sinclair had warned her to do whatever she could to try and protect Lily from infection. With her compromised breathing as a result of the collapsed lung, along with her enlarged heart and poor oxygen levels, even the slightest cough or cold could result in another sojourn in the ICU.

So she did everything she could. Her hands felt like sandpaper from all the washing. She washed them with antiseptic soap dozens of times a day and even the expensive hand cream she'd bought didn't help. She hardly ever had to remind Imran to wash his hands either. They both wore masks if she suspected they had even the vaguest sign of a sniffle. She kept Leo away from his little sister if he so much as sniffed – which wasn't always easy because Leo loved to play with her as much as she loved having her big brother tickle her and show her his toys and watch Barney on TV with her until she drifted off to sleep. But there was always a chance that a persistent, sneaky bug would find its way into Lily's lungs.

That night, Kerry hardly slept. Lily was restless and miserable, and her fever wasn't abating. But her breathing seemed fine. She wasn't gasping; she wasn't turning blue. Kerry turned up the oxygen a little, just in case.

Morning dawned. If anything, Lily was even more miserable, whimpering from exhaustion. Kerry felt like whimpering too. She heard Imran going through his morning prayer ritual and tried to tune him out. She gave Lily another dose of Panado syrup. The baby was too listless to protest and the green analgesic/anti-inflammatory liquid "most recommended by doctors" slipped easily down her throat. Kerry checked her temperature a short while later: it had subsided – slightly.

"Go to work. I'll manage," she told Imran.

"No, I can't go and leave you alone with her when she's like this. Besides, I don't expect to hear back from Mrs Levinson just yet. I only sent the quote to her yesterday."

Kerry tried to smile encouragingly at him. She knew how much this contract would mean to Imran – and to their rapidly emptying bank account. It wouldn't be a fortune – Imran had told her he'd cut his costs, and his potential profit, to the bone to try and win the contract. Competition was getting more and more fierce. He hoped he'd done enough, but until he got the go-ahead from the Sandton housewife, who had an enormous circle of friends who might also want to have their kitchens renovated, there was nothing he could do. So he may as well stay home and help her with Lily.

A couple of hours later, Lily was burning with fever again. It was too soon to give her another dose of Panado. Kerry gently sponged her with cool water. Lily yelled her indignation. Kerry rocked her gently, trying to get her to sleep. Lily cried even harder.

"What is it, baby?" Kerry crooned. "Tell me what's wrong. Is your tummy sore?"

Kerry popped her finger into Lily's month and felt her gums. Nice and soft – no sign of an erupting tooth. She lay Lily on her back, the pressure sore protected by the heart-shaped pillow – and moved her head sharply from left to right, and back again, trying to determine if the baby didn't perhaps have an ear infection.

"Mama, Mama, Mama," Lily sobbed.

Kerry choked back her own sobs. She took her temperature again. Her heart turned over. It was over 40 degrees – far too high. Dangerously high, especially for a baby in a physically compromised condition like Lily. The time for messing around was over: Kerry gave her an anti-inflammatory suppository.

She called Imran who was playing outside with Leo. Together, they bundled Leo, Lily and the portable oxygen cylinder into the car.

"Do you think we should rather go to Sunninghill?" Imran asked.

"I don't think so. Her chest seems fine – she is breathing okay. Her pressure sore also looks okay – well no worse than before so I don't think it's infected. I phoned Dr Sinclair. She isn't in today but her receptionist said it'd be okay to let a doctor at Zamokhule Hospital see her. They have an emergency room there. They'll know what to do," she said, praying she was doing the right thing.

The wait in emergency rooms seemed interminable but eventually they were ushered into an examination room. As Kerry placed her on the examination bed, Lily started to wail, but without much conviction.

"She really isn't well," Kerry told the young, harried-looking doctor. "If she was, she'd be screaming the place down."

The doctor grinned. "I can imagine," he said.

He took her temperature, listened to her chest, checked her ears, and felt her neck and behind her ears. Then he peered closely at her face and neck, nodded, and turned her over to look closely at her back.

"Well, that explains it," he said. "Look here – can you see that?" He indicated her rosy cheeks.

Kerry looked, and looked again. How could she have missed it?

"I thought she was just flushed from the fever – but that's a rash," she said.

"That's right. And you can see it is just starting to spread to her back and tummy. Her eyes are a little red too."

"I thought it was from all the crying and because she is so tired. Oh no. I'm so sorry. What is it?"

"Rubella. German measles," the doctor said.

"German measles? Where on earth did she pick up German measles? I don't know anyone who has it," Kerry said, panic threatening to overwhelm her.

German measles was dangerous – that's why children were

vaccinated against it. Leo had been vaccinated when he'd had the MMR vaccine a few years before. But Lily hadn't. She really hadn't been well enough and she'd only just turned one, the age at which the MMR vaccination was recommended. To be honest, Kerry didn't want to do anything to compound the pain Lily was going through with the pressure sore. Until that was healed, she didn't need the trauma of another injection. But she'd had her other vaccinations – for polio, and TB and whooping cough and diphtheria (whatever that was) and all the others before her second open heart surgery. Because of Lily's compromised health and susceptibility to infections, Kerry had made sure Lily – and Leo – had all their vaccinations on time.

"Unfortunately, we're finding that a lot of parents don't vaccinate their children," the doctor said grimly. "Either they don't know, even though we try to remind them whenever we see them. But more and more of them seem to think that diseases like measles, mumps, Rubella and chicken pox aren't very serious. And for most healthy children, they aren't, although measles kills several thousand children around the world every year, including here in South Africa. There have been reports of several cases of measles in Gauteng recently but fortunately, no deaths. Not yet. It's really only a matter of time."

The doctor paused and shook his head. Then he continued: "Unlike measles, German measles, generally, is a pretty mild disease and is probably only dangerous for pregnant women – or rather for their unborn babies. I've actually seen several kids with German measles in the past couple of months, and a few adults as well. It's unfortunate that your baby has caught it. If everyone vaccinated their children, it would help to protect our most vulnerable children, like Lily, never mind the unborn children who are at risk."

The doctor sounded so indignant Kerry would have smiled had anger not been surging through her too. It wasn't fair! Poor little Lily had been through so much – and now she had caught a disease which was entirely preventable because some parent somewhere had chosen not to vaccinate their strong, healthy child. It just wasn't fair. It wasn't right.

"What can we do? Will she need to go to ICU? Should we call her cardiologist?" she asked.

"At the moment, we should just watch her and try to make her as comfortable as possible while the disease runs its course," the doctor replied. "There's nothing else we can do. It will probably only take a few days now that the rash is coming out. I'll give you something for the itch and to help manage her fever – the last thing we need is for the fever to rise too high as that could result in convulsions. But for Lily, the real danger will be if she develops any secondary infections, like bronchitis or pneumonia. You must watch her carefully for that."

Kerry went cold. "Not pneumonia! Please, please not pneumonia, or bronchitis," she prayed silently.

"There must be something more we can do. Why can't we give her some antibiotics, just in case, so she doesn't get pneumonia." she said, fighting back tears.

"Prophylactic antibiotics is not a good idea. She could develop resistance to them if she takes them when they are not needed. So, for now, just keep her cool; sponge her down; give her plenty of fluids and it should all clear up by the end of the week. But watch her and come back or call your cardiologist or pediatrician if you are concerned – about anything."

Chapter 15

From the kitchen, where she was preparing lunch for Leo and Lily, Kerry could hear her daughter chortling as the familiar lyrics filled the house:

"I love you, you love me, we're a happy family ..."

Yes, we are, Kerry thought. *We have so much to be thankful for.*

She opened the fridge and stared ruefully at the shelves, mostly bare if you didn't take account of all Lily's medication. Kerry grinned when she saw the medication right in the front. Sildenafil. She hadn't known what it was when Dr Govender added it to her long list of chronic medications. The pharmacist at the hospital had told her it was to dilate her blood vessels so that her blood would be able to carry more oxygen around her body. But when the doctor at Zamokhule Hospital had asked about Lily's medications before writing out the prescription for something to control her German measles-induced fever, he had burst out laughing when Kerry said *"Sidenafil"*.

Kerry had been more than a little annoyed. "What's so funny," she'd demanded. As far as she could see, there was nothing amusing about her daughter's condition – not the fever, not her discomfort, and certainly not her enlarged and damaged heart.

"Don't you know what *Sildenafil* is?" he'd laughed.

"Of course I do – it's to dilate her blood vessels."

"Quite right. And Lily's cardiologist has prescribed it as it was originally intended. But it also has another use – a very popular use."

Kerry had stared at him, bewildered.

"It's more commonly known as *Viagra!*"

Kerry hadn't been able to help herself – she'd started laughing too, not quite sure what to feel about the fact that her baby daughter was on medication for erectile dysfunction.

Imran, however, hadn't been as amused. "How on earth am I ever going to ask for it again at the pharmacy? What will the pharmacist think of me? I'm only thirty!" he'd muttered as they left the hospital.

Kerry giggled again at the memory as she closed the fridge door on its almost-emptiness.

Still smiling, she walked quickly into the lounge and laughed again. Lily was sitting on her blanket bed on the floor gazing up at the TV.

"More!" Lily shouted. "More!"

"Did Palesa put Barney on again for you?" Kerry asked and Lily turned her head, giving her mother a rapturous smile that showed off her two new gleaming white teeth.

"Barney, Barneeey, Barneeeeey," Lily shouted before turning back to the TV to watch, yet again, the antics of the purple dinosaur.

"Palesa, Lily seems to be okay at the moment. Can you please watch her a little longer – I have to go to the shops for a few things before Leo gets home from school," Kerry said.

She didn't like leaving Lily with anyone. And most people, including Lily's grandparents, were not comfortable being left alone with her. It was too much of a responsibility, her mother had said when Kerry, against her better judgement but desperate to have some alone time with her husband, had phoned her to ask if she'd please babysit Leo and Lily so that she and Imran could have a very short "date night".

"I'd be delighted to have Leo. He can even sleep over if he wants. But," Gillian had hesitated and Kerry knew what was coming. "But Kerry darling, I love her. You know I do. But, well, Lily … I mean … what will I do if something goes wrong? What if there's a power failure?"

"She has an oxygen cylinder, Mom," Kerry had said through gritted teeth. "Oxygen cylinders don't need electricity to function. That's why we got one. And we won't be long. We only want to go and grab a burger or something."

"There's no need to be sarcastic, Kerry-Anne. Your father would be in a state from nerves and my blood pressure would go through the roof. I'm sorry sweetheart but no. I can't. I just can't. We can't. Anyway, I really don't think it's fair of you to ask us. I don't like to harp on it but as I told you when you took up with him, as you make your bed, so you must lie in it."

"His name is Imran. He's my husband and in case you forgot, Lily is also your grandchild. But forget it. I'm sorry I asked." Kerry had jabbed viciously at her smartphone, ending the call.

Now, as she reached for the car keys, she consoled herself that Palesa was getting used to being alone with Lily for short periods. She was, Kerry assured herself, as level-headed and responsible as her mother. It had been such a relief when Triphina had sent her daughter, fresh out of high school and hoping to earn enough money to study to be a nurse, to help out. Although Palesa's job was just to clean the house and help with the washing and ironing, she always sat with Lily when Kerry needed to get something done – like cook, or run to the shop, or just take a shower. It was easier to get to the shops too, now that Imran had bought a little second-hand panel van from someone at his mosque.

"It's a good investment. I can't keep transporting kitchen cabinets in the car; it's not very professional-looking," he'd said when Kerry had demurred at the cost. Now, he drove off to work every morning in the pale blue van with 'I & K Kitchens' emblazoned on the side; and Kerry had access to the Toyota. But even with the car, running to the shops quickly had been all but impossible before Palesa arrived on the scene.

Kerry would never leave Lily alone with Palesa if she wasn't well – she'd never leave Lily alone with anyone when she wasn't well. But today was one of Lily's 'better' days, and Kerry had learned to take advantage of these rare opportunities to get some chores done.

As she closed the front door behind her, she smiled happily, and then laughed at herself. It was crazy to feel so excited about a trip to the supermarket, but she couldn't help it. She tried to recall the last time she'd been out of the house. It was when she'd taken Lily to Dr Govender for her belated routine monthly check-up, the first following her diaphragm plication surgery.

Imran hadn't wanted her to go.

"Phone Dr Govender and postpone the visit. There's going to be trouble in Sandton," he'd said.

Every news broadcast was warning that the service delivery protests in Alexandra were going to spill over the highway from the desperately overcrowded black residential township into Sandton, arguably the richest few square kilometres in Africa that the protest leaders sneeringly called the very heart of 'White Monopoly Capital'. The Alexandra protest had turned violent; the protestors had chased away the Mayor of Johannesburg, refusing to allow him to address the people. Fortunately, they had stayed away from Wynberg where Imran's little factory was in full production for the kitchen installation at Mrs Levinson's big house in Sandon – the first contract he'd had in months. His profit would be wafer-thin, and any disruptions would push the entire deal into the red.

The news reports made it clear that having effectively shut down Alex, the protest leaders were determined to do the same to the Sandton CBD.

"I'll be fine and we can't postpone her check up again," Kerry had argued. "We are already overdue because of her German measles. Anyway, the protests are going to focus on the stock exchange area. I won't be going anywhere near there."

"But you have to drive past Alex on the highway. They may decide to shut down the highway too. The minibus taxi drivers have done that before. I've even told my guys not to come in today. I can manage without them."

"It'll be okay," she'd said. But she'd been nervous as she drove to the hospital. It was only once she'd got Lily and the heavy portable oxygen cylinder past all the curious stares and quickly averted eyes of all the people in the hospital foyer and was able to collapse into a chair in Dr Govender's waiting room, that she was able to relax.

Dr Govender had been pleased at how well Lily had recovered from her surgery and German measles. He was less happy when he placed her on the scale.

"Hmm. She really needs to eat more," he said.

The familiar guilt washed over Kerry and she bit her lip. She was trying. She really was doing her best. But Lily was becoming more and more difficult, sometimes even refusing to drink her bottle. Mealtimes were a constant battle that left Kerry exhausted and Lily tearful and limp.

"She's starting to catch up on her milestones. She can sit again," Kerry said, not sure who she was trying to reassure – the cardiologist or herself. She proudly itemised the changes this had made to her daughter's overall disposition. Lily was blossoming – pun intended. She could sit up and play: it was so much better because she could use both her hands to try and build a block tower, or cuddle her purple Barney and orange Tigger, or turn the pages of her books. She hadn't been able to do that when she was lying on her back or side on her makeshift blanket bed in the lounge.

"And she loves being able to watch the television properly. She claps and sings along with her favourite Barney tunes. And she's so happy to be able to see what's going on all around her. She can even turn and look at whoever comes into the room behind her. Before, when she was lying down, she had to twist her neck to see."

Dr Govender nodded indulgently and let Kerry rattle on. "Of course, she still can't crawl or roll or pull herself up from a lying to a sitting position, but she's at least back to where she was in terms of movement and development before her open-heart surgery and the diaphragm plication."

"She's doing well, very well," Dr Govender agreed. "I think you can try to wean her off her supplementary oxygen. Take it slowly over the next few months and see how she goes."

Imran was overjoyed when Kerry told him the good news. And Kerry started the process immediately. She reduced the flow on the oxygen concentrator to just 0.5 litres – and waited. And watched. Nothing happened. Lily coped beautifully.

After a few days, Kerry removed the oxygen cannulas from Lily's little nose, and held her breath. She glued her eyes to her daughter's face. It didn't change. No signs of blueness; no gasping for breath. After thirty seconds, Kerry put the cannulas back.

Every day, Kerry removed Lily's oxygen support for a little longer. This morning she had removed the cannulas for four minutes; this afternoon, after lunch and her nap, she'd keep them off for four-and-a-half minutes. And one day, in the not too distant future, Kerry was sure the hum of the big electric oxygen concentrator that was a constant background noise in their home would be quiet for most of the day – possibly all day, and hopefully at night too.

After stopping in the half-empty supermarket parking lot, Kerry got out of the car and turned her face up to catch the rays of the soft autumn sunshine. For the first time in months she was starting to feel human, her exhaustion that had been fed by Lily's misery and discomfort from the pressure sore and the German measles, a fading memory.

She felt free. And guilty. She always felt guilty when was away from the house – alone. Her place was with Lily. Her job – her priority – was to take care of her daughter. She also had a house to manage; another child to care for; a husband. She told Jason Brown that every time he called to ask if she was ready, if not to come back to work, to at least take on a little work that she could do from home. She'd always fight down the temptation, and the feelings of deep regret, and remind herself that she had her priorities right.

Right now, regrets and guilt were far from her mind. The sun was shining; there was a warm, fresh breeze; Leo was thriving; and Lily was so much better. There was no question about it: Lily was on the road not only to recovery, but to living a happy and fulfilling life. It would take time, and a lot of effort from Lily and everyone around her. But one day, one beautiful day when the sun was shining and the sky was blue, Lily would walk, and talk, and play outside with her brother. One day, Lily would be able to do most things every other child could do.

Kerry hurried into the store wondering what to buy that would tempt Lily to eat. Perhaps some apple Purity baby food – she'd always loved that – even though, technically, she was too old for Purity. Perhaps an ice cream; perhaps something with a bit more nutritional value – mac and cheese? Kerry grabbed a trolley and hurried up and down the aisles, throwing this and that into the cart. She didn't have much time – Lily would soon get tired; she'd become grumpy and miserable and want to lie down. And that mustn't happen – not before she'd had her lunch. If she was too tired, there was no chance she would eat. She might not even take her bottle. It was really worrying. Lily needed to eat to grow and get strong. Kerry hurried to the checkout.

It served her right, Kerry admonished herself. She should never have left Lily alone with Palesa. She should never have allowed a stranger into the house and Palesa was a stranger, even if she'd known her since she was a child and had even played with her when Triphina had her come and stay in her little room – flatlet, Gillian called it – during the school holidays. But Palesa had to travel in overcrowded taxis to get to Kerry's house, and heaven only knew what germs and bugs she'd pick up that way.

But Palesa had seemed quite healthy. Not even the slightest indication of a sniffle. Leo had had a slight cold, but that was only to be expected. All kindergarten kids got colds – they caught it from each other.

She should have kept Leo away from Lily. She should have ... she could have ... she hadn't done enough, she hadn't taken enough care.

"There was nothing you could have done, don't blame yourself," Dr Govender said when she ran into him as he was leaving the paediatric ICU two days after Lily had been admitted in the middle of the night with a raging fever and gasping for air.

Perhaps. Perhaps if they'd taken her to hospital at the first indication of a change in her breathing, perhaps if they hadn't driven all the way to Sunninghill Hospital and had rather gone to Zamokhule Hospital in Tembisa, perhaps then Lily wouldn't have had to be intubated. Sedated and intubated – again – because Lily had pneumonia and couldn't breathe on her own.

"She'll be okay," Imran said. "She's a little tiger. She'll pull through."

Kerry nodded automatically. She didn't need hollow reassurances. She didn't need platitudes to lessen her guilt. What she nccdcd was for hcr daughter to recover and continue to improve.

"How's Mrs Levinson's kitchen going? Shouldn't you be there?" Kerry asked.

"I need to be with my daughter. The guys can manage without me for a few days," Imran said.

Kerry bit back the retort that came unbidden to her lips: Imran couldn't and shouldn't leave the most important contract he had had in ages to the two casual workers he had employed a couple of weeks ago to help him with the tiling and plumbing. What if they messed up?

"I'll go check on them tomorrow."

"Lilly is holding her own. I'm here. You really should go and check that the guys are doing what you told them. You haven't been on site for three days – not since Lily was admitted."

"I said, I'll go tomorrow, Kerry. Please don't nag. I need to be here with you."

But I don't need you here, Kerry thought. I need you to make sure Mrs Levinson's kitchen is perfect so that she'll recommend you to all her friends so that we actually make some money to pay for all Lily's medical bills. *And the van. And the rent.*

She bit her lip and looked away.

Imran strapped Lily into her seat at the back of the car. Kerry hurried to the front passenger seat and turned to smile at her daughter, who beamed back at her. She looked fine – and her cough was almost completely gone. Who would have thought that just a week before, Lily had been on the critical list? Imran lifted the oxygen cylinder onto the back seat and adjusted the cannulas in Lily's nose.

"Let's go. Let's take our Tiger home. Leo can't wait to see her again," he said. He started the car and pulled out of Sunninghill Hospital parking lot.

Kerry smiled automatically at him, but she didn't feel like smiling. Not really. It *was* a relief that Lily had been discharged after two long weeks. Travelling backwards and forwards to the hospital twice a day had been draining, for all of them, including poor Leo for whom the ICU waiting room had become his personal playroom, when Mrs Reddy wasn't able to watch him.

The traffic wasn't too heavy and they were soon speeding along the highway.

"What do you think – about what Dr Sibanda said?" she asked Imran. She didn't really care what he thought about what the pulmonologist had said, but she had to say something to break the silence between them.

"What do you mean?" Imran asked.

"About the oxygen. He said Lily would need to use supplemental oxygen for quite a while longer. Dr Govender agreed."

"So, she'll have to be on oxygen. She was on oxygen before."

"But she was doing so nicely without oxygen too. Now I'll have to start weaning her off it all over again. If it's even possible. Dr Sibanda said it could take a long time for her to get back to where she was."

Imran frowned. Silence descended again.

"Well, at least now Lily is home, you'll be able to focus on finishing Mrs Levinson's job," Kerry blurted.

"It's finished," Imran said.

"What? When? How – you haven't been to the site since ... oh, I don't know. Last week? You didn't tell me. So has she paid you already? Why didn't you tell me?"

Imran flushed. He was angry, Kerry could see.

"I'm sorry," she said quickly, soothingly. "I didn't ... I wasn't prying. But I wish you'd told me. I was so worried about how we were going to pay ... things are so tight. But now the job is finished, well, now everything will be okay. Won't it?"

"No. It won't. The old cow hasn't paid."

"What? Why not? You put in such a lot of effort ..."

"She fired me. Just after Lily was admitted to hospital. She said ... well, she said a lot of things. She said I wasn't ever there. She was just looking for excuses not to pay, I swear. She said the work we'd done was shoddy. Shoddy! It wasn't that bad. We could have fixed it but she never gave us a chance ... You'd think she'd understand that I have a sick child – you'd think she'd make allowances for that," Imran said.

"She did," Kerry said through gritted teeth. "She gave you extension after extension. She probably had just had enough."

As I *have*, she added silently.

Chapter 16

"Did you hear the news?" Imran asked as he came into the kitchen where Kerry was preparing dinner.

"What news? Is Lily okay? Who's with her?"

They'd had to let Palesa go, for now. They didn't really need her now that Imran didn't have any jobs and could help Kerry around the house and with the shopping.

"She's playing with Leo. They're fine. They just said that Eskom is warning we are going to be having a lot more load shedding in the next few months."

Kerry continued slicing the cucumber and added it to the salad bowl. She didn't know why she kept making salad – she was the only one who ate it. But she had to try, if only to set a good example for the children, especially Lily. Imran was no help at all. He said salad was alien to Indian culture and that if she really loved him, she'd feed him spicy mutton curry swimming in fat and without any visible vegetables except perhaps a potato and yellow rice for breakfast, lunch and dinner every day. She scraped the last pieces of cucumber off the board into the bowl, and put down the knife carefully, trying to control her anger.

"So, what else is new? Are we supposed to be grateful that they've warned us that we won't have any electricity for hours at a time because they wrecked the power stations? I'll be grateful when there is no load shedding at all. I get nightmares about it. I keep picturing Lily suffocating and the oxygen concentrator just laughs at me and ... it's horrible."

"Well, I was thinking. Perhaps we should get a second oxygen cylinder. Just so that we always have a full one – in case the electricity goes off for longer. You know – it's happened before."

And so it had. The planned rolling power outages sometimes went on for far longer than the scheduled four hours because, when the time came to switch the power back on, electrical substations all over the city tripped out.

"I don't know," Kerry said. "The oxygen cylinder is so heavy and awkward to carry around. And I never really know how much is left. I wish we could get one of those portable little concentrators. They're light and easy to carry. Apparently, they can last for hours when they're fully charged. But they're really expensive."

Imran shook his head doubtfully. "Perhaps, if I sell the van?"

"No, you'll need it when things pick up again. We could ask the medical aid to pay for one."

"Huh – fat chance of that! They refused to pay for the big concentrator, remember? They said Lily didn't need it because she has a problem with her heart, not her lungs. That's why we got our own."

"I know, but things have changed since then. I'll asked Dr Govender for a letter motivating for a portable concentrator. That should help," Kerry said.

"I don't know. Why would they pay for a portable if they wouldn't pay for the big one? They won't even pay for the cylinder. Perhaps we can get a second-hand portable concentrator. I'll see what I can find."

Kerry smiled at her husband and blew him a kiss as his phone rang and he walked out of the kitchen to take the call. It was so difficult for him. He was doing his best, he really was. I & K Kitchens and Cupboards would come right. Imran was trying to find new contracts. It was really tough trying to grow the business with all the disruptions and additional expenses that came with having a desperately sick child. It wasn't fair of her to hold it against him. He was doing his best. He tried to pretend things were looking up, but Kerry couldn't help but hear when he phoned the medical aid to argue with them about unpaid claims.

"That was the anaesthetist's lawyers," Imran said when he returned to the kitchen. His face was pale and his hands were clenched. Kerry had never seen him as upset and angry.

"What anaesthetist? What lawyers? What do lawyers want with us?"

"It's nothing. Don't worry about it," Imran said.

"It can't be nothing. Lawyers don't phone for nothing. Tell me."

"There's nothing you can do about it. I don't want to upset you."

Kerry exploded. "I don't need protecting. And I'm already upset. For heaven's sake, Imran, we're married, we're supposed to be a team. What's the point of trying to hide things from me?"

"Okay, if you really want to know. It's from the Glen Shunt and plication surgeries. Medical Aid said they only pay one hundred percent of the prescribed rate and this anaesthetist charged six hundred percent of the rate. So now, the lawyers are demanding that we pay the R25,000 the medical aid won't pay. They want the money immediately – actually, it's now R27,000 because we also have to pay their fees. So now you know. What do you suggest we do about it?"

Kerry stared at her husband's taut face. "I don't know. I just don't know. Oh Imran, what are we going to do?"

She hated the medical insurance company. When they ran out of excuses not to pay claims, they found reasons not to pay the full amount claimed – not even for blood tests. Lily had had 163 blood tests while she'd been in hospital, and the medical aid had covered only a fraction of those costs too. If only she was also able to contribute to the family's meagre finances – she'd never intended to be a fulltime mom. She'd gone back to work when Leo was tiny. But with Lily, that was impossible. She felt so useless, helpless – and so frustrated.

Her hands shook as she took the fish fingers out of the oven and saw Imran grimace.

"Fish fingers! I hate them," he complained.

"Oh shup up. Please, just shut up," she hissed. "The kids will hear you!"

Imran flushed.

"Oh god, Imran. I'm sorry. Look, I know you don't like fish

fingers – they're not exactly my idea of a good lunch either. But they're cheap and these ones are quite nice. At least they've more real fish than most of the others we've tried. Anyway Lily loves them – well, she used to so perhaps she'll eat one. And they're Leo's favourite. So just eat them, okay? You can drown them in relish – there's a bottle of hot and spicy in the fridge."

Imran shrugged, opened the cupboard and took out four plates then rummaged in the drawer for knives and forks.

"Did you hear Cyril Ramaphosa asking young white South Africans not to leave the country. He said South Africa needed their skills," he said.

Kerry was relieved Imran had decided to ignore her little explosion and change the subject. "What? Why – I mean I know there's an election coming but why did he suddenly decide to talk about white emigration?"

"I don't know. But it's good that he's making an effort to address all the anti-minority racism. To say we're all welcome here – well, I'm presuming he means Indians and Coloureds as well as whites. Maybe he will be able to change things ... maybe we should vote for the ANC again. I mean, he understands business and the economy. We should give him a chance to turn the country around."

"Maybe. I'm not so sure. I think he knows the ANC has lost a lot of support under Zuma and now he's just trying to get votes from anywhere. But I don't know – the country is such a mess. When they fix the public hospitals and the healthcare system, so that babies like Lily can get the treatment they need and we don't have to pay a flipping fortune for medical aid that doesn't pay for blood tests or oxygen for a baby who can't breathe without it, then I may vote for them. But until then ... No."

"So, who will you vote for?"

"I don't know." Kerry picked up the salad bowl and the plate of fish fingers and placed them on the kitchen table. "You?"

"I'll see," Imran said.

Kerry woke with a start. Something wasn't right. The oxygen concentrator was humming away in the passage outside the bedroom. Imran was breathing quietly in the bed next to her. Lily was lying nice and still in her camp cot at the foot of the bed, her breathing was …

Kerry scrambled across the bed to the cot and peered at her daughter through the darkness. And listened. And then Lily coughed. A rasping, raking cough. Kerry reached out and touched Lily's face. It was damp – and hot, burning hot. The images of the burning Notre Dame cathedral in Paris she'd seen on the news earlier that night flashed through her mind.

She jumped off the bed and turned on the light.

"Wasa matter?" Imran sat up, rubbing his eyes.

"Lily. She's got a fever again – and she's … she's coughing. Her breathing is also funny … something's wrong."

Even in the dim light – two of the bedroom light's three bulbs were not working – Kerry could see that Lily's lips were bluer than normal. Her mouth was open and she seemed to be gasping for air between the coughs.

She opened the wardrobe and pulled out some clothes. "Get up, get dressed," she said. "We have to get her to hospital."

"It's the middle of the night. Are you sure we need to go now? She might be better in the morning," Imran protested.

"No. This is worse than before. Something is really wrong. Get up – or you stay in bed and I'll go."

Imran got out of bed and pulled on a pair of jeans and a sweater.

"Go get Leo, we'll have to take him with us," Kerry said as she lifted Lily out of the cot. The baby was limp.

"No, I'll take him across the road. Mrs Reddy won't mind. She said we should wake her in an emergency."

By the time Imran got back from handing over the still-sleeping little boy to Mrs Reddy, Kerry had settled Lily in the car with the oxygen cylinder on the seat next to her. She mentally berated herself – she really should have had it refilled during the week. She couldn't remember how long they had used it for when they went to the shop last weekend. She prayed there was enough oxygen to last for the 30-minute drive to Sunninghill hospital – but they'd probably get there faster. Imran would drive like the wind, and there'd be no traffic at 3am.

Two weeks later, Dr Govender indicated the chair in his office. Kerry sat. Imran stood, as he always did, behind Kerry with his hand on her shoulder.

"Well, your little one has come through this infection nicely. She really is amazing. Quite amazing. But this was a bad one so her rapid recovery has been pleasing, very pleasing. But her heart is still very enlarged. You can take her home today but she must stay on supplementary oxygen. I know you want to wean her off, but I don't think that's a good idea. At least for the foreseeable future."

"The medical aid won't pay for oxygen for Lily. We had to buy our own concentrator. But we can't afford to buy a portable and we really need one. So, we were wondering if perhaps you could write a note to them, to motivate for the portable?" Kerry asked.

Dr Govender frowned. He pulled his prescription pad towards him and scribbled a note.

"Here, this should help. Let me know if it doesn't," he said.

Kerry started to stand but Dr Govender motioned to her to sit down.

"Although your little one is over this infection, I am concerned. So is Dr Sinclair, your paediatrician. She's lost even more weight since she was admitted, which is to be expected, I suppose. But the nurses tell me she won't eat anything – not even her bottle. We've had her on a drip here but ... Perhaps she will eat better when she gets home?"

Kerry shook her head glumly. "We've been struggling to get her to eat. It's been getting worse and worse. I just don't know what to do."

"Well, I was talking to Dr Sinclair and we were thinking. Perhaps, to make things better for her growth and to take strain off her heart and her body, perhaps we should consider putting in a peg."

"A peg?" Kerry asked.

"A feeding tube," Dr Govender said.

Chapter 17

"Well that's it – the ANC has won again," Imran said.

"Surprise, surprise," Kerry responded distractedly. She really wasn't interested. She had far more important things to worry about. Anyway, everyone had known that the ANC, the party of Nelson Mandela, would win the general election – despite the best efforts of former ANC President Jacob Zuma and his cronies to turn the country into their personal fiefdom to be looted and pillaged at will. She hadn't even bothered to go and vote. She was still trying to get used to feeding Lily through her new peg feeding tube.

It had been yet another nerve-wracking, anxious wait outside the operating theatre while the peg was inserted, just above her bellybutton. Kerry hadn't been worried about the actual surgery. She'd googled it and it seemed simple enough. But she'd almost changed her mind about allowing the whole procedure to go ahead when Dr Sinclair had mentioned, almost in passing as they were wheeling Lily into the theatre, that her baby would be ventilated while the peg was inserted.

"But ... but ... a ventilator is bad for her. She struggles to come off it ... what if she can't ... what if she doesn't start breathing again on her own?" Kerry had spluttered.

"We'll remove the ventilator in theatre as soon as the procedure is complete. If she struggles a little, we'll leave it in for a while. But don't worry. She'll only be on the ventilator for an hour, no more than two. She should be fine," the paediatrician had smiled reassuringly.

Now Kerry swallowed her irritation as the sounds of the SABC

News anchor droning on about the election results wafted through the house. Much to Leo's and Lily's dismay, Imran had insisted the TV stay tuned to the 'live' broadcast from the Independent Electoral Commission's command centre since ballot counting had started two days before. Kerry carefully measured out the new medication that had been added to Lily's already long list of meds. This one was to reduce her stomach acid levels. Dr Sinclair had explained that with the peg in place, Lily's brain was constantly receiving messages that there was something in her stomach that needed to be digested and so was instructing her stomach to produce too much acid.

She was also coughing a bit, so cough medicine had been added to the mix too. Lily was lying on her back on her little blanket bed on the lounge floor watching Leo play with his cars. Kerry squirted the cocktail of meds directly into the tube hanging out of her tummy. And it was done. Finished. So much easier giving her all her meds through the peg, rather than trying to persuade her to open her mouth to swallow it. Before the peg, as soon as Lily had seen the syringe with medication approaching her mouth, she'd clamped her lips together and refuse to open them, not even to yell her objections.

"Did you hear that?" Imran demanded. "The ANC's support has dropped, a lot!"

"Uh huh," Kerry said.

"I mean, it's a really big drop!"

"Well, what did you expect – after Zuma and everything?" Kerry said and sat back on her heels, her eyes fixed on Lily's face for any sign of discomfort. Lily gazed back at her with her customary curious expression in her big, brown eyes.

"Not that! I thought that Ramaphosa would turn things around."

"He probably did. If it hadn't been for Ramaphosa, the ANC might have lost." Kerry didn't really believe that, but she'd heard it said repeatedly by all the experts who'd been pontificating endlessly about the election.

"Nah, the ANC will never lose," Imran said firmly. "But if they do, it'll be to the EFF and that'll be a disaster. And the EFF is really growing. They're going to have a lot more seats in parliament."

"Well then they'll just have to increase the number of security people they need to drag the EFF out of parliament when they disrupt the proceedings again."

Imran laughed. "I suppose so. But did you see how much support the DA lost? Seems like a lot of white voters decided to rather vote for the Freedom Front." He paused, then looked speculatively at his wife. "Who would you have voted for?"

Kerry looked up from carefully pouring Frebini, the most nutritionally dense supplement she'd been able to find, into the feeding tube. It was expensive, and Lily had to have four bottles every day but if anything could build their precious baby's body and strength, this was it.

"What? Who would I have voted for? I don't know. I didn't think about it. Who did you vote for? Oh no – oh shit!"

She quickly lifted Lily into a sitting position as a fountain of white vomit shot out of her mouth onto her blanket.

"Quick, pass me that cloth," Kerry yelped.

She grabbed the proffered cloth from Imran and wiped Lily's mouth. Some of the vomit coated the tube that fed oxygen via two little plastic cannulas into her nose. Kerry gently removed the cannulas and quickly wiped them. Then she hurried to the kitchen to get an antiseptic wipe to disinfect the cannulas. By the time she returned to the lounge, cleaned the oxygen tube and had reinserted the cannulas into her nose, Lily's pallor had darkened and there was a distinct bluish hue around her mouth and nose.

"Damn! Look at her, Imran. She was without oxygen for not even half a minute and look at her! She's blue already."

Kerry and Imran watched anxiously as Lily's colour slowly returned to normal now that the supplementary oxygen was in place once again.

"Thank heavens," Kerry said. "I wonder why she keeps vomiting like that. I hope she's actually keeping some of the supplement down."

"Do you think it's too rich for her little stomach? Should we try another supplement?"

"Let's wait and see. Things might get a bit better when they change this peg for the low profile one. And hopefully that one won't leak as much."

Kerry sighed. She cringed when she had to clean the peg wound which had not yet fully healed. It seemed to leak constantly – sometimes there was blood, sometimes stomach acid, and sometimes just stomach contents and gunk. And even when it wasn't leaking, she still had to clean it with salt water, at least twice a day. Lily would cry whenever Kerry touched the wound. There had to be a simpler way – but at least some nutrition was getting into Lily's tummy. Apart from her bottle, Lily would no longer put anything in her mouth at all, not even her once favourite cheese puffs. Not even ice cream.

Chapter 18

It was the click that woke Kerry. Imran often joked that even while she slept, her ears stayed alert for the slightest sound – or lack of sound – that shouldn't be there. The click itself wasn't alarming. It was the silence that followed that caused her heart to pound. Kerry pressed the switch on her bedside light. Nothing.

"Shit!" she swore softly. Power outage. Which meant Lily's oxygen concentrator wasn't working. This was the second outage in three days. The previous one – the result of a tripped generator at the nearby electricity substation – had lasted for five hours but it had at least been during the day. Kerry had hooked Lily up to the oxygen cylinder and waited for the power to return.

And then Kerry's heart stood still. She realised she had no idea how much oxygen was left in the cylinder. Nor did she know how long this outage would last. It could be anything from five minutes to five hours – or more. But Lily couldn't be without supplementary oxygen for two minutes.

She scrabbled for her cellphone and swore again when she saw that she'd forgotten to recharge it when she went to bed. The battery was at forty percent – hopefully enough to last until the sun came up and she'd no longer need its flashlight. She quietly slipped out of bed and shivered her way across the room to the oxygen cylinder. Her threadbare flannel pyjamas offered little protection against the freezing Highveld winter night. She quickly unhooked Lily's now useless oxygen cannulas from the electric oxygen concentrator and attached them to the oxygen cylinder. She turned it on and the reassuring hiss of oxygen flowing from the cylinder to her daughter's nose sent her crawling back into bed, resisting the temptation to warm her icy feet on Imran's warm body. She listened. Neither Lily nor Imran stirred. Leo was also quiet. Kerry prayed he wouldn't wake up. He'd be terrified if he found himself in total darkness, his Goofy nightlight another victim of Eskom's corruption and City Power's inefficiency.

Kerry glanced at her phone. It was 2am. She closed her eyes. She listened. She was too tense to sleep. She got up and checked that there was still oxygen flowing from the cylinder to Lily. She got back into bed. She lay, eyes wide open, staring into the blackness of the bedroom.

And then she heard it. The silence. The cylinder was empty.

She scrambled out of bed once more and by the light of her cellphone flashlight, darted into the lounge where the recently acquired, second-hand portable oxygen concentrator was lying, close to the wall plug where Imran had put it for recharging. She carried it back to the bedroom, switched Lily's cannulas once again, turned on the new concentrator and saw, to her horror, that its battery was about to die.

"What on earth?" Kerry swore. "Why the hell hasn't it charged?" She glared at her sleeping husband, tempted to wake him and scream at him. But what good would that do? Lily needed oxygen – and fast. Fighting with Imran at two o'clock in the morning would simply wake both children. It wouldn't help. Nothing would help – except for the electricity to be restored.

Panic threatened to choke her. How long before the portable concentrator's pathetic battery died? Then what would she do? Should she phone her mother? Ask if they had electricity? Gillian wouldn't be impressed at being woken up in the middle of night. She'd never let Kerry forget it. She'd lecture Kerry about being irresponsible for not investing in a generator. But she wouldn't offer to pay for it, not even to save the life of her own grandchild. Anyway, what was the point of involving her parents? It would take too long to drive all the way to Norwood.

Drive! That was it!

Kerry ran back to the lounge and ripped open the portable concentrator's carry case. There it was. She raced back to the bedroom, pulled on slippers and a warm dressing gown, picked up the (fortunately) still sleeping Lily, bundled her in several blankets and carried her – and the portable concentrator – outside into the freezing night air. She barely felt the stones on the path to the driveway through her thin slippers as she moved as quickly as she could to the parked car.

She settled Lily on the back seat, hooked her up to the portable concentrator, trying to ignore the flashing red of the battery warning light and plugged the special recharge cable into a car's cigarette lighter. She started the car and held her breath. The battery's warning light turned from red to orange, an indication that it was charging. She glanced at the car's fuel gauge – just under half. Enough, at least till morning. After that – well she'd make another plan then.

She settled down in the driver's seat. It was going to be a long night. It was bitterly cold, but she didn't want to turn on the heater in case it made her drowsy. She'd heard that sitting in an idling car could be dangerous, it could lead to carbon monoxide poisoning. Or was that only in a closed garage? She opened her window slightly. Better the cold air than poison gas. Lily whimpered but didn't wake. Kerry felt her forehead – it was cold. She felt the back of the baby's neck – nice and warm.

It wasn't as dark as she'd thought it would be, albeit the streetlights were out. There were no lights anywhere. The stars and moon shone brightly in the cloudless sky.

She waited. And watched. It was probably not very safe to be sitting in a stationary car in a quiet street in this area. They were only a few streets from the hostel – and the township. She checked the car doors again. She watched. She waited. She hoped Imran had remembered to chain and padlock the driveway gate, but she wasn't going to get out of the car to check.

It got even colder. The sun would be rising soon. It was always coldest just before the dawn. She shivered and pulled her blanket tighter. The sky began to lighten. She dozed.

Imran was knocking at her window.

"What the hell are you doing? Why are you in the car with

Tiger? It's dangerous out here."

"The portable concentrator. You didn't charge it."

Even in the dim light, Kerry could see Imran's face flush.

"Why didn't you wake me?" he demanded.

"What for?" she asked.

Chapter 19

"She is better, isn't she? I mean she's out of hospital, she's home."

"Yes Mom, she's home," Kerry said, and glanced over at Lily who was propped up on some pillows, her eyes glued to the television where Barney was singing and dancing. She looked just like any other baby, she was just like any other baby if one ignored the oxygen cannulas in her nose. And the nebuliser mask she was holding in place over her nose and mouth. What other fifteen-month-old baby knew how to hold a nebuliser mask in place? It was a new trick she had learned in the two weeks she'd being in hospital fighting her latest infection. The ICU nurses had thought she was the cutest little thing when she held the mask while the steam and medication helped to ease the tightness in her chest. It eased her breathing. The pulmonologist had said they should continue to nebulise her at home, even after she was discharged. So three times a day, Kerry handed her baby the mask, and Lily held it to her face.

"So why is she having another surgery?" Gillian demanded.

"It's not exactly a surgery," Kerry interrupted her mother. "It's more of a procedure."

"A procedure, surgery – whatever, it's still ..."

"It's called a bronchoscope. Dr Govender said they need to see why she still can't manage without supplementary oxygen and a bronchoscope will help them find out what's going on."

"What does that mean? Will she have to be admitted again? Will Dr Govender do it in his rooms? Seems to me the man doesn't know what he is doing. I mean, it's been months and months since he cut open poor little Lily's chest – twice – and he still can't get it right. And she keeps getting sick. How many times has she landed up in hospital this year? Three? Four? That can't be right. I think you need to get a second opinion before you let him cut her open again."

"Mom, I told you. It's not surgery. They're not going to cut her open. Anyway, Dr Govender isn't a surgeon. He doesn't cut ..."

"That's not the point, and you know it!" Gillian said. "I just think your Dr Govender clearly doesn't know what he's doing. Lily isn't getting better. In fact, from what you tell me – or don't tell me because you never tell me anything but it's perfectly obvious to anyone with even half a brain – Lily is getting worse. So either it's because your doctors don't know what they are doing, or Lily isn't going to get better and you are subjecting her to all kinds of operations – sorry, procedures – for no good reason."

Kerry's fingers whitened around the phone and she bit back the retort that was forcing its way past her lips. No good reason? Was trying to give Lily the best possible chance of a normal life 'no good reason'? What did her mother expect her to do? Just give up and let her child die? Not a chance! Not now. Not ever. While Lily still had a chance, even the slightest chance, of getting better, of ... of living, she – her mother – would be right there with her every step of the way. As Lily's mother, wasn't it her duty – no, not her duty ... wasn't it the natural, normal response of any mother to do everything she could, whatever it took, to give her precious daughter every possible chance? Why couldn't *her* own mother, Lily's grandmother, understand that? Why couldn't she support her daughter, and her granddaughter, just once? What kind of mother, what kind of grandmother, just gave up? What kind of mother would *she* be if she gave up on Lily? Especially now. Especially after all Lily had gone through. Especially when Lily was such a fighter. While Lily could fight, she would be right there fighting alongside her. Imran had named Lily well. She was a little tiger.

"Mom," Kerry said through clenched teeth. "Lily's team of doctors – not just Dr Govender, but the whole team at Sunninghill – is the best at this sort of thing in South Africa. They are doing everything they can for Lily. Dr Govender – and Dr Sibanda, her pulmonologist – say the bronchoscope is necessary. Dr Sinclair agrees. So as I said, she will be going into hospital tomorrow for the *procedure*. Not surgery. Procedure."

"There's no need to shout, Kerry-Anne. I just want to be sure you have considered all your options and that you know what you're doing. Let me know what your Dr Govender finds out – and more importantly, what he's going to do about it. More surgery, I suppose."

"I'll call you when ... when I can. I don't know how long it will be so don't worry if you don't hear from me."

"If you don't want me to call me, you can just say so, Kerry-Anne. I know how much you dislike it when I phone you at the hospital, so I won't. But then don't go accusing me of not caring."

"Bye Mom."

Kerry ended the call and resisted the urge to throw her phone against the wall.

She was tired. So tired. Lily's check-up at Dr Govender's rooms today had been one of the worst Kerry could remember. Lily hadn't fought and screamed the way she usually did when Dr Govender scanned her little chest or listened to her laboured breathing. She hadn't yelled when the nurse had stuck the little electrodes to her chest for her ECG; she hadn't screamed when her blood pressure was taken. She hadn't even objected when she'd been put on the scale and weighed. She had just lain there, like an inert little doll.

And then Dr Govender had started ticking off all the things that were worrying him, shaking his head from side to side as he went through the list: Lily wasn't gaining weight; Lily wasn't making progress towards her milestones; Lily was still in heart failure – her heart was still far too enlarged and didn't show any signs of getting smaller, let alone returning to normal; Lily's liver was a little enlarged too, indicating possible – or the start of – liver failure; Lily's breathing was getting worse; Lily's collapsed lung hadn't reinflated

"I don't know, Mrs Patel. I just don't understand it," he'd said.

Kerry had winced as Imran's fingers dug into her shoulder. She'd shrugged his hand off and glared at the doctor. "What do you mean? How can you not know?"

"I'm so sorry. It's been six months since she had the Glen Shunt and she should have made more progress. She's not responding to the medications. In all my years as a paediatric cardiologist, I've never seen a case quite like your little one." Dr Govender sounded tired, defeated.

Surging anger forced Kerry to her feet. "Are you saying there is nothing more you can do for her. You can't just give up on her! I won't let you. I won't!"

"Mrs Patel, no. I'll never give up on a patient. I'd like to bring her in for some tests. I've spoken to her pulmonologist about her breathing and he'd like to do a bronchoscope to see what's going on with her lungs."

"What's that?"

"It's a fairly routine procedure," Dr Govender had said. "Dr Sibanda will just pass a little camera down her trachea – her windpipe – into her lungs and take a little look around. It shouldn't take very long."

"But ... but ... if you're putting a camera down her windpipe, how will she breathe – she'll be terrified!"

"No, no don't worry. She won't be awake. She'll be lightly anaesthetised and if necessary, we may have to put her on a ventilator for the duration of the procedure."

Kerry's blood ran cold. A ventilator – again. She hated that breathing machine with a passion. It terrified her. What if they were unable to get Lily breathing again without it? What if Lily had to stay on a ventilator forever? What if something went wrong? So much could go wrong. Lily was doing okay on high flow oxygen. Was it worth the risk, just to 'look around'? She realised Dr Govender was still talking.

"... and then I'd like to do an angiogram to check her heart. Check that the Glen Shunt is holding – that sort of thing."

Kerry's heart leaped into her throat. "You think there might be something wrong with the shunt? How is that possible?" she squeaked, her mind immediately flashing back to Lily's very first surgery which had required a revision the next day.

"No, no, no, Mrs Patel. I am not saying there is anything wrong with the shunt – it all looks fine on the scan. But ... but scans don't always show everything. I think we need to go back, check everything ... try to see ... it's a very complicated case. I've discussed it with my colleagues, the Professor too. The whole paediatric cardiology team is working together on this. Once we know more, once we have all the facts, then we will have a better idea of what course of action we should take."

"Isn't there another way to do this? Do you have to put her on a ventilator again? Can't she just have another scan? I read somewhere about these really advanced, sophisticated scans."

"I'm sorry, Mrs Patel. I understand how nervous you are. But really, at this point in your little one's treatment, this is our best – our only – real choice. If we could avoid it, we would. But we can't. And the longer we leave it ..." he shook his head sadly.

"When would you like to do it?" she whispered.

"As soon as possible. There's no point in waiting. We can do the bronchoscope early tomorrow, then the angiogram. Bring her in at 6am. Nothing to eat or drink after 10pm tonight and ..."

"Yes, I know the drill," Kerry said. Dr Govender handed her the consent forms. She hesitated, and passed them to Imran for signing. He signed.

Chapter 20

Kerry carried Lily outside, trailing the extra-long oxygen tube behind her. She sat her down on the blanket on the lawn and placed some of her favourite toys within easy reach around her. The sky was just turning from winter's pale, washed-out blue to the bright, deep azure so characteristic of a Highveld summer. The sun too was losing its winter weakness, bathing the little garden in a pleasant warmth. It was a perfect early Spring day. It was a day to be treasured. It was Lily's first day outside in the fresh air since coming home from hospital after her bronchoscope and angiogram.

"To recuperate," Dr Govender had said. "She's had quite an ordeal. We need to give her a little time to get over it."

Watching her daughter play, Kerry felt lighter, as if a massive weight had been lifted off her shoulders. Lily had blossomed since coming home. She was definitely more alert. She was interacting more with everyone, especially Leo. She had even learned a few new words. Perhaps that's what she needed – just to be at home with her loving family. To be given a chance to get over the trauma of all her surgeries and procedures and infections. Lily was a little tiger. She hated being told what to do. She would get well in her own, sweet time. She just had to be given a chance.

Leo came charging over and threw himself down on the blanket next to his baby sister.

"Boo!" he said.

Lily beamed at him. Leo tickled her distended tummy. Lily chortled, the deep infectious sound bringing a smile to Kerry's lips. Leo picked up a plush purple dinosaur and made it jump up and down in front of his sister, occasionally tickling her face with it.

"Barney, Barney, Barney can jump. Jump Barney," Leo sang.

"Barneee, Barneee, Barneeee," Lily echoed.

Lily's chortle morphed into a booming laugh. She laughed, and laughed, and clapped her hands, and laughed some more and wheezed and gasped for breath.

Kerry almost staggered as the weight came crashing down again. She watched, alarmed, as Lily's lips turned blue, the sparkle in her eyes faded, and she waved her hand weakly at her brother before flopping over onto the blanket where she lay, gasping like a stranded fish.

And Kerry knew. She and Imran had been agonising over it for two weeks. From the time Dr Govender and Dr Sibanda, the pulmonologist, had come to the ward together to tell them what the bronchoscope and angiogram had revealed.

"The good news," Dr Govender had said, "is that the Glen Shunt is holding beautifully."

"That's wonderful," Imran murmured and squeezed Kerry's shoulder.

"And the bad news?" Kerry demanded. She ignored Imran's almost imperceptible shake of his head. He didn't want to hear bad news. He never wanted to hear bad news. But Kerry knew there was bad news coming. She could see it in both doctors' faces.

"Well, yes. I'm afraid ... the thing is ... it's because of the little one's heart," Dr Govender said.

"What about her heart?" Kerry asked, dread flooding through her.

"It's too big," the cardiologist said.

"Well, yes – but we've known that for ages," Kerry said, not bothering to hide her annoyance and impatience.

"That's true, but we were hoping it would revert, get a little smaller, but it hasn't and now it is pushing on her trachea – her windpipe, you see, and that's why she is having trouble breathing."

"It's also the reason her left lung has not reinflated since collapsing. To all intents and purposes, she is functioning on only one lung," Dr Sibanda chipped in.

A dozen questions immediately swirled around Kerry's brain. She stared speechlessly at the doctors. Imran's hand had dropped from her shoulder. Kerry could sense him standing motionless behind her; she could hear his strained breathing. She stared at Dr Govender, then at Dr Sibanda. The silence stretched endlessly.

It was Dr Sibanda who finally spoke. Softly. With quiet authority. "But we think we have a solution," he said.

What? Somehow there was suddenly a way to make Lily's heart shrink?

"There are several options available to us," Dr Govender said. "We've discussed it with the team and we've looked at each one carefully. I must be honest with you, none are without risk. And we cannot guarantee their outcome. But we've taken everything into consideration and we think you should consider the option we feel would be most effective."

Kerry shook her head. The words 'risk', 'no guarantees', 'solution' reverberated.

"What are our options?" she whispered.

"Well, we could do nothing – or nothing new. We could continue with her medication and hope that will start to bring her out of heart failure. If that happens, and her heart starts to shrink, the problem with her breathing should ease."

"And if it doesn't? The medication hasn't helped yet, has it? What are the chances that it suddenly starts to make it difference after so long?"

"Not good, I'm afraid," Dr Sibanda said. Dr Govender nodded.

"So, what are the other options?"

"Well, the team has looked at everything and we suggest ... you might consider ... I know you are hesitant to have your little one undergo more surgery but ..." Dr Govender muttered.

Dr Sibanda interrupted: "We recommend Lily have a procedure called an Aortapexy. What we'll do is take her aorta – that's the main artery in her body – and pull it to one side which should relieve the pressure on her trachea."

"How will you do that? Will you have to cut her chest open again?" Kerry demanded.

"I'm afraid so. There's no other way. We will go in through the side of her chest, put a little stitch in her aorta, gently pull it to one side and attach it to her sternum – her breast bone, or perhaps her rib."

"And that will sort out all her breathing problems?"

Dr Govender and Dr Sibanda exchanged a glance and Kerry's blood ran cold.

"As we said, there are no guarantees. But we're hopeful," Dr Govender said.

"And if we don't do it? If we just wait and see ..."

"If we do nothing, the chances are that Lily's breathing will deteriorate. She is likely to become even more susceptible to lung infections and the strain on her heart will in all probability increase. The prognosis is not good," Dr Sibanda said.

"Take your little one home," Dr Govender had said. "Give her a chance to recuperate. Think about it. You don't have to make a decision now."

"But don't leave it too long," Dr Sibanda had added.

Kerry looked at her baby now lying limply on the blanket in the warm sun. She watched her gasping for air. She turned to Imran who had just emerged from the house carrying a tray of snacks and drinks for an impromptu outdoor picnic.

"I'm going to phone Dr Govender. I'm going to tell him we're going ahead with the Aortapexy."

She tried to block out her mother's strident, disapproving, nagging voice in her head: "Another surgery, Kerry? What are you thinking? How can you put your child through yet more pain and suffering? For a highly risky procedure that may not help."

"We don't have a choice," she told Imran – and herself.

Lily lay spread-eagled on the bed in the cardiothoracic ICU attached to tubes and monitors: one on her big toe on her right foot; one on her left ankle; two ECG sensors on her chest; the oxygen tube taped to her cheeks. Pink dummy in her mouth. Dark lashes fanned across her pale cheeks.

"It's time, Mrs Patel, Mr Patel. We have to take Lily to theatre now," the nurse said cheerfully. "You can come along to the theatre doors, if you like."

"Thank you," Kerry said, biting back the retort: "Yes, we know. We've done this before. Lots of times. Too many times."

Imran took her hand as they followed the cot carrying their sleeping baby along the familiar corridors to the operating theatre. Kerry bent and kissed Lily's forehead before the cot disappeared through the doors. Imran did the same. The doors closed.

"Let's get some coffee," they said simultaneously. And smiled at each other weakly. It was all so familiar. So routine. Yet somehow it didn't get any easier.

Their table in the coffee shop was unoccupied. A *good omen*, Kerry thought. Imran ordered a scone with cheese and jam on the side. Kerry watched him convert it into a pile of crumbs. She watched him lift his cup halfway to his lips, and carefully replace it in the saucer. She lifted her cup and stared at it, surprised. Empty. When had she drunk it? She couldn't remember. They waited. They didn't speak. There was nothing to say.

Chapter 21

It went well. The operation went well. The procedure went well. It went well ... Kerry silently chanted Dr Govender's and Dr Sibanda's words like a mantra as she gazed at her baby's tiny little body, draped in her blue theatre gown, lost against the huge white sheet in her hospital cot.

It would take a while, a few days, an unspecified amount of time for the effects of Aortapexy procedure to become apparent, they'd said. Her lung, and her pulmonary vessels which had been compressed for so long could take some time, a while, a few days, to reinflate. They couldn't predict how long it would take. But the procedure went well. It all went well. Lily had come through it all like the tiger she was.

Except her temperature had soared. Sponge baths, cool wet cloths changed regularly were helping. A little. For a short while. She was resting on an icepack. That was helping too. But then her fever would spike again. Another sponge bath. More cool cloths. A new icepack ...

But her vital signs were stable, as long as the oxygen pressure was maintained at three litres per second. She didn't seem to be in pain. She wasn't sedated.

It went well. The procedure went well. It would take time. She was holding her own. Kerry repeated the mantra.

"She is a remarkable little girl, your daughter," Dr Govender said a few days later. "Look how peacefully she is sleeping. Look how nicely she is maintaining her vitals. Look how her temperature has subsided. Her breathing seems much easier. It's been a week since her surgery and she is ready to go home."

Kerry beamed at the cardiologist. "She's a little tiger, our Lily. She is a fighter. She'll never give up," she said.

Dr Govender nodded and almost smiled. "Indeed she is. I think you should take her home tomorrow. That's the best place for her right now."

∾ ৩

"I don't think we should have brought her here," Kerry told Imran as they stood looking down at their daughter lying like a rag doll in her cot in the paediatric ICU at the Zamokhule Hospital in Tembisa.

"It was closest. We wouldn't have made it to Sunninghill in time. You know that. We agreed it was best!"

Kerry nodded reluctantly. She'd never forget that mad dash, in the middle of the night, with Lily gasping for breath in her arms despite the portable oxygen machine turned up to its highest level of six litres per second.

There had been no indication that anything was amiss when they'd brought Lily home from Sunninghill Hospital that morning with Dr Govender's blessing and assurances ringing in her ears that all was on track and she would soon be so much better.

Or had there been signs? What had she missed? She was Lily's mother. She knew her better than anyone. Had she been so determined to believe that the Aortapexy had worked, that Lily was on the road to recovery, that she'd overlooked a tiny, almost imperceptible clue that something was not right.

Leo had been so overjoyed to have his sister home again. Lily had been so excited to see him too. Her booming laughter had enveloped the house like a warm hug, lifting everyone's mood. The children had played happily together on Lily's makeshift bed on the lounge floor. Well, to be honest, Leo had played, egged on by his sister's exhortations and chortles, and Lily had watched, her breathing laboured and slow, her lips and fingertips blue.

Kerry had convinced herself to ignore the signs. It was too soon to expect much. Lily had been through so much – the surgery, the fever. She had only just been discharged that morning. She needed time to settle down at home. She would be fine, just fine.

Except that night, Lily's distress was so obvious that Kerry couldn't ignore it a moment longer. Imran's face as he carried a sleeping Leo across the road to Mrs Reddy's house had been pasty and pale.

"She needs more oxygen than we can give her. We have to get her to hospital as quickly as we can. Zamokhule Hospital is only ten minutes away. We have to take her there. They can stabilise her and then, if necessary, we can transfer her to Sunninghill," Imran had said.

And now, two weeks later, Lily still hadn't stabilised. She'd been hooked up to the CPAP machine immediately on her admission to the hospital. Kerry had protested, but the paediatrician on duty had assured her that CPAP – continuous positive airway pressure – wasn't the same as the invasive ventilators she hated so much. With CPAP, Lily would have to initiate all her breathing on her own; she wouldn't become so dependent on a machine breathing for her that it would be difficult to wean her off it. But it would keep her lungs' little alveoli open while she recovered from whatever it was that was affecting her breathing in the first place. Except, they didn't know why but she wasn't getting any better. They didn't even know what was wrong. What they did know, after umpteen blood tests which the medical insurance would probably refuse to pay for, again, was that Lily didn't have an infection. She didn't have bronchitis. She didn't have pneumonia.

"I've spoken to her cardiologist and pulmonologist at Sunninghill," the Zamokhule Hospital paediatrician said. "We believe it will be best if we transfer her there, and let them take a look at her. They know her. They're the best people to take it from here."

"They took her off the ventilator after the Aortapexy too soon. They discharged her too soon," Kerry said bitterly. "They should never have sent her home so soon after the Aortapexy."

"They took her off the ventilator because she was able to breathe on her own. The longer she was kept on the ventilator, the harder it would become to wean her off it," the paediatrician said

"I know that. But ... things keep going wrong. My mother was right. They don't know what they are doing!"

"They're doing the best they can," Imran said.

Kerry turned away. She wasn't about to let the paediatrician – or Imran – see the tears of helpless rage in her eyes.

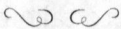

"Thank you Triphina, that will be all," Gillian said. Triphena put the tray on the dining room table, smiled kindly at Kerry, and disappeared back through the kitchen door to watch over Leo. Kerry wished she could go with her. She wished she'd stay. She wished Triphina would take her in her arms and comfort her, just as she'd always done when she was little and had been upset or frightened or worried.

"Right, who wants tea? Coffee?" Gillian rose to her feet, raised the Royal Albert teapot that was only brought out from the depths of the 'good crockery' cupboard for special occasions, and glanced around the table. The whole family was there, thanks to her summons that morning to an 'emergency family meeting' scheduled for after Kerry returned from visiting at Sunninghill. This was the third such meeting for which she had been directly responsible, Kerry mused. The first was when she had moved in with Imran. She'd been subjected to nearly three hours of haranguing (from her father); tears and high-pitched threats (from her mother); concerned, if reluctant, support from Eliot; and stony-faced disapproval from Neville. The second of these meetings had taken place when she'd announced her intention to marry Imran. If anything, it had been worse than the first, with tears, recriminations, declarations of unconditional, undying love, and promises of support for her – and the unborn child – if only she'd come home and not ruin her life forever.

Kerry glanced around the table and noticed that the three Aarons siblings – Eliot, Neville and herself – and her father,

Stephen, had automatically taken up the seats they had occupied for as long as she could remember. Imran – at his first such meeting – was perched on a hastily added kitchen chair at her side. Gillian was in her customary place at the head of the table, closest to the kitchen, and Stephen was at the foot, closest to the liquor cabinet.

With teas and coffees dispensed, the customary Devonshire Cream cake from Cookies Bakery sliced and shared, Gillian settled back in her chair and glared at Imran.

"Kerry-Anne, explain it to me," she said. "What exactly did that doctor of yours say he was going to do to Lily this time?"

"I've already told you, Mom."

"Well, tell me again. I want your father and your brothers to hear it too. It doesn't sound right to me. I can't believe you'd even consider it. I can't imagine how you are expected to take care of a baby like that."

Kerry clenched her fists. Next to her, Imran sat motionless, his head bowed but Kerry heard his sharp intake of breath.

Sucking in as much air as she could, as if she were preparing to dive into a pool at the start of a 400-metre medley race, Kerry straightened in her chair and opened her mouth. The voice that emerged wasn't hers. It was whispery, wavery, weak ...

"Lily is still on a ventilator. It's been two weeks since she was admitted to Sunninghill and they can't extubate her."

"What does that mean?" Gillian demanded.

"Mom, don't interrupt. Let Kerry finish," Eliot said.

"I just want to make sure we all understand everything," Gillian snapped.

"It means she can't breathe on her own. It means she is stuck on a ventilator. And they want to ... they have to ... they may have to ... we may have to keep her on it permanently. Forever."

"That's ridiculous, they don't know what they are doing," Gillian said, her voice grating like fingernails on a chalkboard.

"Gillian! Shut up. Just shut up!" Stephen said.

All heads swung in Stephen's direction. He seemed to shrink into his chair.

"I … I … just meant … this is hard enough for Kerry. And … and Imran." Then suddenly, he sat upright and glared at his wife. "You called this so-called family emergency meeting to hear what Kerry … and Imran … have to say, about Lily. About what's going on. So for heaven's sake, will you … can we all just shut up and listen for once. I need a drink."

Stephen deliberately settled his delicate Royal Albert teacup in the saucer and stood up. "Anyone else want one?" he asked, opening the liquor cabinet.

"It's only five o'clock!" Gillian objected.

"I'll have whisky, neat," Eliot said.

"Same, with a splash of water in mine," said Neville.

"No thanks," Imran muttered. Kerry shook her head.

"Sorry about the interruption," said Stephen, settling back into this chair swirling a hefty shot of golden liquid in a crystal tumbler, ignoring his wife's baleful glare across the table.

"That's okay Dad," said Kerry.

Having refilled her teacup, Gillian slammed down the teapot. "Well go on Kerry. Don't keep us all in suspense."

"Okay. So Dr Sibanda – that's Lily's pulmonologist. He says they can't keep her in ICU on a ventilator anymore. They can't keep her sedated any longer – it isn't good for her. She isn't … they say … they can't …" Kerry swallowed, blinked and forced the words out in a rush: "They say she will have to be ventilated at home. That means she will have to have a tracheotomy. That's a tube they'll put in her throat and … and when they do that it means … it means …"

She blinked again, and again, but she couldn't stop the tears from overflowing and spilling down her face. This was her worst nightmare. The last thing she wanted was to cry in front of her mother, her father, her brothers … and Imran. Poor Imran who she knew was also battling to hold it together. If she gave in, if she showed weakness now, it would destroy him. She felt Imran's hand on hers, she felt him squeeze her fingers. She turned and looked at him. He gazed back at her with such love, such deep compassion and understanding, such sadness, that Kerry lost it.

She cried. She felt Imran's arms go around her. She turned to her husband, buried her face in his chest and sobbed. Imran held her, rocked her, made soothing comforting murmurs in her ear. She howled. The rest of the world receded. It was just her and Imran, bound together in a pain so deep, so visceral, nothing else mattered.

Eventually, the crying storm abated. Kerry hiccupped, gulped, sniffed. Her father handed her a white serviette.

"Blow," he said. Visions of her mother's horrified face drifted before her as she blew into the damask. Having already ruined one of Gillian's prized pieces of linen, she used a clean corner of it to wipe her eyes.

"I'm sorry," she gulped, sitting down again. "It's just ..." She stopped. She couldn't say it.

Imran took over. "What's Kerry's trying to explain is that if they do the tracheotomy, it could damage her larynx – her voice box. It could be permanent. But even if it doesn't cause permanent damage, the tube would go over her vocal cords. So she wouldn't be able to ..." Imran faltered.

Kerry continued: "She won't be able to talk. Or cry. Or laugh. She won't be able to laugh. Her voice will be gone. We'll never hear her, not while she is ventilated. She could end up being silenced. Forever."

"Oh no. That's dreadful. Are you sure?" Stephen asked.

Kerry was horrified to see tears running down her father's face.

"My poor, poor Kerry. What a terrible situation for you ... and Imran of course .... Is there nothing else that can be done? When are they going to do this?"

"They've said ... probably tomorrow. Imran and I, we haven't made up our minds yet what to do. They gave us the consent forms to sign. But really, Dr Sibanda made it pretty clear. There's nothing else ... we have no choice, really."

"Oh Kerry. How awful. But please know this, sweetheart. Whatever happens ... whatever you and Imran decide, we will support you. Won't we, Gillian?"

"Of course I'll support her. Don't I always?" Gillian said.

Stephen ignored her. "Kerry, it may not be so bad. I'm sure they can do it without damaging her vocal cords. Lily is a fighter. She's a tiger. She will roar again, you'll see," he said.

"Oh Dad, thank you," Kerry said, tears welling again. "I'm sorry to make such a fuss. I'm just so scared, so frightened."

"We all are," Gillian muttered.

Chapter 22

Dr Sibanda listened to Lily's chest, stared at the oxymeter readings on the monitor above her cot in Sunninghill cardiothoracic ICU, shook his head and frowned.

Seated on the other side of the cot, Kerry's stomach churned. She watched him carefully, trying to read something – anything – from his inscrutable expression. Behind her, Imran lightly squeezed her shoulder. The pressure of his hand felt comforting, reassuring. She rested her head against his arm. She could never have made it through the past two weeks since her meltdown at the family meeting without him.

"Well?" said Dr Govender, bustling across the ICU towards them. "How's our little patient doing today?"

Dr Sibanda shook his head again and folded his arms. A grimace of a smile cracked his usually dour face.

"You were right," he said to his beaming colleague. "She's holding her own nicely."

"She's more than holding her own," Kerry wanted to shout. "She's getting better!"

It had been Dr Govender who had persuaded Dr Sibanda to hold off on the scheduled tracheotomy that would have placed Lily on the road to home ventilation and perpetual silence.

"I know this little patient," he'd said when Kerry and Imran had joined him in Dr Sibanda's office, the still unsigned consent forms for the tracheotomy in her handbag. "She's a fighter. She has confounded me time and again. Every time I've thought 'this is it', she turns the corner. Let's give her more time."

Dr Sibanda had eventually agreed, making his reluctance

to wait even another day stubbornly obvious. "One week," he'd growled.

"Two!" said Dr Govender.

"Okay, two more weeks. And that's it! We really cannot keep her sedated on this invasive ventilation for longer. It's already been too long. If she's not breathing on her own in two weeks, we'll do the tracheotomy. There's no alternative. We shouldn't even be waiting that long."

The two gifted weeks had been the longest two weeks of Kerry's life. Every day she'd sat by Lily's cot, watching, waiting, pleading with whatever amorphous, unnamed gods there were for a sign that Lily was improving. Imran had taken to going to the new mosque near their home for his daily prayers. He said Imam Omar there was amazing, the support of his fellow devotees comforting.

And then it came. The miracle that Imran had been imploring Allah for in his daily prayers. Lily started to turn the corner. Slowly she was weaned off the ventilator. Slowly she was woken from her sedation. Slowly, so slowly, she woke up.

"Mama," she'd murmured when Kerry approached her cot on day twelve following Dr Sibanda's ultimatum. It was said so softly, in such a hoarse, broken little voice that Kerry wasn't sure at first if she'd imagined it.

"Mama," Lily whispered again, with a sleepy smile and a glimmer of a twinkle in her big brown eyes.

Kerry didn't bother to hide her tears.

Spring day. Imran and Kerry drove to Sunninghill Hospital at 7am. The car ate up the kilometres on the almost deserted multilane highway. Kerry retuned the radio to 5FM. It usually played good music on Sundays. But the radio was silent – not even a crackle. She switched to Metro FM. Also silence.

"That's odd," Kerry said.

"Let's just listen to 702."

"I don't want to listen to news and talk today. It's always so depressing," Kerry said. But Imran had already changed the radio station, in time to hear the newsreader report that many of the national broadcaster's radio stations, including 5FM and Metro FM were not on air because of a power failure in Auckland Park where the SABC's head office was located.

And in other news, the newsreader continued, a man had been arrested in connection with the disappearance last Saturday of University of Cape Town student Uyinene Mrwetyana, although it still hadn't been officially confirmed whether the body of a young woman found in Kyalelitsha, the overcrowded, high-density shackland outside the city, was hers.

Kerry turned off the radio. "No, I don't want to hear about young women being murdered. It's the first day of Spring. The sun is shining. The blossoms are blossoming. And we're going to fetch our baby girl home, for the first time in weeks. No, not weeks. It's been nearly two months! Today is a good day. I don't want anything to spoil it."

"Nothing can spoil it," Imran said, but he didn't argue. They drove on to the hospital in contented silence.

Dr Govender was already doing his rounds when they walked into the ward. He saw them at Lily's cot and bustled over.

"Ah, perfect timing," he said. "I was just about to discharge your baby. She has done very well, far better than we could have anticipated in the circumstances."

Kerry's ebullient mood evaporated. She could sense a 'but' coming. Dr Govender was smiling, but his eyes were sombre.

"She's done incredibly well! She's such a little fighter. I knew we shouldn't ever give up on her," Kerry said, determined to be cheerful – for Lily, and for Imran.

But Dr Govender wouldn't co-operate. He shook his head sadly. "Although we're sending Lily home, you must understand, she is still a very, very ill little girl."

"But she's getting better. She's going to get better. Isn't she?" Kerry asked. The familiar knot of anxiety tightened around her heart.

Dr Govender hesitated. "It's too early ... there's no way ... she may. She could. But from a medical, from a surgical perspective ... I'm sorry Mrs Patel, we've done all we can for her," he said.

Kerry gripped the side of Lily's cot, her knuckles whitening. "What do you mean you've done all you can? You can't give up on her. I won't let you!" She could hear the note of rising hysteria in her voice, but she couldn't help it.

"We're not giving up on her," Dr Govender said, his soothing, reassuring tones sending Kerry's rapidly fraying nerve endings into jangling overdrive. "Your little one has to get stronger. She needs time to get stronger. We have to give her a chance ... time .... You must understand. She has been through so much."

"But ... but we can't just do nothing! We have to do something – you have to. You're her doctor!"

"Mrs Patel please, try to understand. We'll keep her on her medication of course – and monitor her regularly. And she will continue to need supplementary oxygen. But other than that ... there's nothing more ... our surgical options are ... she will have her next surgery, as scheduled, when she is older. And stronger. We discussed all this before. Until then ..."

"But her medication isn't helping. You said so yourself – her heart is still enlarged, so is her liver. She still battles to breath. There has to be more we can do – there must be. We have to do something ... anything."

A black cloud of impotent despair engulfed her. Kerry tried to shake it off, but it clung to her like a shroud, transforming her from the strong, determined, optimistic mother she knew she should be into a pathetic, whining, pleading excuse for a human being.

"I'm sorry. I'm truly sorry. I wish we could do more. But we can't. All we can do is wait for Lily to get stronger. We have to help her to get stronger. Perhaps ... you need to try and get her to eat solid food again. And perhaps, some exercise. Perhaps you should consider some rehabilitation therapies – physiotherapy. That may help, also with her milestones. But the main thing is to keep her safe and well. Away from infection – the type of infections she could so easily pick up in a hospital environment."

Kerry stared at him. She opened her mouth to speak. Closed it. She looked at Imran. He appeared to be as stunned as she was.

"Take Lily home, Mrs Patel, Mr Patel. Keep her safe. Bring her back in a month for a check-up."

"He sounded like he was sending Lily home to die!" Kerry fumed, after settling Lily down to sleep in her camp cot at the foot of their bed.

The humming of the large oxygen concentrator filled the house. Oh, how she'd missed that sound all the while Lily had been in hospital. And oh, how she hated that sound with a passion. It was the aural manifestation of Lily's frailty, and of her own maternal failure. That hum followed her day and night, in the bathroom; in the kitchen while she tried to conjure up something, anything, that Lily might eat; in the lounge where she watched her poor, neglected son trying to play with his adored sister. It was the last thing she heard before falling into an exhausted sleep at night and the first thing she heard when she woke a few hours later. It was a constant reminder that Lily was ... that Lily wasn't ... that her baby daughter was broken and she couldn't fix her.

"No, no. I'm sure that's not what Dr Govender meant. Of course they're not sending her home to die," Imran said.

"Well, he said they can't do anything more. He's giving up on her."

"I don't think he meant it like that. But perhaps ... perhaps," Imran hesitated. He stroked his beard. "Kerry, perhaps he's right. Perhaps we need to leave it in Allah's – in God's hands. Perhaps we need to prepare ourselves ..."

"No! No. What's the matter with you, Imran? You can't believe this is all there is for Lily. That after all she's been through, everything she has overcome, that she is just going to ... that we're ... that I am just going to let her fade away. No! It's not going to happen. I won't let it happen."

In the lounge, Leo was watching Barney on TV – again. Ever since they'd told him that Lily was coming home, he'd refused to watch anything else. "Lily likes Barney so I like Barney," he'd said.

The happy tunes, the cheerful voice of the purple dragon plucked at her nerves. The sound of the oxygen concentrator drilled through her brain. She opened her mouth, gasping for air like a stranded fish. She felt the walls crashing in on her.

"I can't ... I just can't," she said and pushed past her husband, fleeing from the prison that her home had become. She had to get out. She had to breathe. She had to think. She had to figure out how to be the mother that Lily deserved.

Chapter 23

Kerry glanced at the clock on the lounge wall. Three o'clock. One hour to go. Just an hour. She strained her ears, then smiled ruefully. All she could hear were the usual sounds: the oxygen concentrator puffing away in the bedroom. Lily's faint murmurs as she slept fitfully on her makeshift bed on the lounge floor. The TV was silent. Leo was playing across the road. She moved into the kitchen and wiped the counters down again. Three thirty. Time to change, except she was already changed. She opened the fridge. She closed the fridge. She went into the bedroom. She straightened the bed. Lily cried out. Kerry hurried back into the lounge. Lily whimpered. Kerry hurried back into the kitchen and got a bottle of Lily's Frebini nutritional supplement. Back to the lounge. She lifted Lily's pink dress, exposing her distended little belly with its jutting peg feeding tube. She carefully cleaned the feeding tube and poured in the liquid. Lily smiled up at her – and vomited, the projectile spray hitting Kerry's T-shirt. Grabbing the towel she always kept close at hand, Kerry lifted Lily into a sitting position, wiped the baby's mouth and dabbed ineffectively at her T-shirt. She'd have to change. Again. She swallowed her annoyance. It wasn't Lily's fault. She shouldn't have poured the Frebini so quickly. She shouldn't have been so impatient. She should have been paying closer attention. She shouldn't have been distracted by the silence. She glanced at the clock. Almost time. She strained her ears for the sound of impending freedom. Oh, how she missed Palesa, whose recent acceptance into nursing school had relieved Kerry of the trauma of having to tell her, once again, that they could no longer afford to pay her the pittance they had been giving her since she'd agreed to come back in exchange for her transport costs, food, and pocket money.

"I am getting good experience helping with Lily. This will help me get into nursing school," she'd said.

"Mama! Mama. Barney," Lily demanded.

Kerry sighed. She turned the TV on, and the purple dragon's gratingly cheery voice drowned out any chance she'd have of hearing the car coming down the road. She hurried into the bedroom, pulled off her soiled T-shirt, replaced it with a fresh one from the wardrobe, and hurried back into the lounge. And groaned. Lily had vomited again. No wonder she wasn't getting any stronger – she hardly kept any of the very expensive supplement down. Perhaps it was too rich. She'd phone Dr Sinclair in the morning. Clearly the medicine the paediatrician had prescribed to try and prevent the vomiting wasn't working. Perhaps she should try and call now, but ... but it was too late. It was already after four o'clock. Her annoyance bubbled up. This time, she didn't even try to suppress it. Imran was late. He'd promised he wouldn't be late again.

She wiped up the vomit and carried the soiled towel into the kitchen. She'd soak it later. She opened the fridge. Nothing had changed. Everything was still ready for dinner. All she'd have to do was pop it in the microwave when she got back. She heard the key in the front door and flew back into the lounge. Imran was home.

She pecked him on the cheek, blew a kiss in her daughter's direction, grabbed her cellphone and flew out the door into the warm Spring afternoon.

Kerry's heart pounded. Sweat poured down her face, dripping into her ears. Her straining mouth sucked at the air, trying to force oxygen into her constricted lungs. She couldn't go on. She stopped, gasping as she bent over and pushed the 'pause' button on her Fitbit. She had protested when Imran had proudly presented the smart watch to her. They couldn't afford it, she'd reminded him. Imran was doing his best, but it seemed that demand for kitchen renovations and built-in cupboards had dropped even more over the past year. And the lousy review of I & K Kitchens on the *Hello Peter* website from Mrs Levinson wasn't helping matters much. There were contracts to be had, but these were getting smaller and smaller, customers more demanding, complaints more frequent. Or perhaps the problem was that Imran just wasn't paying as much attention to his business as he should, especially when Lily was stable, as she was now. But he was stretched to the hilt, trying to do it all: sales, marketing, project management, admin. And going to mosque to pray, every day. She'd offered to help but he'd turned her down. She had enough on her plate, he said. And he was trying, so hard, to be the best father, the best husband, the best entrepreneur he could be. Kerry didn't want to do anything that could make him feel even more inadequate than he already did.

"You don't have to come with me to Dr Govender for Lily's check-up," Kerry always said.

"You can't manage alone. And I want to be there – Lily's my daughter too. You can't do everything," he always responded.

"Neither can you," Kerry wanted to reply, but never did. Imran troubled her. His face was gaunt and pale, his eyes sunken. He never laughed. He hardly smiled. Well, he did smile – at Lily and at Leo. Sometimes. At night, he tossed and turned. When she got up to check on Lily, she could feel his eyes following her every move. When she got up in the pale predawn, heading to the kitchen to prepare Lily's medications for the day and pack lunches for Imran and Leo, Imran got up too – to pray. She wished he'd stay in bed longer. He needed to rest, to sleep.

He was anxious about her too, she knew it. It was her fault. She didn't want him to worry. He had enough to be worried about. But how was she to know he'd come home to pick up those papers he'd been working on all weekend? For the Khumalo's kitchen. A big contract, if he got it. So he'd walked in while she'd been curled up on the couch, snivelling like a two-year-old, the house looking like it had been hit by a tsunami.

The next day, he'd arrived home and with a rare smile, handed her a little box, beautifully wrapped in red paper, with a silver bow.

"What's this? It's not my birthday," she'd protested.

"I want, I want – let me!" Leo had insisted, making a grab for it.

"It's for your mother," Imran had said, picking up his son and cuddling him. "It's to help her cope with all of us."

Swallowing her misgivings, Kerry had carefully unwrapped the box. The silver smartwatch had winked at her.

Now it glinted in the bright sunlight. Four kilometres done. She smiled. Imran knew her so well. Her daily runs were saving her sanity. She knew it was wrong that Imran had to leave work early to give her a chance to get out of the house, to go and run off her frustrations while it was still light. She knew this was putting more strain on her kind, caring, thoughtful, stressed-out husband. But she was grateful, so grateful for the hour she could spend pounding the streets.

It had been hard, at first. Years of no exercise, two babies, too much weight and general exhaustion had taken their toll on her athletic prowess. But the Fitbit drove her on. She couldn't allow Imran's reckless generosity to go to waste. And it hadn't. She'd done it. Four kilometres. And in a pretty decent time too. She grinned. Tomorrow, she'd do four-and-a-half.

She pushed open the gate and walked slowly to the front door, trying to suppress the knot of dread that tightened again in her stomach.

Chapter 24

Kerry smiled at the pretty young woman sitting on the floral couch opposite her. Risa smiled back.

"I'm so glad we finally got together, what with all the holidays and Christmas and everything," Risa said. "The kids are having a great time, aren't they?"

Kerry nodded and grinned. Lily's chortles grew even louder as six-year-old Anesta made a white stuffed bunny hop into Lily's lap and out again.

"Boo!" said Anesta.

"Bunny ... more bunny," Lily giggled.

Anesta got up from the blanket on the floor and skipped to the other side of the room. She picked up a pink teddy bear, skipped back and flopped down next to Lily again.

"Teddy," Anesta panted through darkening lips. "Here Lily ... a teddy ... for you ... to play."

Kerry looked anxiously at the child's mother, but Risa seemed to be quietly unperturbed at the sudden deterioration in her daughter's condition.

"Risa – is Anesta okay?" Kerry asked quietly, although it was patently obvious that she wasn't.

"It'll pass," Risa said, but Kerry noticed that her eyes were glued to Anesta's pale face. "She just needs a bit of time to catch her breath after all that exertion. That's all. She'll be fine. She'll be fine."

"Shouldn't you ... we ... shouldn't her oxygen be increased?'

Risa shook her head. "It's as high as it can go. Don't worry. She'll be fine. In a few minutes – she'll be fine. It's just – it's just that it's getting harder and harder for her to do anything, even walking quickly across the room. I try to remind her to take things slow, but she forgets. I forget sometimes too. Please excuse me – I'll go put the kettle on again. I'm sure you'd like another cup of tea – or coffee?"

Risa hurried out the lounge but not before Kerry had seen the glint of tears in her eyes.

On the floor, Anesta seemed to have regained her former perkiness. She sat up and bounced the teddy on her lap while Lily did the same with the bunny. Then she got up and hopped around Lily, inadvertently knotting her oxygen tube with Lily's. As Kerry hurried to disentangle them, the new friends shrieked in unison. Kerry laughed with them, relieved that no harm had been done. Their oxygen concentrators – Lily's small and portable, and Anesta's large and powerful – seemed to be working just fine, pushing life-preserving oxygen through their nasal cannulas into their tortured bodies.

This was the first time, outside of the hospital, that Lily had met a child who was also hooked up to an oxygen machine. It was a first for Kerry too. She hoped Risa hadn't noticed how she'd stared when she'd walked into the lounge and saw the little girl with her long, dark hair so like Lily's, sitting quietly on the floor paging through a large picture book.

"It's great to meet you in person at last," Risa had said, leading them into the lounge.

Kerry looked around. "You have a beautiful house. It's so bright and airy. And you've decorated it so nicely. Did you do it all yourself?"

"Yes, thanks. But we're selling it – so if you know anyone who's looking? You can plug Lily in there – do you need an extension cord or is the cord on your concentrator long enough? Anesta, put your book away and come and say hello to Lily."

"I'll put Lily on the floor next to you, shall I?" Kerry said.

"Okay. Are you also PH?" Anesta asked Lily, tilting her head and staring hard at her.

"PH?" Kerry asked.

"You know, like me. Pulmonary Hypertension."

"No, Lily's lungs are okay," Kerry said.

"Oh. Then what's wrong with her? Why is she on oxygen?"

"It's her heart."

"Oh. Okay." Anesta had clearly lost interest in the conversation with Kerry and turned back to Lily who was staring at her with enormous eyes. "Do you want to see my room? Is your oxygen long enough?"

"Lily can't walk – or crawl yet," Kerry said.

"Oh. Okay. We can play here. Do you want to hold my bunny? It's my favourite. It was my brother's but now it's mine," Anesta said.

The two children played and Kerry and Risa chatted. Kerry felt as if she'd known her forever. It had been a stroke of inspiration to join that Facebook group for mothers of children with congenital diseases. She'd been feeling so low, so frustrated and out of her depth. And then she'd met Risa. They discovered they lived only a few kilometres away from each other and regularly promised to get together. But something always intervened.

"Perhaps we'll run into each other at Dr Sinclair," Risa had joked when they discovered they shared the same paediatrician. And Dr Sibanda had been Anesta's pulmonologist too, for a while, when her own pulmonologist had been away.

For the first time, when talking about Lily, Kerry felt as if she'd found a kindred spirit. Risa understood. She knew what it was like to watch your child battling to breathe and being stared at – sometimes with pity, more often with morbid curiosity – in supermarkets and shopping malls. She understood the terror that gripped you when your child got an infection. She knew how the ICU smell permeated your very pores and followed you home. When Lily got a sniffle, it was Risa who could calmly remind her that not all sniffles were dangerous, and Kerry would know she was right.

Certainly, their individual circumstances were not the same. Risa had not endured the nail-biting terror of waiting out multiple surgeries. But, as far as Kerry was concerned, she had experienced far, far worse. How Risa maintained her air of equanimity, of poise and quiet self-assurance was beyond Kerry – especially after having lost her two sons to the same horrific condition that could take her little girl too.

"You must come again, when we get back," Risa said as she ushered Kerry and Lily to the door later that afternoon. "I haven't seen Anesta this happy for ages. She really loves Lily."

"Get back? You didn't say that you were going somewhere." Kerry stopped and stared at her new friend. Something in Risa's tone made her realise that this was about more than just a short holiday. Was this why their house was on the market? Were they emigrating? No, they couldn't be emigrating – they were coming back.

Risa hesitated then blurted: "We're going to India. I'm sorry. I didn't mean to say anything about it."

"India? Why on earth would you go to India? How long will you be away?"

"I don't know. A few months, perhaps."

Kerry's heart dropped. She'd just made a friend, a real friend. Their online chats had been fun, but not the same as sitting in the same room and watching their daughters have fun together. In the few hours they'd spent together, Kerry had felt a connection – a real connection to Risa. Risa got her. And Lily had just found a friend – her first real friend. And now they were going away – to India of all places. For a few months.

"But ... but ... can Anesta travel? I mean – I'm sorry. It's none of my business but why are you going to India? I mean it's so far. And there's that mystery new disease in China – I was reading about it. They say it's dangerous to go there now. They say people shouldn't travel and ..." Kerry's voice faltered.

"We're not going to China. China isn't anywhere near where we're going. Anyway, the stories about that disease have been blown out of all proportion. You know how the media loves to sensationalise everything. It's just a flu virus. It's no big deal."

"So why didn't you tell me?" Kerry demanded, and then, realising how harsh and accusatory she sounded, she reached over and touched Risa's hand.

"I didn't want to upset you."

"Why would I be upset?" Kerry asked, ignoring the little voice in her head that confirmed Risa's concern: she was upset. She felt as if she were about to cry.

"Look, let's sit. I don't want to talk about this while we stand here in the doorway."

Risa led the way back into the lounge. Kerry sat and held Lily tightly on her lap.

"So, why are you going to India, of all places? And for so long?" she blurted.

"It's Anesta. The doctors here can't do anything more for her," Risa said softly, glancing over to where her daughter now lay limply on the couch. "But there's a doctor in India. I found out about him from a British woman I met on an international PH site. She took her son to see him and ... and he's better. Her son is better! So I got in touch with him and after he'd seen all of Anesta's medical records – my doctor wasn't happy about giving them to me but eventually I got them out of him and sent them to India – anyway, the doctor there said they'd probably accept Anesta onto their programme. They have to do their own tests, of course."

"So, you're saying that there's a treatment for PH in India that isn't available in South Africa? Well then, of course you have to go," Kerry said.

Risa eyes filled and overflowed. "It's not that easy. You see, the only – the only hope for Anesta is a double lung transplant. The doctors here haven't said that but I know. I watched both my sons die, I watched them suffer. I can't let that happen to Anesta. But I can see that she is going exactly the same way. She is going to die. We're having to resuscitate her more and more often. I can't lose another child, I just can't. I won't."

"What? Resuscitate her? What do you mean?"

"Oh I'm so sorry. I didn't mean to talk about it ... it's not un-usual for PH sufferers. Her heart just stops sometimes – it just happens. There's no real reason – it's just part of her illness, you see. And then, I have to resuscitate her."

"What happens if you don't – I mean, what happens if you're sleeping or ... or taking a shower or something ..." Kerry stared at her friend in horror.

Risa's mouth twisted. "I never leave her alone during the day and at night – well, we've one of those cot death alarms hooked up in her bed. So, when her heart stops, it wakes us up."

"You mean it's happened before? At night, when you're sleeping?"

"Yes – a few times. And as I said, it's happening more often now so that's why we have to get her a double-lung transplant as soon as possible. Before it's too late. Before I can't resuscitate her. But her chances of getting a transplant here are slim – non-existent probably."

"So that's why you're going to India. For a lung transplant? Do you have a donor? Is that why you're going now?"

"No, of course not. We just have to go and wait for a donor. It sounds dreadful – waiting for another child to die so mine can live. But what's the alternative?"

Kerry nodded. "When do you go?"

"Sunday. I'll fly with Anesta and my husband will come as soon as the house and everything is sold."

Realisation dawned and Kerry wanted to weep for the woman sitting on the couch, stroking her daughter's hair.

"You have to sell your house to pay for it all, don't you?"

"We don't have a choice. The medical aid won't pay for it – they say the surgery can be done in South Africa – if it's really necessary. Of course it's necessary! Oh, her doctors don't say that, of course. They say perhaps when she's older. But she won't live till she's older. You'd do the same thing, I'm sure you would."

Kerry nodded again. Of course she would – if she had a house to sell, and if that would save her daughter, she'd do it in a heartbeat. But she didn't have a house, and anyway, Lily was holding her own. She hadn't had a spell in hospital for a few months. She wasn't getting better – her heart was still enlarged – but Dr Govender had said she was holding her own when he'd cleared her for their holiday in Umhlanga.

She had almost hoped he would say the eight-hour drive would be too much for Lily. But that was selfish of her. Yes, she was dreading the trip but Imran was so excited about it. So were the kids, especially Leo. His first words, every morning since Imran had told him that they were going to Umhlanga, were: "Can I swim in the sea today?" Lily, who didn't really understand what was planned, nevertheless knew something exciting was in the air.

"Well then – we'll see you and Anesta when you get back," Kerry said as she settled Lily into her car seat and plugged the portable oxygen concentrator into the car lighter socket.

"See you," Risa smiled.

Risa presented a lonely, frail figure in the rearview mirror as Kerry drove away. So small and yet so strong. So much tragedy in her life – yet still filled with hope. *An inspiration,* Kerry thought.

Chapter 25

The drive down to Umhlanga had been horrible. The drive home was even worse – but, Kerry thought as she mopped sweat from her face, travelling 700km in heavy traffic with two unhappy, rapidly dehydrating kids crammed into the back of the over-loaded Toyota Corolla with its non-functional air conditioning, was a breeze compared to the previous five days.

How her heart had soared the night before last when the newsreader made the sombre announcement that the provincial borders were to be closed. She'd smothered a grin when the newsreader added that South Africa was about to enter what the government was calling a Level Five lockdown designed to give the country's hospitals three weeks to prepare for the coming tsunami of Covid-19 cases.

"Oh no," she'd wailed, metaphorically crossing her fingers behind her back. "We have to cut our holiday short. We have to get back before the borders close. I'd better start packing so we can leave first thing tomorrow."

"There's no need to rush. We've got a few days before the lockdown starts," Ammi Patel said. "Imran needs this holiday. He works so hard for you and the children."

Kerry forced her lips into a grimacing smile as she turned to her mother-in-law.

"I don't think we should take a chance," she said, hoping her tone conveyed concern rather than jubilation. "I'm worried that the roads will be really busy if we leave it to the last minute to go. And what if something goes wrong and we're delayed? We also need to make sure we have enough of everything before the lockdown starts. I mean, I need to order Lily's meds – I'd better phone and order more to pick up when we get home. And I must get another oxygen cylinder just in case – and food. I must stock up on food, and toilet paper … they say there's going to be a shortage of toilet paper … and …" Kerry rambled on as she headed into the tiny bedroom she and Imran had shared with the two children for the longest four days of her life.

It appeared that Ammi Patel suffered from claustrophobia and needed the big main bedroom with the floor-to-ceiling windows that overlooked the sea.

"Don't say anything – not a bloody word," Imran had hissed at her when they arrived at the timeshare unit and his mother ushered them into the small bedroom that the resort's designers had clearly intended for occupation by no more than two very small children. It commanded a great view of the corridor and the happy holidaymakers trooping past on their way to the noisy lifts.

"It's their timeshare so it's only right that they get the better room," he'd whispered.

"But how are we all going to fit in here? Where are the kids going to sleep?" Kerry had hissed back.

"We'll manage. Lily's camp cot can fit at the bottom of the bed there, and we'll organise a mattress for Leo to put between our beds."

"If we put Lily's cot there, we won't be able to open the cupboard. And I'll stand on Leo if I have to get up to see to her during the night. And where are we supposed to put her oxygen concentrator?"

"Kerry please. Don't be like that. My parents are trying to do something nice for us. We wouldn't have been able to afford this holiday … please. I know Ammi can be a bit – well you know – but at least she's making an effort."

"About bloody time," Kerry muttered.

Frantic wailing from open-plan living room cum kitchen area cut short the impending argument and sent Kerry flying out of the bedroom to see what had happened to Lily who she'd deposited on the floor while she'd been in the bedroom trying to figure out where to fit everything. Lily was lying on her back screaming; Ammi Patel was standing over her, a look of utter terror on her face. Baba Patel seemed to be oblivious to the racket, his full attention focused on helping his grandson build a tower of plastic blocks.

"What's wrong? What happened?' Kerry demanded, swooping her daughter into her arms. "Shhh, shhh, shhhh. It's okay, it's okay." She turned to her mother-in-law. "What happened? Did she fall? Did she hit her head on the tiles? It's okay Tiger, shhh. Shhhh."

"I don't know what's the matter with her. I was talking to her and then I picked her up and she just started screaming so I put her down."

"She doesn't like strangers touching her – I told you that," Kerry spat.

"I'm not a stranger. I'm her grandmother!"

"Well, Lily doesn't know that, does she?"

"Kerry!" Imran yelped. "Don't speak to Ammi like that. Ammi we're sorry. We're all just tired after the long drive. Kerry didn't mean it."

Oh yes I did. Every bloody word! Kerry thought as she stormed back into the tiny bedroom, fighting down the fury that surged through her. She sat and jiggled Lily not too gently on her lap. How dared Imran? How dared he reprimand her as if she were a child – and in front of his parents too? How dared he grovel and simper at them, and take their side over her and their children? His parents had said not a single civil word to her – actually not any word – ever. Not one. They'd never invited her to their home, and Kerry could count on one hand the number of times they'd come to visit her and Imran. Two, maybe three, if you included their fleeting inspections of their little Kempton Park house as a 'visit'. They'd just stand at the front door and stare at Lily lying or sitting on her makeshift bed on the floor of the lounge. Then they'd leave with Leo, and just drop him off at the gate an hour or so later.

She hadn't wanted to come on this holiday. She'd been absolutely stunned when Imran had excitedly informed her that his parents had invited them to join them on their annual holiday in Umhlanga in their stunning, luxury two-bedroom timeshare unit right on the beachfront.

"We all need a break," Imran had said. "We need to get away – *you* need to get away. You'll be able to relax and just enjoy yourself for once – and the kids will love the beach and the sea."

Yeah right. She'd fallen for Imran's soothing persuasion hook, line and bloody sinker. She'd swallowed her apprehension when President Ramaphosa had declared a State of Disaster just five days before their scheduled departure. She'd agreed that the limit of 50 patrons in restaurants wouldn't affect them too much – and she'd been right. They hadn't eaten out once. They hadn't even had takeaways. Because she had been the designated cook – and cleaner, and dishwasher, and general skivvy. She hated cooking but there she was, at the stove, every day. All three meals – breakfast, lunch and fucking dinner. She cooked while Imran joined his parents in their daily prayer rituals. She cleaned while they were at the beach or out for a walk on the promenade in the afternoons. She cooked even though Ammi criticised her curry-making efforts with a clucking sound that indicated she hadn't expected anything better from a girl like Kerry who had tricked her beloved son into a disastrous marriage.

Kerry had tried to object – but Ammi's withering stare and Imran's imploring gaze had stifled her protests.

Anyway, it wasn't as if she could have done anything about the situation. Someone had to stay home with Lily who hated the beach – or, more particularly, the sand. Even seating her on a towel hadn't done the trick on their first – and only – beach outing because beach sand had a way of creeping in where it wasn't wanted. And when Leo had excitedly flopped down on Lily's towel to show her a shell he'd just found, and had accidentally kicked sand onto her stick-like legs, Lily had screamed and screamed, her lips turning a purplish-blue.

"Seeing you're not going to the beach today you may as well prepare lunch – and dinner. Oh, and please clean the main bathroom. Leo messed some beach sand on the floor," Ammi had instructed Kerry as she'd ushered her husband, son and grandson out the door the next day. And all the days thereafter until the President's proclamation of the three-week, country-wide lockdown had liberated her.

Home at last, Kerry breathed a sigh of relief as the Toyota turned into their Kempton Park street and shuddered to a halt outside the house. Their house. The one she shared with her husband and her two precious children. Their sanctuary from the malignant forces of family – hers and his. And right now, his more than hers, if she were to be honest. In fact, if she never saw Imran's parents again, it would be too soon.

"What's going to happen with the workshop during the lockdown?" Kerry asked Imran later after finally getting their exhausted, irritable, filthy, sweaty children bathed, fed and put to bed.

"I'm not sure. I've a meeting with the Khumalo's tomorrow to talk about it all. We can't do anything about their kitchen during the lockdown – but I'd like to get everything finalised so we can start as soon as lockdown ends."

"But that's three weeks away! We were banking on your being able to start work on it this week – that's why you said we could afford to go to Umhlanga. You said the money from the Khumalo contract would be in by the end of March – mid-April at the latest. Now we're going to have to wait ... until when?"

"Well, three weeks of lockdown – then probably three weeks to complete the job. So ... mid-May. Maybe. But I'm sure the Khumalo's will pay the deposit tomorrow – I'm going to ask them for fifty percent. That should see us through."

"And what if they won't give us the deposit now? What are we going to do? I have to get to the shops tomorrow to stock up on everything ... Imran, what are we going to do?"

She stared at her husband. He stared back, then dropped his eyes. Silence sliced between them.

Chapter 26

Kerry jumped as her phone rang – a jarring jangle in the noisy chaos of the lounge. Imran was slouched on the couch opposite, gazing as intently at the antics of Barney the purple dinosaur on the television screen as Lily who was smiling and laughing and clapping along to the gratingly cheerful song. Leo was listlessly rebuilding the tower of wooden blocks, which he'd just knocked down. He'd loved those blocks as a toddler. As an energetic four-year-old, the blocks had lost their appeal – but then so had all the toys in the house. And after four weeks of being cooped up – the three-week lockdown having been extended for a further two weeks – Kerry had run out of ideas to keep him entertained indoors. If only they could go for a walk; if only they could go to the little park down the road with its swings and slides. If only they could go somewhere – anywhere – even for a short break. Just to get out of the house. Kerry had thought about taking a shopping bag and going for a walk, pretending to head to the shops – going out to buy essential groceries was still permitted. But what if she was stopped on the way home with her shopping bag still empty? Hundreds of people had already been arrested for violating the lockdown. She certainly didn't want to be one of them.

She glanced down at the caller ID on the phone and her heart gave a little hop. Then she glanced across at Imran, who hadn't stirred. He never did. He left the couch only to go and pray, or – despite the lockdown restrictions – to visit his parents with whom he seemed to have grown inordinately close since their return from Umhlanga. He always went with a bag of groceries in the car in case he was stopped. He'd tell the cops, or the army, that he was taking them to his elderly parents who were unable to shop for themselves. In the first few days of the lockdown, he'd insisted on laying out his prayer mat in the lounge. But Lily's screaming objections to having the television turned off even for a short while to allow her father to pray in peace, had swiftly ended that practice. Now – to Kerry's silent relief – Imran did most of his praying in their bedroom, or at his parent's house.

"I need to take this," Kerry muttered, heaving herself off her chair and scooting out the front door, carefully closing it behind her. She forced herself to take a long, slow breath to steady her shaking hands – and her heart. *This is crazy*, she thought as she tapped the green icon.

"Hello?" she said.

"Hey Kerry – sorry, did I disturb you? You sound out of breath."

"No, no, it's fine. I left my phone in the kitchen and had to run to get it," she muttered.

"Oh. Good. Listen, I just wanted to thank you for the last set of reports. They're fantastic – you're brilliant!"

"Thank you!" Kerry said and could feel her face burning. "I mean, it's a pleasure. I'm glad you're pleased."

"I'm more than pleased. You're a lifesaver, Kerry. Honestly, I don't know what I would have done – what I would do – without you."

"Thank you," she breathed again and mentally kicked herself. She sounded like a simpering teenager instead of the professional, efficient, no-nonsense businesswoman she was – or at least wanted Jason to regard her as.

"Kerry ..." Jason said in his deep, slightly husky voice and Kerry's heart fluttered again. She loved the way his voice caressed her name. "... I need you."

"You ... *need* me?" she squeaked.

Jason gave a husky chuckle. "To do more work for me, I mean. Do you have time? I don't want to impose."

Kerry took a deep breath and forced herself to keep her voice steady.

"Of course. No problem. It's not as if I can go anywhere, or do anything. So sure. Just email me whatever you need, no problem. No problem at all. It'll be fine. I'll just shut myself up in the bedroom – my bedroom – mine and Imran's – oh, and Lily's of course. She sleeps in my, our bedroom so I can keep an eye on her just in case, you know?"

Oh god – Kerry's face flamed. What was wrong with her? She'd known Jason for years. And here she was prattling on, sprouting inane garbage whenever she spoke to him. But just thinking of him – which seemed to be all the time lately – sent her heart rate through the roof. It was crazy. Lockdown was making her crazy. But she couldn't help it. Perhaps it was because she'd been – she *was* – so grateful that he'd contacted her early in the lockdown, begging her to help him keep the business going.

"I can't rely on Thembi," he'd said when he'd called the first time. "She doesn't have wifi at her house – not her fault of course – but she's never been the most efficient assistant around. Now that she is supposed to work from home – well, it just isn't working out. It's not going to happen. She needs supervision, you see, and I can't supervise her from home, now can I? So I thought of you. I hope you don't mind."

Mind? She'd been overjoyed. And not just about the extremely generous amount that Jason said he'd pay her. Imran's business would effectively be closed for the foreseeable future – the list of Covid level restrictions published by the government indicated that any domestic construction and renovations would only be permitted under Level Two. And as the Level Five restrictions had just been extended along with the State of Disaster, who knew how long it would take to reach Level Two? So of course she had jumped at the chance to earn some much needed money – and, to work with Jason. And to speak to him every day – sometimes two or three times a day.

She knew she was being stupid, and childish to make more of this than it was – whatever *this* was. It was nothing. He just needed someone to help him with Browns and she needed a job. That was it. Anyway, she was too old, too tired and had far too many responsibilities with a sick child and a son – and a husband, let's not forget the husband – to behave like the heroine in a second-rate bodice-ripper.

Pull yourself together, she berated herself and realised that Jason was still speaking.

"... so I'll send it through," he said.

"What? Um, sorry Jason – you broke up there. I didn't hear you. What are you sending through?"

"The sales reports. I'll set it all out in an email. If you have any questions, just give me a ring – or mail me if you prefer."

"I can call you? Oh – yes, of course. I'll call you."

"Kerry – are you okay? You sound a little distracted?"

"Sorry Jason – I can hear Lily crying. I have to go and see to her. I'll call you later. Bye."

Kerry ended the call and sank down to the ground, resisting the urge to press her burning cheeks onto the cold stone of the front veranda. It was eerily quiet. No passing cars; no sounds of children playing; no chatting pedestrians walking by. The lockdown had transformed the world into a giant, post-apocalyptic prison with people everywhere forced to cower in their homes while the novel coronavirus rampaged without, bringing death and destruction on a scale not seen, it seemed, since the Black Plague or the Spanish Flu. At least overseas, especially in China and Italy. Videos of wildlife wandering around once bustling cities – including three intrepid penguins waddling along the streets of Cape Town – had gone viral. Facebook, Instagram and WhatsApp groups were flooded with videos and selfies of users' recently acquired cooking and craft-making prowess; there were videos of people using their stockpiled supplies of toilet rolls to build pirate castles or obstacle courses; yet more videos of hastily devised home-based, almost-like-the-gym exercise routines; and hundreds of how-to videos for making everything from homemade pineapple liquors, wine and brandy to beat South Africa's illogical booze ban to fail-proof, exotic desserts and elastic-waisted pants and skirts. There were poorly coded and widely shared messages about which pharmacy was willing to turn a blind eye to illegal purchases of hair dye for hiding greying roots now that hairdressers were closed; and which friendly dope dealer-cum-tobacconist had stocks of real, brand-name cigarettes rather than the dubious counterfeits that had flooded the market in the wake of the equally nonsensical cigarette ban. But there was nothing – not a shred of advice – on how to deal with an absurd and inappropriate crush on one's boss. Or how to hide that crush from one's husband – one's kind, considerate, thoughtful, patient, caring, handsome (before the beard covered half his face) but oh, so boring, inert, ineffectual, increasingly devout husband.

The sound of Lily's cheerful chortling wafting through the closed front door jerked Kerry back to reality. Sighing, she got to her feet, straightened her back, lifted her chin, opened the door and went in to face her life.

Chapter 27

Kerry's fingers flew over the keyboard. The report was coming together even better than she had hoped. Jason would be delighted. It just showed how much she could achieve when the house was quiet and peaceful, when she wasn't being disturbed and distracted by constant demands for her attention from her children – and her husband. From the impromptu workstation she'd managed to squeeze into a corner of the bedroom, she glanced over to where Lily was napping in her camp cot at the foot of the bed. Through the open door she could see Leo was still playing happily with the Lego set she had ordered online. It had been expensive – but worth every cent. Leo loved it and it kept him occupied for ages. And Imran wasn't back from mosque yet – or had he gone to his parents' house to pray this time? She hadn't really listened to what he had said as he'd headed out the door. The mosque was not supposed to be open but Imran said Imam Omar said the government had no right to stop people from praying together.

"Prayer will protect us from the virus," he'd said.

"And what if you get infected? What about Lily – you could infect her too!"

"It won't happen. We all sanitise our hands and social distance."

"So why do you bother if you believe Allah will protect you?" The words slipped out before Kerry could stop them. She found Imran's deepening faith disturbing – and irritating – but it wasn't worth arguing over. Unless it endangered her child. And Imran wouldn't deliberately risk Lily's life. He loved her. And if prayer was what he needed now to cope with the strain of the lockdown, and the feeling of powerlessness and uselessness now that he couldn't work, well she should support him. Or at least tolerate it.

"I'm sorry. I didn't mean it," she added quickly, but Imran had turned his back on her and left the room.

∾ ∽

Kerry heard the front door open. She bent over the keyboard again and continued typing.

"I'm back," Imran said from the open doorway.

"Shh. Lily's sleeping," Kerry whispered. She glanced up but Imran had already disappeared, probably back to the lounge and his usual position on the couch. No, she could hear him in the kitchen, probably rummaging for something to eat. Any second now he'd be back asking what she was going to make for supper. She hadn't given it a thought. She just wanted to get the report finished and email it to Jason. It would give her an excuse to call him. Not an excuse – she didn't need an excuse to call him. She'd just discuss the report with him. That was all.

Her cellphone rang. A WhatsApp call from an unknown number.

"Hello," Kerry said, annoyed at the interruption, but curious as to who would WhatsApp her.

"Kerry, hi. It's Risa."

"Risa! Hi. I've been trying to call you. I left messages but they never went through. Do you have a new phone?"

"I'm so sorry. Yes, I had to get a new number – it was just easier."

"Well, at least we can chat now. So how are you? Where are you? How's Anesta?"

Silence.

"Hello Risa – can you hear me?"

"Yes, I can hear you Kerry. I'm sorry. I ... I should have called you before but ..."

Risa's voice faded again. Kerry glared at the phone in frustration.

"Risa – can you hear me? Where are you? This connection is dreadful! Should I try call you back?"

"No ... no, there's nothing wrong with the connection. I'm in India and ..."

Silence.

"Risa? Risa – are you okay? What's wrong? How's Anesta? Has she had her transplant yet?"

Silence.

"Risa – are you there?" Kerry could feel panic rising in her throat.

"I'm here," Risa said, so softly Kerry barely heard the words. "Oh Kerry, Anesta didn't have the transplant. She ... she ... her heart stopped again. On the plane. They couldn't revive her you see. They tried. But ... but they couldn't. It was too late. We'd left it too late. I'd left it too late."

Kerry stumbled into the lounge, tears streaming down her face. Imran looked up at her, and jumped to his feet, alarmed.

"What on earth – Kerry – what's wrong?"

She shook her head mutely and flung herself at him. His arms closed around her. She pressed her face into him and sobbed. Leo abandoned his Lego and wrapped his arms around her legs, trying to comfort her. Kerry sniffed and picked Leo up, hugging him tightly.

"Mommy?" the little boy asked, tears trembling on his thick, dark lashes. "Mommy, are you hurt?"

"No Leo, I'm fine. I just got some very sad news. I'm sorry I upset you. Go back to your Lego. You can show me what you've made later. I just need to talk to Daddy."

Taking Imran's hand, Kerry led him into the kitchen and closed the door.

"I don't want the kids to hear," she explained.

And then, between sobs and sniffs, she told him about Risa and Anesta and how Risa had already lost two children and she and her husband had sold up everything to try to save Anesta but they had left it too late and now Risa was stuck in India alone and couldn't get back because there were no flights ...

"It's terrible. I feel so sorry for her. I don't know how she can bare it," Kerry said, and the sobs overwhelmed her once again.

Imran held her and rocked her, making the comforting noises he always made when Lily or Leo were upset.

"Imran," Kerry said when her sobs abated. "We can't let that happen to Lily."

"What happened to Anesta was Allah's will," Imran said.

"No! I don't believe that. We can do something. We can't just wait and wait and wait – and then regret it when it's too late. That's what Risa said. She said the only thing she regrets – well, not the only thing, obviously – but she wishes she hadn't waited so long to get Anesta a transplant. She said I – she said we – you and I – shouldn't make the same mistake."

"Lily is not Anesta. Lily doesn't have a problem with her lungs. Her case is nothing like Anesta's," Imran protested.

"But what if – what if her heart failure doesn't reverse? What if – I read that the only solution for chronic heart failure is a transplant. What if Lily needs a transplant? What if we have to take her to India too? How will we be able to afford that? What if we leave it too late? What if Lily also ..."

"Lily isn't Anesta. Allah will take care of her. I pray for Lily, every day. I pray for her five times a day. Allah will hear my prayers. If he wills it, Lily will live."

"But what if she needs a transplant?" Kerry insisted.

"I will speak to Imam Omar. I will ask his advice. And I will pray. Allah's will be done."

Chapter 28

"Pull over!"

Imran looked at Kerry in the rear-view mirror. She stared back at him and then down at Lily lying limply in her arms.

"Pull over! Now!"

"Oh shit! Now what?" Imran said and coasted to a halt in the emergency lane of the deserted freeway but left the engine running. One set of flashing blue lights pulled in behind, another skidded to a halt in front of them, cutting off any chance of escape.

Lily coughed and wheezed. Leo whimpered quietly on the seat next to her and was silent again. The portable oxygen concentrator hummed.

A large shadow loomed outside the driver's seat window. Another smaller shadow appeared at the passenger side and shone a flashlight around the car's interior. The large cop on Imran's side did the same. Imran wound his window down and bitter night air flooded in. Lily coughed again. Kerry pulled the blanket tighter around her.

"You're breaking curfew," the large cop said.

"Yes, I know officer. But it's a medical emergency," Imran said.

"Where's your licence?"

Imran opened his wallet, removed his driver's licence and offered it to the cop, who trained his torch on the wallet before taking the licence and examining it closely. He then shone his torch on Imran's face before examining the licence again.

"This isn't your licence," he said.

"Of course it is! I have a beard now, that's all."

Kerry held her breath. That bloody beard! It was going to get

Imran arrested. But it seemed the cop had other ideas.

"Why aren't you at home? You know you are not allowed to leave your home." The harshness of the words, the aggressive, accusing tone, made Kerry shudder.

"Yes, officer. We know. We're going to the hospital," Imran said politely but Kerry detected the nervous tremor behind the soft, reasonableness of his words.

"Looks like a family joyride to me," the cop sneered, training his torch on the backseat. "Where are you going?"

"I told you – it's a medical emergency," Imran repeated.

"I wasn't talking to you, I'll deal with you just now," the cop snapped and shone his torch directly into Kerry's eyes. "I'm talking to your madam."

"You heard my husband," Kerry said, bristling. "It's a medical emergency. We're taking our daughter to the hospital."

Having leisurely checked the car's licence disk on the front windscreen, the smaller cop, a woman, came around the car and joined her colleague at Imran's window.

"Which hospital?" she demanded, aggressive, threatening, disbelieving.

"Sunninghill," Kerry and Imran chorused.

"Where's your permit to be out during curfew?" This from the male cop.

"We don't have a permit – I told you, it's an emergency," Imran said.

"I wasn't talking to you. I was talking to the madam. Tell your driver to be quiet," the woman cop said.

"He's not my driver, he's my husband!"

"Then why you sitting there? You're a white madam too good to sit next to the coolie – um Indian – Uber driver."

"I'm holding my daughter – our daughter. She's sick. We have to get her to hospital – to Sunninghill. Please. It's an emergency."

"Why do you have to take her to Sunninghill? Where's the letter from the doctor that this is an emergency? Why you go to a private hospital? You white people, you think you can do what you like. You think curfew's only for black people. Right? You lying. There's no medical emergency. Show me the emergency? Where's the blood?" the woman cop said.

Imran interrupted. "I'm telling you, this is an emergency."

"Shut up!" The male cop turned the blinding beam of his torch directly into Imran's face. "We're talking to the madam."

Leo woke with a start and started crying. Lily wheezed and whimpered.

"For God's sake," Kerry shrilled. "I'm not his madam. I'm his wife. And this is our daughter – and our son."

"Don't you shout at me. Who do you think you are?" the woman cop yelled.

Leo's sobs rose in unison. Kerry awkwardly patted his head and held Lily closer. They should have left Leo with Mrs Reddy. But they'd delayed long enough, debating about whether to take Lily to the hospital when she first started wheezing. There hadn't been time to take Leo across the road. And it was so late – midnight. How could they wake Mrs Reddy in the middle of the night? Anyway it was against the lockdown regulations for Mrs Reddy to have Leo in her house. And what if Lily had that dreaded coronavirus virus – even though everyone was saying that it only affected old people? What if Lily had infected Leo and Leo infected Mrs Reddy? They hadn't had a choice. They'd had to take Leo with them. He'd wait in the ICU waiting room as always while they settled Lily – if Lily had to go to ICU. But she was burning with fever, her breathing was laboured and her saturation levels frighteningly low, even for Lily. Kerry just knew that Lily was destined for another sojourn in the ICU – once they got her to the hospital.

"I'm sorry, I'm sorry" Kerry said. "But please. My daughter is really sick. Please. She has an infection. See? She's burning up with fever."

"Turn off your engine and step out of the car," the male cop growled at Imran

"I can't – it's ..."

"Turn off the fucking engine. Get out of the car or I'll arrest you. Now!"

"Please listen. If I turn off the engine, the oxygen machine will stop working," Imran said.

Kerry interjected: "Our daughter has a heart condition. She can't breathe without oxygen. She has an infection that is making it even more difficult for her to breathe. If we don't get her to the hospital quicky, she may die. Please. Please – let us go."

"Turn off the engine," the cop said again, but not as forcefully this time.

"Please," Imran said. "It's true. Our daughter needs to get to the hospital."

"How do we know you won't just drive off and laugh at how easy it is to fool us stupid black cops?" the woman cop demanded.

"Why don't you just escort us to the hospital then?" Kerry said.

The cops looked at each other.

Kerry pressed on: "Listen, you can make sure we go there – you can escort us right into the emergency department if you want. You can even ask the doctors if Lily really is sick. If this is really a medical emergency. If it isn't, you can arrest us. Please. Just let us go."

"Get out!" The male cop pulled open Imran's door. "Get out."

"No," said Imran.

The cop pulled out his firearm and pointed it at Imran's head. "I said, get out!"

Imran clambered out. The cop pushed him towards the front of the car and slid into the driver's seat. He switched off the engine and the oxygen concentrator died. Kerry stifled a scream. She had to remain calm – for the children's sake. She tried to recall how much money she had in her purse. Not much. Probably not enough. She wondered where the nearest ATM was. Not that that would help – their bank account was virtually empty.

"What do you want?" she asked.

"I'm arresting you. I'm going to drive you to the police station."

"What about my husband – we can't leave him here!"

"He's under arrest too. It's illegal for Uber drivers to carry passengers in the lockdown. My partner will bring him to the police station."

Kerry shuddered. From what she'd heard about these types of shakedowns, Imran might not make it to the police station, at least not in one piece. Sensing his mother's distress, Leo's wails intensified. Lily coughed, choked and gasped for breath. The cop stared at her, alarmed.

"What's wrong with the kid?" he demanded.

"I told you. She has a heart condition – but we think ...," Kerry decided to improvise: "We think she may have caught the coronavirus from ... from my mother. My mother has it, she is in hospital and now Lily seems to have it. I'm also not feeling well," She coughed delicately. "So that's why we're all going to the hospital. I hope you don't catch it." She coughed again.

"You're lying," the cop said.

"I'm not! Look at my baby. Feel her forehead – she has a fever. She can barely breathe. I'm sure she has the virus."

"Children don't get Covid," the cop muttered. "Only old people."

"Are you sure about that?" Imran asked from outside the car.

As if on cue, Lily emitted another series of barking coughs followed by more wheezing gasps. The cop scrambled out of the car, almost falling in his haste to get away from whatever dreaded lurgy was being transmitted by the obviously sick child. He backed away, and his female colleague followed.

"Go, just go," the cop said. "Get away from us."

"Please could you move your car," Imran said as he slid back into the driver's seat. He started the engine and Lily's oxygen concentrator resumed its reassuring hum.

As the police cars drew away from them, Imran let out a shaky laugh. "That was close. All set, madam? Let's go!

"It's not Covid-19," Dr Sinclair said when Kerry finally managed to get her on the phone the next day.

"That's a relief. So what is it?"

"It's just pneumonia – it's not too bad. She should be out of ICU in a couple of days."

"Can we visit her?" Kerry asked. Lily's anguished wails when she'd been forced to hand her over to a nurse swathed from head to toe in blue scrubs at the entrance to the emergency department still haunted her.

The nurse's kind eyes – the only part of her face visible above her strange, cone-shaped mask – had narrowed as she'd taken Lily's temperature and heard Lily's barking cough.

"I'm so sorry," she'd said. "You can't come in. Only patients are allowed inside. I'm so sorry, we'll contact you ..." the rest of her words had been drowned by Lily's screams as she was borne away and the glass doors closed behind her.

With tears streaming down her face, Kerry had walked back to the car where Imran had been waiting with Leo.

"That was quick," Imran said as Kerry slipped into the seat beside him. "She surely couldn't have settled so quickly? Shouldn't you still be with her?

"They won't let me in. They wouldn't even let me through the doors. They told me to go away."

"How could you just let them take her? You should have objected. You know how she hates strangers."

"For god's sake Imran – I tried," Kerry hissed. "What the fuck was I supposed to do? Stand outside in the fucking cold and let Lily freeze to death while I argued with a fucking nurse? The rule is only patients are allowed into the hospital. That's it."

"Don't swear. You should have tried harder. I should have taken her and you should have stayed with Leo. I wouldn't have let Lily go."

Leo whimpered.

"Now see what you've done – you've woken him," Imran whispered. "You deal with him. I'm going to see what's going on with Lily."

Kerry moved to the back seat and took Leo into her arms. "Sssh," she crooned, and watched her husband disappear in the direction of the emergency department.

A few minutes later he returned, got into the driver's seat and started the car.

"Where are we going?" Kerry asked quietly.

"Home."

"Is Lily okay? Did you see her?"

"They wouldn't let me in."

                               ∽ ∾

"Can we visit her?" Lily asked Dr Sinclair again.

"No, I'm sorry. Hospital rules. But don't worry. We're taking good care of her. We're keeping her well away from the Covid patients. Fortunately there's only a few of them but we're taking every precaution to keep your little one safe."

"Why does she keep getting sick? How can we prevent this from happening again?"

Dr Sinclair hesitated. "I don't know. She's not responding to the medication we're giving to treat her heart failure. And while her heart is so enlarged ... she'll remain susceptible to infection, I'm afraid. I'll be honest with you Kerry-Anne, Dr Govender and I agree, we've never seen a case quite like this before."

"What are you saying? That there's nothing you can do for her? That this will keep on happening?"

"I'm saying that this is a very difficult ... I'm saying that perhaps ... perhaps you need to look into the possibility of a transplant. If you like, I can ask Dr Govender to make some enquiries."

"Yes please," Kerry whispered.

Chapter 29

Lily sat on her oversized skateboard at the open front-door, looking through the security gate towards the house across the road. The September sun was shining brightly, warming the house and wiping away the memories of the long, cold, fearful winter.

"Hello!" Lily shouted in her gruff, booming voice that belied the frailty of her body. "Hello!"

"Hello Tiger," Mrs Reddy called back. "Are you going to come and visit me? Mohammed also wants to play with you!"

"No!" Lily yelled emphatically, furiously shaking the short, thick black bob of hair that Kerry had managed to trim in an effort to keep Lily's hair a little more tidy – even if her home cut was somewhat ragged. Lily hated having her hair tied up, so keeping it short was the only option. But with visits to the hairdresser still prohibited, Kerry had done her best which, as Imran had pointed out, wasn't very good. Too bad.

Kerry watched with bated breath as the little girl's delicate fingers gripped the gate's bars. Would the child succeed in pulling herself to her feet this time?

Kerry knew that Lily was probably too tired for such a strenuous undertaking. She had almost fully recovered from her last bout of pneumonia but she still tired very quickly. And she'd had a very busy morning. Since medical professionals had been able to resume home visits, Kerry had taken Jason's – and her mother's – advice and set up a full schedule of therapy for Lily.

"That child is not making any progress," Gillian Aarons had said during one of her infrequent phone calls. "From what you tell me, she can't walk, she can't crawl, she can't talk and she can't – or won't – put food in her mouth. How do you expect her to get better if you just let her sit there like a lump and watch television all day because it sounds to me that that's all she does?"

"Mom – that's unfair," Kerry had protested. "Lily is making progress. It's actually quite amazing. But when – if – she gets sick and has to go to hospital, it knocks her right back."

"Well, she's not in hospital now, is she? So what you doing about helping her to live the normal life you say you want for her? You say you'll do anything for that child, but it seems to me you have given up on her."

Kerry gasped. Even from her mother, the accusation was monstrously unfair and patently false.

"Mom! You don't know what you're talking about. I do everything I can to make Lily comfortable, to keep her safe. You don't see how hard it is; you never visit – and don't use the pandemic as an excuse. You never visited before and you have no idea ..."

"Stop whining," Gillian snapped. "Of course it's hard. But because it's hard doesn't mean you give up. Honestly Kerry-Anne, you're always saying you'll do whatever it takes to give Lily a normal life. But you're not doing very much at all are you? Be honest about it. And in the process, what are you doing to Leo? He's also your child and it seems to me he is being made to suffer because of ..."

Kerry had ended the call in a fury. But, much as she hated to admit it, there was a tiny grain of truth in her mother's harsh words. She had to do more for Lily, and somehow make more time for Leo.

She'd broached the subject with Dr Govender and he'd said some professional therapy for Lily could be a good idea. But with Covid – and therapy was so expensive. Dr Govender had written a letter of motivation for the medical aid company to pay for therapy. It had been only partially successful: the medical aid had said they'd pay for the standard number of therapy sessions, to be taken from their medical savings. Once that money was depleted – and there wasn't much left – what would happen?

"Browns will pay for it," Jason had said when she'd told him. "Consider it a token of our deep appreciation for your invaluable contribution to keeping the company going."

Today's session with the physiotherapist had been a nightmare. As usual. Lily had started screaming the moment Glenda had walked through the door and she hadn't stopped until Glenda disappeared through the front door again with a cheery wave.

"I can't stand this," Imran had muttered as the physiotherapist had tried to get Lily to bend her knees. "This is just cruel. It's enough already."

"It's important. Lily will never learn to walk without therapy – you know that."

"She's torturing her!"

"She's not. It's just Lily being dramatic. If you can't take it, then leave," Kerry snapped. She hated it when Imran made her feel like a heartless monster. She also hated it when Lily cried during her therapy sessions. But she sucked it up because she knew it was for Lily's own good. It would help her catch up on her milestones, help her get to live a normal life one day.

But Imran had slammed out the front door, and Lily's wails had grown even more anguished.

After a nap, Lily's afternoon session with the speech therapist was happy and noisy. The therapist, Kris, a pretty young woman who Lily liked immensely, tried – unsuccessfully once again – to persuade her eat something. But not even the tiniest piece of carrot, or cucumber, or even the soft, cheesy, all-taste-no-nutrition puffed snack that she had loved when she was younger went anywhere near her mouth, let alone into it. She sat on her red plastic chair at the little plastic table with the therapist on one side and Leo, at four years old, very conscious of his big brother status, on the other, and fed bits of this and pieces of that into the hungry, gaping mouth of Kris's toy monster. As usual, Leo ended up scoffing most of the carefully chosen and prepared food. But progress was being made. At least Lily now touched the food with her fingers. And she was becoming quite adept at spearing some pieces with a toothpick and a fork.

It was worth it, Kerry reassured herself. She wished Imran had been around to see, but he hadn't come back. She wanted him to see just how much progress Lily was making. Yes, she hated her physiotherapy sessions, and her occupational therapy sessions too. But she was getting stronger. Anyone could see that. Perhaps, perhaps her oversized, damaged heart was finally starting to respond to the new medication regime Dr Govender had started her on.

At the end of her session, Kris started walking towards the front door, but Lily objected.

"No! See. See me!"

Balancing uncertainly on her skinny little feet while holding on to the long ottoman in the lounge where she had insisted her mother place her, she cruised slowly along its length, determined to reach the stuffed purple dragon at the other side. Her big brown eyes danced with excitement and a beaming smile lit her pretty round face.

"Here's Barney, Barneeee," she chortled in triumph as she reached the toy.

"That's wonderful, Lily," Kris said.

"Bin," Lily said, holding up a scrap of paper she'd found under the toy.

"Do you want to take the paper to the bin?" Kerry asked.

A vigorous nod of the dark head, accompanied by a huge smile. "Walk!" she demanded.

Kerry's heart swelled with pride. "She wants to show you how she can walk. Do you mind waiting?"

"Of course not," Kris said.

Clutching her mother's hands for support, Lily tottered, stiff-legged across the room to the bin. She balanced carefully as she opened the lid and deposited the paper inside. Then she turned, grasped her mother's hands again and started making her way back to the ottoman – only to be distracted by the giant skateboard.

"There," she insisted. "Go. Go mama."

Kerry helped the child to sit on the edge of the skateboard, her little legs stuck out as straight and stiff as two pale matchsticks. Then pushing with her feet, she slowly began to move the skateboard forward, chortling with unadulterated pleasure and excitement.

"She loves it," Kerry said. "It took her a little while to figure out how to move it, but now she rides it as often as she can. It's amazing. She's never been mobile, never even crawled or rolled. Now she can move all over the house. Oops, watch out."

The wheels on the skateboard appeared to become entangled in the long, clear, plastic tube that fed the life-saving oxygen from the electric oxygen concentrator in the bedroom, through plastic cannulas into the child's nose. Lily just kept pushing and the skateboard bounced over the tube and kept going.

"Wow," Kris said. "What progress! I can't believe how much she's improved since I first started working with her. It's really amazing. You are such a clever girl, Lily! But I have to go now. I'll see you next week – if we're not in for another crazy lockdown when the President does his thing on TV again on Sunday night."

"Surely not again?" Kerry stared at Kris. "No way! I mean they've even lifted the ban on cigarettes and booze. Things are starting to get back to normal. I know the State of Disaster has been extended again but I think that's a bit over the top. I mean, new cases of the virus are right down. So I'm sure we'll see you next week. Lily, Leo, say goodbye to Kris."

As Kerry locked the security gate behind Kris, Lily scooted across the lounge to shout her goodbyes and wave and call to Mrs Reddy across the road. Leo remained at the little table, eating the last of the baby carrots.

Kerry held her breath. watching as Lily pulled on the gate. Her baby was growing up so quickly. It was as if, like Sleeping Beauty, she'd awoken slowly from a long, long sleep and was now doing her utmost to make up for lost time. Dressed in a cream denim shirtwaist-style dress, with pale blue flecks and shiny silver buttons, Lily looked like any other happy two-and-a-half-year-old little girl. But the harsh series of battle scars on her chest and under her arm, hidden now from view by her pretty dress as was the peg feeding tube in her tummy, and the oxygen cannulas in her nose, all told a different story.

She wasn't like most other children her age. She wasn't even like other children with the same congenital heart defect. She was one in a million – perhaps more. But she was a fighter. She was a tiger, a true heart warrior. She would surprise everyone. She would prove Dr Govender – and all the other doctors – wrong, yet again. Kerry just knew it.

Chapter 30

The tension in the car on the drive to the Sunninghlll Hospital was palpable – at least to Kerry. In the back seat, Leo gazed out the window and Lily dozed, her portable oxygen concentrator humming quietly beside her; the back-up oxygen cylinder on the floor at her feet. In the front seats, the silence crackled.

"There's no need to come. It's just a check-up now that we're down to Level One and restrictions at the hospital have been lifted," Kerry had said to Imran as she prepared to take Lily for her pandemic-delayed monthly check-up. "You stay home with Leo."

"I'm coming," Imran said.

"But then we'll have to take Leo along. Mrs Reddy's in quarantine – her brother has Covid. Leo can't stay there."

But Imran had walked out of the room. It had been like that for days – weeks if she thought about it and was being honest with herself. Since before she'd asked him not to go to the mosque. She'd spent days formulating the request to make it as obsequious and unconfrontational as possible. She needn't have bothered.

Imran had erupted: "I won't get infected. Why would you think I'd get infected at the mosque? Are you saying we're dirty? That we're not careful?"

Kerry had stared at him, stunned at his anger at what was, after all, a perfectly reasonable request.

"No – it's got nothing to do with dirt. It's spread through the air, like the flu – you know that. That's why we have to wear masks now."

"So, if it's like the flu why shouldn't I go? You've never objected to me going out because I might catch flu. Anyone, only old people are getting sick and dying. I'm not old, in case you hadn't noticed. In fact, I'm younger than your precious boss and I don't hear you telling him what he can and can't do."

"It's not you I'm worried about. It's Lily! What if you infect her?"

That had been the spark, and it blew the lid off the insecurities and frustrations that had been bottled up over the weeks and months of enforced, round-the-clock proximity. They skirted around each other in the too-small house, with neither having anywhere to go, even after lockdown restrictions eased. The row – that row – had quickly escalated into a heated, hissed litany of allegations and accusations about Jason's monopoly of her time – and affections. Her furious, guilty denials and counter-jabs about his obsession with his religion, inability to revive his moribund business, and neglect of his family had merely added fuel to the fire. Her brain had instructed her to withdraw, let things cool down, not allow his insecurities to get under her skin – but her mouth seemed to have taken on a life of its own and venom had flowed until Leo's distressed sobs had brought them both to their senses and ushered in a grudging, paper-thin truce.

Lily sat on the examination table in Dr Govender's darkened office and beamed at him, her screaming objections to every routine aspect of the preliminary examination by the harried nurse seemingly forgotten. She'd started yelling the moment the nurse lifted her little shirt to attach the ECG sensors to her chest; she'd screamed blue murder when the nurse placed her on the scale to weigh her; and she'd roared in rage, kicking and flailing her arms as the nurse tried to take her pulse. The nurse had soldiered on, shaking her head in awe at the fury emanating from Lily's frail, scarred little body.

Her frustrated outrage seemingly spent, Lily had sniffled quietly as Dr Govender spread gel over her emaciated chest and distended tummy to conduct the echocardiogram scan that would reveal how well, or badly, her heart was functioning. Kerry stared at the grainy image on the monitor. She could see the image of Lily's heart beating, but she couldn't tell if it was better – or worse – than at her previous examinations. Dr Govender's face gave nothing away: he just stared intensely at the screen. Kerry glanced over at Imran standing motionless in the shadows on the other side of the examination table. His face too was inscrutable.

At last Dr Govender put down the probe wand he'd been moving over Lily's chest and gently wiped off the remaining gel with a pink tissue. Then he pulled down Lily's shirt and helped her to sit up. Lily's whimpers immediately stopped. She smiled at him and raised her eyebrows questioningly. Kerry suppressed a giggle – it was almost as if Lily was encouraging the doctor to pronounce on her vastly improved health and wellbeing.

Except he didn't. He turned up the lighting in the examination room, sat back in his chair and looked through his notes, the hum of Lily's portable oxygen unnaturally loud in Kerry's ears.

After what seemed like an age, Dr Govender looked up.

"Is the little one having any rehabilitation therapy?" he asked.

"Oh yes," Kerry said. "Well, we thought about having her admitted to Milpark Hospital for intensive rehabilitation but it was lockdown and we didn't want to leave her there without being able to visit. But as soon as we were able, we arranged for the physiotherapist and occupational therapist to come to the house every week – the speech therapist too. Lily is making fantastic progress. I've also tried to keep on with her exercises on the days they don't come. It's hard but she is doing so well. She can stand and walk a bit if she's supported. She scoots all over the house on a skateboard-scooter thing the physio gave her. I'm sure she'll soon be able to pull herself up to stand on her own, and her speech is so much better."

Dr Govender nodded understandingly as her litany of pride finally petered out.

"Good, that's good," he said and smiled at Lily who beamed back proudly. "And eating? How is that going?"

"Well …" Kerry hesitated. "Actually it's still a battle. She won't eat anything solid. She takes her bottle sometimes and I'm giving her Frebini every two hours through her peg feeding tube. Although she does sometimes vomit it up. She just doesn't seem to want food, not even her old favourites. I'm not sure why – it's as if eating is just too much of an effort. I try … I really do."

Dr Govender stroked his chin. "She is very underweight for her age … how old is she now?"

Kerry suppressed the familiar guilt that surged through her and forced her voice to remain steady. "Two and a half … and a bit. She'll be three in February."

"Hmmm. And when did she have her last admission to hospital?"

"Oh not since she had that bout of pneumonia – you know – it was a couple of months ago. During the lockdown, remember? Since then she's been fine – great actually. She's been making such good progress as I've already said. I mean the different is noticeable, it really is. Don't you think so?"

"Two months, you say? Ah yes, I see it here in my notes. Nothing since then? That's good. Very good. Is she sleeping better?"

Kerry hesitated. Why couldn't the doctor just acknowledge that Lily was improving instead of looking for something else to find wrong?

"No, she still doesn't sleep well. Not really," she admitted.

"Ah, so if she's awake at night, that means you are too?"

Kerry nodded. "It's okay, I'm used to not having much sleep. It doesn't take as long as it used to, to settle her after she wakes. I'm getting more sleep lately – we all are."

"Hmmm. Yes, Well. Let's take a moment and review where we are. Don't you want to sit down?" Dr Govender said looking at Imran who was still standing on the far side of the examination table, cradling the emergency oxygen cylinder in his arms, the back-up should the battery on the portable concentrator die.

Imran shook his head and shifted the oxygen cylinder slightly.

"No? Okay. So let's recap and then look at where we are now.

As you know – and it's very clear on the scan, your little one now has only one atrium and one ventricle. That's what we did during her last surgery. The problem now is that the deoxygenated blood from the lower part of her body is still mixing with the oxygenated blood in her heart. That's no good. In most children with Lily's condition, we'd sort it out in the third surgery around the time the child is three or four years old. After the second surgery they usually get better, stronger – and the third surgery can go ahead. But Lily hasn't responded like other children. Unfortunately, her heart muscles have been weakened, probably by infection but perhaps it's something else. It could be from the condition itself. She hasn't responded to treatment – she's been in heart failure for a long time. Cardiomyopathy, you know. That's why her heart is so enlarged. I had hoped that by now this might have begun to reverse. But that hasn't. I don't know why. I just don't know. I've discussed this case with the team ... with the professor ... we just don't understand why."

Kerry stared at the doctor in dismay. Dr Govender sounded so ... defeated. So sad. And she'd hoped – she'd prayed – that Lily's enlarged heart would have started to recover. She'd been so confident, especially since Lily was so much better. Surely that was a sign that she'd started to turn the corner? Kerry glanced at Imran who seemed to have turned to stone. His face was grim. His knuckles were white. He didn't look back at her. His eyes were glued to Dr Govender's face. Lily, as if sensing the change in mood in the room, stopped smiling and looked up questioningly at her mother.

"But," the doctor continued hurriedly, "that's not necessarily a bad thing. I mean her heart has ... her cardiomyopathy hasn't deteriorated. It's the same as it was. It isn't worse."

"So that's good news, isn't it?" Kerry demanded.

"Yes, yes it is, if her heart stays as it is – if it doesn't worsen – it's a good sign. But I can feel her liver too – it's also very enlarged which is another sign that she is still in heart failure. The muscles of her heart have not recovered – her heart is still very weak. But if the muscles were to get stronger – well, that could reverse the heart failure."

"So you're saying that it could still happen?" Kerry pleaded, trying to find the bottom line in Dr Govender's ramblings.

"Yes, it could. It could. But ..." Dr Govender hesitated and then continued, quietly: "But after so long ... I'm not very hopeful."

"And what if it doesn't? What then?" The question slipped past Kerry's lips before she could stop it. She didn't want to know. Not really. Once before, the doctors had said there was nothing more they could do for Lily – and look how much progress she'd made since then.

But the question had been asked, and it hovered in the air like the sword of Damocles. And shrugging off his characteristic dithering, Dr Govender grasped it and plunged it into Kerry's soul.

"Then the only option that we have for your little girl is a heart transplant."

As if on cue, the portable oxygen concentrator started beeping, warning that its battery was about to die.

Chapter 31

Across the examination table, above the beeping of the dying oxygen concentrator, Kerry heard Imran's sharp intake of breath. She glanced at him again, but he was gazing intently at his shoes.

"I'm sorry, we need to change Lily's oxygen to the cylinder. Imran!" Kerry said.

Imran stirred, as if emerging from a trance, and quickly detached the plastic tube from the concentrator and affixed it to the cylinder. He then resumed his statue-like posture with the cylinder in his arms.

"I'm so sorry," Kerry said again. "You were saying?"

From behind his desk and computer screen, Dr Govender continued.

"Yes, of course. A heart transplant. It seems your little one may need – we need to think about it. But it's not that easy. A heart transplant for this kind of condition is not ... there's a very high risk to it. And also, in South Africa in general, we haven't had kids of less than five years who have had transplants. Our transplant programme is very weak, in general. Oh not the doctors who do transplants – they're excellent, world class ... world class. But the problem is there is not a lot of awareness about transplants. I have discussed transplant with parents before but we've never pursued it."

"Why not?" Kerry demanded.

"Well, we have a transplant programme here, at Sunninghill, but with the lack of awareness ... Anyway, a transplant here – it's probably not an option now."

"Why not?" she demanded again, her voice shrill, strained.

Dr Govender looked at his notes, then looked up at her again. "The surgeon who does our transplants is emigrating to New Zealand soon. So I suppose we'd have to send our transplant patients to Cape Town where they still have a very small programme. I'm not sure if they'd even accept a child from Gauteng again ..."

Kerry interrupted his musing; "Doctor, just to get this straight. You're saying that if Lily's heart doesn't improve – and the chances are that it won't – then despite all the risks, despite everything – her only real hope is a transplant. Is that right?"

As she said the words, her mind flashed back to that afternoon when Lily had played so happily with Anesta. Her mother, Risa, had known that a transplant had been Anesta's only hope, Her last hope. But Risa had left it too late.

Kerry had no intention of making the same mistake. If Dr Govender said that a transplant was what was needed to give Lily her only chance of a 'normal' childhood; if a transplant was her best hope of growing up into the very special young woman Kerry knew she would be, then a transplant was what Lily was going to get, even if she had to cut out her own heart and put it in her daughter's chest herself.

"No, no, no Mrs Patel. I'm not saying ... we're not there yet. Not yet. Not yet. A transplant for your little one ... it would be risky. Very risky. We've never transplanted a child so young. So small – and you must remember – it is important to understand that a heart transplant is not a cure. It is a palliative procedure. It helps you to be better."

"How many transplant patients have you dealt with?" Kerry asked.

"We don't have many. Two ... three at the moment in my practice who have had transplants. We had another one – the transplant was done elsewhere – but for some reason she didn't survive long. She rejected the heart."

"Does that often happen? That the heart is rejected?"

"No, not often. But it does happen. Sometimes. Sometimes I think ... perhaps ... I think some transplants are just not meant to be."

"What do you mean?" Kerry demanded. "Are you saying we shouldn't even consider a transplant for Lily?"

"No, no not at all. Not at all. We need to consider it. We do. We must. But it's not simple. It's not simple at all. I can tell you that the waiting for a heart in South Africa can be long, very long, extremely long. I had a child, a kiddie, who waiting for a heart for six years. And then eventually they found a heart. And it was … the kid lived in Polokwane and the parents had to drive for more than two hours to get him to Johannesburg and then they had to fly to Cape Town – this was before we set up the transplant unit here in Sunninghill. And they just managed to get on the last plane to Cape Town – and the kid had the transplant – and then he rejected the heart."

Kerry gasped. Another rejection. Dr Govender didn't appear to hear; he seemed to be focused inwards as if remembering and trying to make sense of what had happened. "After waiting for six years, living a reasonable life for six years – and then he got this heart, and he died, just a short time later."

"But … but … he would ultimately have died anyway – wouldn't he?" she asked. "And with Lily's heart failure, aren't we heading down that same road?"

Dr Govender sat back and looked at Kerry, a little startled by the bluntness of her questions. He seemed to consider his words carefully before responding. "Mrs Patel, your little one has been in heart failure for quite a long time and she has coped. I don't see any signs on the machines that indicate that she is going to deteriorate suddenly."

"So she doesn't need a transplant? But you said …?"

"But unfortunately in some respects you are right, Mrs Patel," the doctor continued as if Kerry had not interrupted.

"If you have heart failure, you can't stay like that forever …" He shook his head: "But … but …" He shook his head again, drew in a deep breath, closed and opened his eyes, and looked hard at Kerry: "But I think, perhaps, in this kind of scenario, we might have reached the point where we should discuss transplant. Just discuss, you understand. Talk about it. Consider it."

Dr Govender shifted in his chair again. He glared at the echocardiogram monitor which still showed an image of Lily's overlarge, weakened, *failing* heart, as if willing it to tell him a different story to the one he clearly was reluctant to share with his little patient's parents.

"I thought that's what we *were* doing. Discussing it," Kerry said with a quiet determination she was far from feeling. "Just tell us what our options are. Don't sugar-coat it. We want the truth. We can take it."

What she really wanted was to scream and cry but that would frighten Lily who was clearly sensing her mother's distress. Her bottom lip was starting to tremble. Kerry lifted her off the examination table and put her on her lap, squeezing her so tightly, the little girl yelped.

Dr Govender clasped his hands together, leaned back and addressed an invisible spot on the ceiling.

"Right. So my view is that in her condition, a transplant would be high risk – very high. So I think ... Look, we've focused very much on conservative treatment so far and she is holding her own. That's important to remember. She is holding her own. But ..."

"But the next infection – it could kill her, couldn't it?" Kerry blurted. "That's what you're worried about, isn't it? And you said ... she isn't going to get better, is she?"

"An infection is always a danger to a child in Lily's condition. So we take care – we take care. As much as we can."

"But will she get better without a transplant? Is a transplant – should we consider it?"

"Yes, yes of course. I don't want you to think transplant is a bad idea. I have a little patient, he was six when we transplanted him – he's seven now, nearly eight, and he's doing well. So we should discuss all options. But Lily – she's so young. We've never transplanted a child of her age in South Africa. And with her it's not so straight forward either."

"What do you mean? What's the problem? Her age? What

else?" Kerry demanded. Across the examination table, Imran shifted slightly. Beneath his beard, a smile – a tiny twitch of a smile – seemed to tug at his lips.

Chapter 32

Kerry stared at her husband. The smile, if there actually had been a smile, was gone. Imran's face was as inscrutable as ever. She had to have imagined it. Imran loved Lily – he adored her.

"Well, there's one other thing that worries me," Dr Govender continued. "The last time we did a catheter – you know, to measure the pressure in her lungs – well the pressure was high. Too high. So the challenge is always that if you need a heart transplant in that situation, the chances are that you will need a lung transplant too. And so it gets very complicated – very complicated ..."

"Wait! Hang on! Are you saying Lily will need a heart and lung transplant? Not just her heart?" Kerry squeaked.

"No. No not at all, not at all. I think we are getting a little ahead of ourselves here. First, we need to establish if your little one would be – could be – a candidate for a transplant. So if you like – she might have to go to Cape Town for an assessment to see if they would even put her on the transplant list. I could make some enquiries?"

Kerry looked at Imran, but he was staring at his floor with his arms still firmly wrapped around the oxygen cylinder. Anger and frustration gurgled up in her chest. Why didn't Imran say anything? Why didn't he – for once – contribute to the discussion? Why had he bothered to come along at all? He could have stayed home with Leo, instead of leaving the poor little mite to the tender mercies of Dr Govender's harried receptionist.

Well, if Imran wasn't going to make a suggestion, let alone a decision, she would just have to carry on alone. As usual.

"I think," she ventured, glancing at her non-responsive husband again, "*we* think that perhaps we should look at making some preliminary enquiries. Because at this point, all we are doing is treading water – and *praying*, which doesn't seem to be helping very much," she added pointedly, glaring at Imran, who ignored her. As usual.

Dr Govender nodded. "Alright. I'm going to see if she can be placed on the programme."

"In Cape Town?" Kerry asked. "Can Lily fly? Wouldn't that be dangerous?"

"No no, it is perfectly safe for her to fly. Not a problem at all."

"So if she can fly, why don't we take her overseas where she'll have a better chance of getting a heart?" As she said the words, Kerry knew that could never happen. She and Imran would battle to raise enough money for the airfare to Cape Town, let alone overseas.

"No, no, no. That's not a good idea – not a good idea at all," Dr Govender said firmly. This was so unlike his usual soft-shoe shuffle approach that Kerry was startled.

"Why not? Why shouldn't we take her to wherever is the best chance of her getting a heart?"

Kerry had heard of there was a thriving black market in human organs overseas and she quickly calculated that if she sold one or two of her own – a kidney, perhaps, or a cornea – she really didn't need two of them, that could help fund Lily's transplant. Although perhaps Imran would have to sell his too. She had no idea of the going rate for black market kidneys and corneas, for even perhaps bits of her lungs, or liver. Did they transplant bits of a liver?

Dr Govender's voice interrupted her musing calculations.

"No, no, Mrs Patel. There are waiting lists for organs in every country, even in those countries where everyone is presumed to be a donor unless one specifically chooses to opt-out – to refuse to have their organs donated for transplant after their death. Several European countries do that, and Canada too, I believe. But somehow there is still a shortage, always a shortage. As a result, every country prioritises its own citizens for any organs that become available – it's highly unlikely they'd consider a foreign child for a transplant ahead of their own."

"What about India? I have a friend ... they went to India for a lung transplant ..."

"Was it successful?" Dr Govender interrupted.

"No – they were still waiting – they left it too late ... she didn't make it."

Dr Govender nodded. "Uh huh. That happens. That happens. And chances are they would have had to wait a very long time. Even in India. The black market for organs was very big in India but I believe the government there has clamped down so even there, there is a shortage. What I suggest is we first look at what we can do for your little one here, at home. And the first step is to find out whether transplant is even a possibility for Lily."

"But you said it is!"

"I said we need to consider it. And we can only consider it ... it only becomes a possibility if the transplant team believes she is a suitable candidate. They would have to register her as a candidate for a transplant. So that's our first step. Just a first step. Would you like me to proceed?"

Kerry nodded vigorously. Imran remained motionless. It was as if he had zoned out of the conversation.

Dr Govender picked up the phone on his desk, dialled and identified himself before launching into one of his characteristically long-winded monologues: "Good morning – oh no, sorry, good afternoon. I have a young kiddie here who is now two years and eight months old. She has a Tricuspid Atresia – it was a 1C. She had a band initially, then a Glen Shunt. But for some reason this kid has some kind of cardiomyopathy. We don't know what caused it – why she developed a myopathic heart. And then, when I did her last cath – the pulmonary pressures were a little high even though we had done a Glen Shunt. Thank god the Glen Shunt took nicely. She has never had an SVC – a Superior Vena Cava – obstruction but she has struggled with the cardiomyopathy. She is in intractable cardiac failure. Uh huh ..."

At the words "intractable cardiac failure", Kerry shuddered. It wasn't that she didn't know Lily was in heart failure, but Dr Govender had always indicated that it might – it could – reverse. Now he was saying it was "intractable" – he was saying Lily wouldn't ever get better. He was implying that Lily *would* die – not could die – would die without a transplant. Imran didn't seem to have picked up on this; he didn't seem to have heard. Was he even listening?

She dragged her attention back to Dr Govender who still had the phone clamped to his ear. Then he continued: "The reason I'm calling? I thought I'd made it clear. The reason I'm calling is because I think my little patient is a prime candidate for cardiac transplant. I need to know if she could be put on the list?"

Kerry caught her breath. Dr Govender had just said Lily was a "prime candidate" for a transplant. So much for all his talk about risk and waiting and caution. He clearly believed Lily needed – and deserved – a transplant. Kerry found herself holding her breath as the doctor listened and nodded. And listened again.

"Okay ... okay," he said after what seemed to Kerry like forever, "So can I tell them ... so how is it going to work? Because I'm thinking with you leaving ..."

Kerry wished he had a speaker phone so she could hear what was being said. It was surreal. This conversation was literally discussing whether Lily would live or die. This was it. If Lily was put on the list, she could grow up and live a relatively normal life – perhaps. If she wasn't, the only question was how soon she would die. Lily whimpered and squirmed on Kerry's lap. Kerry shushed her and strained unsuccessfully to hear both sides of the conversation.

"Okay ... Okay ... okay that ... uh huh ... okay ... uh huh ... no, that's fine. So if you say that then ... uh huh ... so we should ... Okay ... yes ... okay. So we don't have to ... Uh huh. So what about bloods? The last cath? Hmm, let me check ..."

Dr Govender looked at his notes and continued: "It was in December 2018. So that's nearly two years ago. ... uh huh – okay. And at the same time we can ... Okay ... Alright. Thanks very much."

He nodded and put the phone down. And smiled.

"Right. So that was our transplant doctor – the one who is leaving as I told you. But what she suggested is that we maybe do all the preliminary tests here. Now. As soon as possible. And we put your little one on the list – then it won't matter if she leaves because Lily will be listed here and the transplant list – the Cape Town list and our list here in Gauteng – it all gets combined."

A wave of terror, and relief, washed over Kerry. "So Lily can go on the transplant list? And she would have the transplant here, in Sunninghill?"

"No, no – that's still a long way off. All we are going to do now is put her on the list. And then there is the catheter procedure which we will do here. And that's easy because she has had the Glen Shunt."

Kerry switched off as Dr Govender explained in excruciating detail why a catheter procedure on a child who has had a Glen Shunt was so much easier than on one who hasn't. Kerry didn't care. She just wanted Dr Govender to get to the point, to talk about the transplant.

"... and this will help us because if the pulmonary pressure – the lung pressure – is very high, then, if we do a transplant, we would have to do a heart and lung transplant. If the pulmonary pressure is not very high, then we are only looking at a heart transplant. And at the same time, we can take bloods for compatibility ..."

Kerry realised Dr Govender had finally stopped talking and was looking at her, waiting for a response.

"Umm – so we're going to do the cath and all pre-transplant tests here, not Cape Town?" she asked.

The doctor nodded. "Yes."

"And she'll be put on the transplant list here?"

"Yes."

"Great," Kerry said.

Across the examination table, Imran stirred. "No," he said.

Chapter 33

With Lily secured in his right arm and the portable oxygen cylinder in his left, Imran marched across Sunninghill Hospital's lavish foyer, looking neither left nor right – nor back. Behind him, Kerry scurried to keep up but Leo seemed to have grown lead in his shoes. He'd grasped Kerry's hand as soon as she'd rescued him from Dr Govender's flustered receptionist and refused to let go.

"Come on," Kerry begged, pulling the little boy along with one hand while hanging on to the dead portable oxygen concentrator with the other. "Daddy's in a hurry."

He wasn't just in a hurry, he appeared to be in a fury. As she and Dr Govender had gaped at him, stunned by the bombshell he'd dropped, Imran had scooped Lily off her lap.

"I'm taking my daughter out of here," he'd said and stormed out the room.

Grabbing the raft of papers Dr Govender held out to her – "consent forms," he'd muttered – she rushed after her husband, worried he'd leave her, and Leo, behind

But despite her urging, Leo's footsteps slowed even further.

"Do you want me to carry you?" Kerry asked frantically. Imran and Lily had disappeared through the hospital doors, well on their way to the parking area.

"No."

"Well, if you don't walk a little faster, I'm going to have to carry you. Daddy's going to leave us behind."

Leo released Kerry's hand and dropped to the floor, howling. Kerry stared at him in shock. Leo hadn't thrown a tantrum like that since … she couldn't remember when. She actually couldn't remember Leo ever having a full-blown meltdown. He was always such a placid, happy, affectionate little boy who loved nothing more than winning his mother's approval. Ignoring the disapproving eyes boring into her back, Kerry bent down and somehow managed to pull the kicking, twisting, screaming child into her arms while desperately hanging on to her handbag and the concentrator. She staggered as quickly as she could across the last mile of the foyer and out into the hot November sunshine, ignoring Leo's tears and flying snot.

By the time she reached the sun-baked car, she was dripping in sweat. Imran was ensconced behind the wheel, doors closed, engine revving.

"Imran, please help me," she called, struggling to open the back door as Leo's squirms and cries intensified.

Imran got out of the car. "Give me that before you break it," he said, taking the concentrator from her. He slid back into the driver's seat and revved the engine again.

With one hand now free, Kerry pulled the door open and unceremoniously dumped Leo onto his booster seat. The child immediately twisted over and slid to the floor. Kerry dropped her handbag, leaned into the car and tried to pry him from where he had wedged himself between the front and back seats.

"Leo please, get into your seat," she begged.

On the far side of the back seat where she was securely strapped into her baby seat, Lily's face crumpled, her mouth opened and she joined her brother's howling cacophony. Imran sat unflinching in the driver's seat, revving the engine and tapping his fingers on the steering wheel. Near to tears herself, Kerry finally extricated Leo, manhandled him onto his booster seat and strapped him in.

"Don't," she spat as Leo fumbled for the button to release himself. "Don't you dare!"

She scrabbled in her bag for a tissue and dabbed at his face, trying to remove the worst of the damage caused by streaming snot. She'd worry about the mucus and tears that had soaked into her blouse later. Slamming the door on Leo's and Lily's now heartbroken sobs, she hurried to the front passenger door and pulled at the handle. Nothing. She pulled again. The car's engine revved loudly.

"Imran, it's locked! Open it."

Click.

She pulled the door open and scrambled in. She barely had time to close the door, let alone fasten her seatbelt, before Imran released the handbrake and screeched away.

"What the hell's the matter with you? What is going on?" Kerry hissed.

Silence.

On the backseat, the children's cries froze. The car's arctic interior was flooded by a terse stillness. Kerry shivered.

"Where are you going?" Kerry asked as Imran took the car keys off the hook at the front door.

"Out."

"To the mosque? Again?"

As always, Imran ignored her.

"Imran, please – we have to talk."

He closed the door behind him. Quietly for once, considerate enough not to risk waking Lily who had finally settled for her nap in her cot. Exhaustion had finally overtaken her desperate efforts to stave off sleep as long as possible – and her anxiety. Her enormous brown eyes seemed to be permanently tear-filled. At least, when her father was around, which was becoming less and less often.

With Imran 'out', the frigid atmosphere that pervaded the little house lifted. Leo rushed over to where she was folding Imran's blankets and pillows into a neat pile on the couch and wrapped his little arms around her legs.

"I love you mama," he said.

Kerry sniffed. This couldn't go on. It was more than three weeks since Dr Govender had suggested they put Lily on the transplant list; three weeks since he'd handed her the consent forms to sign for Lily's cath procedure; three weeks since Imran had taken to sleeping on the couch; and even longer since he had said a civil word to her. The consent forms lay accusingly on the disused dining room table. Kerry had taken to eating her meals, standing, in the kitchen; Imran ate his on the couch; and Leo had commandeered the little plastic table where Lily's seemingly futile speech therapy sessions were held. Kerry's phone rang and she glanced at the number: Dr Govender's. She ignored it – she was running out of excuses for not returning the signed consent forms or for setting a date for the cath. She knew Dr Govender would want to do it soon, before everyone went away for the holidays. But she was too embarrassed to tell him that Imran refused to sign them. Well, he hadn't exactly refused – he just ignored her when she asked him. She was seriously considering just signing the forms herself. She'd guiltily googled it and it seemed that only one parent's signature was required for a medical procedure that was in a child's best interest. And having the cath procedure and being put on the heart transplant list was certainly in Lily's best interests. Why couldn't Imran see that? But Imran was Lily's father; he loved his daughter. He only wanted the best for her. And Kerry didn't want to antagonise him. She certainly didn't want to alienate him even more than he already seemed to be.

"It's just a cath. She's had them before. Please just sign," she'd pleaded, holding out a pen to him.

"I'm busy," he'd said, resuming his intense concentration on the Barney cartoon that was enthralling Lily. Leo, totally bored by Barney's cheerful antics which he had seen dozens of times before, had continued building a tower of blocks in the corner.

The phone rang again. Jason. Her face flushed. She hoped Leo wouldn't notice.

"Hey," Kerry said, deliberately avoiding using Jason's name in front of her son. It wasn't that she had anything to hide, but if Leo innocently told Imran that Mommy had been talking to Jason on the phone, Imran would probably become even more obdurate about signing the documents – if that were possible.

"Howzit going – you okay?"

Kerry smiled. Just hearing Jason's deep, velvety voice made her smile. He always seemed to know when she needed to hear his voice.

"Yeah, I'm okay. Lily's sleeping, Leo's playing."

"And Imran?"

"Out. Have you looked at the spreadsheet I sent you?" Kerry hastily changed the subject. She didn't want to burden Jason with her personal problems although she suspected he had an idea that things were not great between her and Imran. She hadn't told him. She hadn't told anyone, not even Sandy or Jade, and they always told each other everything. But this was different. And it was easier to hide things from your best friends when they couldn't see your face. Lockdown had its advantages.

Picking up on her cue, Jason's tone quickly became a little more formal, business-like. They chatted on about this and that, all work-related. All perfectly respectable and innocent. Nothing for Imran to get jealous about. Nothing for her to feel guilty about. Nothing at all ...

"Jason, I have to go," Kerry said eventually. "Lily's woken up. I have to feed her."

"Okay, chat soon. Let me know if you need anything – I mean, with regard to the new project. Or anything else," he added.

"Will do. Thanks. Bye." Heart pounding, she ended the call.

Kerry slowly poured the little bottle of Frebini into the peg feeding tube in Lily's stomach, a large mop-up cloth close at hand in case she vomited. It usually helped to pour the liquid food slowly, but not always. It never failed to astound Kerry how Lily could gag and vomit up something that she hadn't swallowed. It was as if her stomach rebelled at having anything in it regardless of how it got there and got rid of it as forcefully as it could. Lily was a campion projectile vomiter, so accustomed to it that she scarcely blinked when she heaved and the white liquid fountained from her mouth. Nothing Dr Sinclair had prescribed seemed to help her keep the liquid food down and it worried Kerry. Lily needed it to grow, to be strong for the surgeries and procedures that lay ahead. One day, hopefully sooner rather than later.

After allowing the last drops from the bottle to drip into the peg, Kerry gently sat Lily up and watched her anxiously. Lily grinned at her – and promptly spewed up jet of white liquid that landed on the cloth Kerry had deftly manoeuvred into place to catch the worst of it. She wiped her daughter's lips and face with a clean damp cloth and left her sitting happily on the floor playing with her Barney toy while she went into the kitchen to rinse the soiled cloths yet again.

A sharp knock at the front door sent her scurrying back into the lounge. She grabbed a face mask and gingerly opened the door. Covid-19 infections had started rising again, just as the summer holiday season got underway. South Africa was officially in the midst of a second Covid wave which would be worse than the first, according to the news – and Kerry was terrified that the virus would find its way into their home and Lily's tortured lungs.

"Kerry-Anne Aarons-Patel?" said the well-dressed man through the still locked security gate, his voice faintly muffled by the black and red mask covering his nose and mouth.

"Yes."

"I'm the Sheriff of the High Court. I have to serve these papers on you."

He pushed a sheaf of papers through the gate at her.

"What ... who ... what is this?" Kerry demanded as her fingers closed automatically around the documents. "I don't want ... I can't ..."

"You need to sign that you have received them. You must sign the top copy – it's the original – and return it to me. The other copy is for you to keep. You just have to sign and date it on the back. You can use your own pen if you like but I did sanitise this one." He held out a black Bic pen.

"What am I signing? I can't just sign documents I've never read!"

"You only have to sign that you've received them. That's all. You can see where you need to sign on the original – it's clearly marked."

Kerry stared at the papers in her hand. They were covered in hieroglyphics. What was this? A million thought fragments flashed through her mind – had she forgotten to pay an account? Were they being evicted? No, their rent payments were up to date, she made sure of that. Had Imran run up a debt she didn't know about? He was always out, he was so secretive. But no, she saw his credit card statement every month – she had to pay it after all. Divorce! Imran was going to divorce her! No, it couldn't be. He'd have told her. And he would have moved out first, taken his things. Wouldn't he? But perhaps not – hadn't she read somewhere that leaving the family home could count against him in court ... Court!

From a million miles away she heard the man's voice: "Ma'am? Ma'am? Please sign the top document and give it back to me. Here's a pen."

Kerry took the pen in her nerveless fingers. She scratched at her page with the pen, a scrawl that bore little resemblance to her usual signature and blindly shoved the document back through the gate.

"Now please sign the back of your copy. And date it."

Kerry scribbled on the back. The papers fluttered to the floor, like petals from a dying flower. The pen followed.

"And my pen, may I have it back please ma'am?"

"What? Oh yes – here." Kerry bent and picked it up. The blood rushing to her head cleared some of the fog that had engulfed her brain. She handed the pen back through the gate.

"Thank you. Have a good day."

She didn't respond. She couldn't. The words that had jumped out at her as she'd retrieved the pen had paralysed her vocal cords.

Chapter 34

"I don't understand. I just don't understand. How ... Why ... it's crazy, crazy!" Kerry sobbed.

She couldn't seem to stop crying, not since the urgent interdict application had been dropped on her by the Sherriff of the High Court. She didn't cry in front of the children, of course. Somehow she managed to hold it together then. But they sensed something was wrong. Leo was uncharacteristically clingy, preferring to stay home and play with his tired blocks than go across the road to Mrs Reddy where he could tag along behind his adored, honorary 'big brother' Mohammed. And she certainly didn't cry in front of Imran, the fucking bastard. Somehow she managed to squeeze out icily polite words to him when he imposed himself on her little family – and on the couch in the lounge. But now he could fold his own fucking blankets. She wished he'd just go away and stay away. She wished he'd just move out, but he wouldn't and she couldn't make him according to Darryl, Jason's old mate from high school and now her recently appointed attorney.

"I'm so sorry Kerry," Darryl had said during their first WhatsApp consultation which Jason had organised "You have no grounds to bar your husband from the family home."

"You can't mean that! It's wrong, all wrong. He's gone nuts – he's been brainwashed or something. I don't want him here. There's got to be something you can do! Can't I get a protection order or something – anything – to keep him away from me and the children?"

"Has he physically harmed you? Has he threatened you in any way at all?" Darryl asked.

"No, of course not. He's … he's not violent."

"I'm afraid a domestic disagreement without the threat of violence is not grounds for a protection order. Sorry."

"But I don't want him here. He's upsetting the children."

"He could argue that it's you that's upsetting them."

"That's not true! I'd never do anything to harm them. He knows that!"

"Well, if his application is anything to go by, it appears he doesn't. And he'll argue that he has to remain in the family home to ensure that you don't do anything that he thinks could be harmful, or at least not in the children's best interests."

"So what can I do?" Kerry demanded.

"You can fight," Darryl said.

He'd obviously been talking to Jason who had said exactly the same when Kerry had called him hysterically after she'd managed to pierce the fog of legalese and jargon in the urgent interdict application the Sherriff of the High Court had delivered. It seemed that Imran had named her as the first respondent and she had just fourteen days to respond.

"The first thing you have to do," Jason had said, "is get a lawyer, a good one."

"I don't know any lawyers – and I don't have the money to pay for one either."

"Don't worry about the money – or about getting a lawyer. I'll help you."

"But I can't take your money. It's not right."

"You can consider it a loan from Browns, if that makes you happier. An advance on your salary. Okay?"

Kerry had reluctantly agreed – she had no choice.

That first whispered WhatsApp meeting with Darryl had been awkward, what with Imran just a few metres away, stationed strategically on the couch from where he could monitor her every move, her every word.

So she'd gone outside into the baking midday sun and shut the front door behind her.

"I've read the application you scanned and sent through to

Jason. I'm going to send a messenger to pick up the original, but in the meantime, we need to get moving. We don't have much time to prepare our responding affidavit."

✄

It hadn't been easy to find a suitable time for a meeting with the advocate Darryl had recommended. It had to be done remotely, but not just because of the coronavirus pandemic. When infections started to rise again so rapidly, the government had imposed renewed restrictions on workplace meetings regardless of whether one sanitised, masked, social distanced or presented with a normal temperature.

"We could meet in a shopping mall. That's still acceptable, even if going to the beach isn't," Darryl had joked, referring to the government's latest irrational ban on sitting, sunbathing or even walking on beaches in the fresh air during the height of the holiday season. So bored holidaymakers packed into closed, poorly ventilated malls in search of entertainment while vast stretches of pristine beaches were empty but for patrolling police officers hoping to arrest errant sunbathers and surfers.

Kerry's acknowledging giggle was half-hearted. She appreciated Darryl's efforts to put her at ease, but she wasn't in the mood. She had three seemingly implacable hurdles to overcome before any meeting could take place: she was terrified of contracting Covid-19 and infecting Lily; she couldn't leave the children alone while she went off to meet with lawyers; and she couldn't ask Imran to stay with them either. He'd probably refuse. She couldn't go out to do anything these days. Leo wasn't as much of a problem – he could go across the road to Mrs Reddy and play outside with Mohammed; but she couldn't leave Lily with her neighbour or anyone else. She certainly wouldn't risk taking Lily with her and put her at risk of catching Covid, or anything else. She also didn't want Imran to know that she was consulting with lawyers, which was pretty stupid really because he must have realised that she would have to do just that if she was to respond to his application. She just wasn't going ask him for help to enable her to do so.

Imran, it seemed, was going to make it as difficult for her as he could. Even before the application she'd not known when he was going to go out, or how long he'd be away. Sometimes he'd disappear for hours, probably, she thought bitterly, to plan his ambush of her, and consult with his lawyers and whoever was financing his application because he certainly couldn't pay for it himself; and sometimes he'd leave and return suddenly just fifteen minutes later, almost as if he'd been hoping to catch her doing something she shouldn't – or he thought she shouldn't. Like speaking to Jason.

But Fridays were different. On Fridays Imran always went to the mosque. Lockdown or no lockdown, it had continued to operate – illegally at times. Apparently, the congregants ga-thered at different locations, in members' homes mostly, for surreptitious, hurried prayer sessions. But on Fridays, Imran usually stayed away for at least two hours for the midday prayers.

Today was Friday.

Imran remained motionless on the couch. Kerry glanced at her watch. It was almost noon. He should have gone by now. But he didn't seem to be going anywhere. Did he know? He couldn't possibly know that she needed him gone. She'd made a point of deleting her WhatsApp chats with Darryl as soon as they were over. She'd listed Darryl in her contacts as Elle Woods, named for the Reece Witherspoon character in *Legally Blonde*, one of her all-time favourite movies which Imran had refused to watch. She hoped Darryl would turn out to be as astute as Elle and find a way to turn the tables on Imran. But so far, Imran seemed to have the upper hand.

Kerry pottered about in the kitchen, banging cupboard doors and clattering dishes as she prepared Leo's lunch, keeping at ear cocked to detect the sound of the front door opening, indicating that Imran was leaving. Nothing.

She carried Leo's plate to the lounge and put it down on the little plastic table.

"It's lunchtime! Come and eat, Leo," she said pointedly. Imran didn't take the hint. He didn't budge.

The seconds crawled by. Kerry waited, panicked bile starting to rise in her throat. Imran stirred. He slowly unfolded his inert frame, looked directly into Kerry's eyes and smirked slightly. Then he bent and kissed the top of Lily's and Leo's heads and opened the front door just as Kerry's phone flashed a reminder that her Zoom meeting with Elle Woods was starting.

Kerry quickly settled the children in front of the television, put on *Barney's Great Adventure – The Movie* which would keep them occupied for at least an hour, closed her bedroom door behind her and booted up her laptop.

She clicked the link Darryl had emailed for the meeting that morning, praying it would work. It did.

"Sorry I'm late – Imran wouldn't leave," she said as soon as she connected.

"That's okay sweetie," said the smiling, squarish-faced woman with butchered grey hair in the left block on the screen. Zoom identified her as 'Hentie'.

Darryl's block was on the right. "Hi Kerry. Good to see you. This is Advocate Henriette Weinberg."

"Hello – um ... Advocate Weinberg – um Ms Weinberg, Mrs Weinberg?" Kerry said. Darryl hadn't told her how to address the advocate, he hadn't really told her anything about her at all, except that he considered her 'the best' and that she'd been brilliant in her defence of Yair Silverman when he'd been accused of killing his fiancée. Kerry remembered the case – who wouldn't? It had been headline news for ages. But Kerry's first impression of Advocate/Ms/Mrs Weinberg was less than reassuring – she looked like a dowdy old bag.

"Call me Hentie. Mrs Weinberg was my long-departed, unlamented mother-in-law," the advocate said in a raspy voice that testified to too many cigarettes and probably too much whisky. Kerry fleetingly wondered how she had survived the months' long cigarette and booze ban.

"But listen sweetie, from what young Darryl here tells me, we don't have much time so let's forget the pleasantries and get to it. I hate this Zoom but it's what we have to work with, so we'll just get on with it. I've found it works best when one person speaks at a time. Right. So – I'll do the talking. And when I want you to speak, I'll tell you to speak. Otherwise you listen. Got it?"

"Um … yes. I think so," Kerry said.

"Good. Right. So. According to your husband's application – nicely presented, by the way. He's got himself some good legal representation there, must be costing him a pretty penny, I thought he was unemployed. That's what young Darryl told me. Is he unemployed?'

"Um … yes. Well, he has his own business but with lockdown he hasn't had any jobs and …"

"Just yes or no will do, sweetie, okay? If I want your life history, or his, I'll ask for it. So, he's unemployed which means he must be getting financial support from somewhere. Do you have a joint bank account?"

"No. Well yes, but he usually uses his own account. I mean the joint account is just for household stuff. We both contribute to that but … well, since Covid, he hasn't really contributed anything, you see. I've been doing work for Jason Brown – you know Jason, Darryl."

"Just yes or no, sweetie. Just yes or no or we'll be here all day and your dear husband will come home and interrupt our little meeting. Okay?"

Kerry nodded. She decided she didn't like Hentie at all. But that was okay, she reassured herself. She didn't have to like her. In fact, it was probably better if she was a bitch. That's what Imran deserved for putting her – and the kids, especially Lily – through this.

"Right. So the application is to ask the court to grant sole guardianship of your minor children to him. From what I under-stand from young Darryl here, it's to prevent you from authorising any kind of medical treatment for or intervention on your minor daughter, Lily Aarons-Patel. He's also named a number of doctors and institutions – Sunninghill Hospital for one, and a Dr Govender,

Dr Sinclair, Dr Sibanda, Dr Patterson ... a couple of others too – as respondents, to prevent them from treating your daughter without his express consent. Who are all these doctors? Do you know them?"

"Yes. I mean no. Not all of them."

"And?"

"And what?"

"Who are they? Come on Kerry. I don't want to have to drag information out of you. We don't have time for that."

"Oh, sorry. Dr Govender is Lily's cardiologist of course, and Dr Sibanda is her pulmonologist, and Dr Sinclair is her paediatrician and some of them are surgeons who have operated on her in the past but I've never heard of some of the others. And he's also even named her therapists – her physio and OT ... he's crazy!"

"Right. We'll get into all that later. Young Darryl is working on finding out exactly who all the respondents are and why they are also part of the application. What I am having difficulty establishing from this application is why? Why is he going to so much trouble to exclude you from any say in your children's care? Is he a closet Jehovah's Witness by any chance? You know – opposed to blood transfusions?"

"No, he's Muslim. And he's never had any problem with authorising Lily's treatment and surgeries in the past. He's always been so supportive. He's been a rock, a wonderful father. He adores Lily. He knows that without the surgeries – the treatments – Lily would ... she wouldn't ... I don't understand what's gotten into him. I just don't understand."

Chapter 35

Kerry furiously dabbed at the tears that were suddenly coursing down her cheeks while Hentie and Darryl waited for her to gather herself together.

"Have you asked him?" the advocate demanded as soon as her sobs subsided.

"What?"

"Why he's doing this? What he really wants?"

"Of course I have. He won't talk to me. But I don't want to fight with him in front of the children, so it's difficult to push him. I've been begging him to sign the consent forms for Lily's cath but he won't."

"Her what?" Hentie and Darryl demanded in unison.

"Her cath – catheterisation. It's a surgical procedure to check the pressure in her lungs. She needs to have that before she can be put on the transplant list. If the pressure is too high it could mean PH – pulmonary hypertension, you see. It would need to be treated now – and it could mean that she'd also need a lung transplant and ..."

"Whoa. Whoa – back up a bit," Hentie said. "Slow down. Now, from the top. In your own words, tell me about Lily's condition – what's actually wrong with her, the treatment she has received to date, and the treatment she is going to need in the future."

"It's all described pretty clearly in Imran's application. Why do you want me to tell you again?"

"Because that's your husband's take on what's going on with his daughter. I'd like to hear it from your perspective – not only the facts of her condition, but how you felt, what you did and, importantly, what your husband said and did."

"Oh, okay. So, when we heard that Lily had a congenital heart defect called Tricuspid Atresia – she was only eight days old. We'd been told she just had a lung infection so it was a huge shock."

Hentie nodded. "Yup, I can only imagine. Sorry, go on."

Both lawyers scribbled furiously as Kerry described the surgeries, the setbacks, the infections, the tests – the long, long list of the good, but mostly the bad that had happened in Lily's short life. They let her talk and talk, interrupting only occasionally for clarification.

"And that's it, in a nutshell really," Kerry said finally.

"Alright," said Hentie, perusing her scribbled notes. "That's quite something, poor little mite. We'll get Lily's medical records from Dr Govender and Dr Sinclair too, of course, but I think you've given us sufficient information to work with for now."

Kerry felt a glow of accomplishment at the advocate's implied praise.

"Right. Now – just to check I understand you correctly," Hentie said, and Kerry felt a frisson of panic. Was she going to be questioned? Cross examined? Surely not, Hentie was her lawyer.

"Right. So. From what I understand, you and your husband have agreed on every aspect of Lily's treatment through everything you've described, until now. He's never objected or indicated that he had a problem with anything – that he'd like a second opinion? Right?" Hentie demanded.

"Yes. There's been nothing, no indication at all. We've been a team, Imran and I. We've worked together to give Lily the best possible chance of a normal life – well, as normal a life as possible. We've always supported each other. He's been my rock, always."

"So what changed?"

"I don't know. I've tried and tried to figure it out but I just don't understand."

"Right. So let's try and work out when he changed and perhaps we'll find an answer there to what's really behind this application. On the face of it, the application is about preventing Lily from being subjected to 'unnecessary and cruel' procedures and treatment. In other words, *you* are subjecting your daughter to 'unnecessary and cruel' procedures. And that's why he's asking for sole guardianship."

"That's totally crazy. I'm her mother!" Kerry blurted.

"Of course you are," Hentie said soothingly. "But as we know, some parents – and that includes mothers – do dreadful things to their kids."

"Are you nuts? I'd never do anything to hurt my daughter! No decent mother would," Kerry said, furious that the lawyer would even suggest it.

"Tell that to the kids whose loving, caring moms have Munchausen syndrome by proxy."

Kerry opened her mouth to object but Hentie forestalled her. "No, no, I'm not accusing you of that but we need to be aware that there are mothers who *do* harm their kids. So, my dear, simply claiming that because you're Lily's mother, and you love her and care for her does not absolve you from accusations that you might deliberately harm her in some way. That argument may not impress the judge. Probably won't, depending on who we get."

"No! Imran would never accuse me of actually harming Lily!" Kerry protested.

"I'm afraid he has. As I said, that seems to be the underlying presumption of his application," Hentie said.

Kerry didn't bother to wipe away the tears that rolled down her cheeks. This was beyond a nightmare. She couldn't, she wouldn't believe Imran thought *that* of her. This horrible woman with her mean face and snake-like lipless mouth was wrong – she had to be wrong.

"Right. Now, let's move on to the facts of the matter and leave sentiment out of it. Right. You say you've aways been a team," Hentie continued in a tone that implied she didn't really believe it. "So tell me what's been happening with Lily recently – say in the last couple of months – that would make Imran do a 180? Why would he go from working with you, to alleging that you are inflicting 'unnecessary and cruel' treatment on your child? Has he really supported you in everything? I mean, has he been a true partner in everything?"

"That's what I said. He has. He's been an amazing father."

"Huh. Really? In my experience, there's usually one parent who takes the lead in dealing with the children, who makes most of the day-to-day decisions – and the other parent just goes along with things."

"Well, it was sort of like that before – before lockdown. Imran was at work and I was home with Lily so I had to make most of the decisions. I know her. I mean, when you are with a sick child all day, every day, you get to understand everything about her. I can hear when her breathing changes, I can tell if she's unwell, just by looking at her. I *know* her so well and Imran knows that. He's always trusted my judgement."

"So you say. But he clearly doesn't any longer. Why?"

Kerry thought hard before answering. "Imran has been around Lily a lot more than in the past, I suppose. Because of lockdown. I mean, he sees what her daily routine is like – every day. It's hard – but he's always known that."

"Has he? How can you be sure of that? Before lockdown, he wasn't here all day, every day, dealing with a very sick little girl 24/7."

"But he knew how much of a strain it was – he's always done what he could to support me. He's come to all Lily's check-ups; he's been there with me every time she was in hospital. We were a team!"

"Well, something changed. So think, Kerry. What's different now?"

"I don't know. I mean Lily has been doing so well. She has made so much progress with her walking and talking. You'd think he'd be happy about it, but it just seems to make him angry."

"Ah. Now I think we might be getting somewhere." Hentie smiled thoughtfully. "I'm a little puzzled ... why is she suddenly making so much progress?"

"It's not really all that sudden. But I think it's probably because she hasn't had as many setbacks as she had before – actually she hasn't had any. Just one or two since lockdown actually, which is pretty amazing. We had to rush her to hospital in, I think it was May or June. We thought she might have Covid but it wasn't. It was just ordinary pneumonia. She's had it before, of course. Three times – maybe four. But she didn't have to be intubated this time and she's recovered really well. It set her back a bit – it always does. But as I said, she's been doing nicely since then. She's such a little fighter. We call her Tiger Lily – that's Imran's name for her. Tiger. Because she's such a fighter."

"Uh huh," Hentie interrupted. "I get that. But the question I'm asking is why – why is it that she hasn't had as many 'set-backs'." Hentie's stubby fingers stabbed the air in an imitation of quotation marks.

"I don't know. Perhaps Covid has something to do with it – I mean we're so much more careful about infection and I sanitise everything all the time and we wear masks when we go out to the shops or whatever, and I don't take Lily out at all."

"So that's it? Masks and sanitiser and isolation have prevented her from getting the infections she was prone to before and that's why she is making such good progress?"

Kerry bristled at the disbelief oozing from Hentie's pores.

"Yes, I think so."

"Well, think harder. Something else must have happened to prompt Imran to object to how you are dealing with Lily's condition."

Kerry hesitated. She didn't want to voice her suspicions. She didn't want to believe it was true. It couldn't be true. If she said it, that would make it real, and she didn't want it to be real. But – what other reason could there be?

"Well?" Hentie snapped. "Spit it out, girl. What aren't you telling me?"

Chapter 36

Kerry couldn't just say it. If she did, it would validate every hateful thing her mother had predicted when she'd first plucked up the courage to tell her parents about this amazing guy she'd met in the queue in the Wits cafeteria and had fallen in head over heels love with. And even more incredibly, he'd fallen for her too.

"He's amazing Mom, Dad," she'd said. "He's smart and funny and hard-working and really, really good looking. You'll love him."

Her mother had sniffed, not bothering to hide her scepticism that any smart, funny, hard-working, handsome young man would give her plain, awkward, not very bright daughter the time of day.

"So why haven't you brought him home to meet us?" Gillian had sneered. "There has to be something wrong with him or you'd have been flaunting him at us. So – what's his problem? Is he a cripple? Is he blind?"

"Of course not! He ... his name," she'd muttered, and then fuelled by anger at her mother, and at her own cowardice, blurted: "His name is Imran Patel."

If she hadn't been quaking inside at the prospect of the ferocity of her mother's – and probably her father's – reaction, she'd have laughed as the blood drained from her mother's face and a throbbing vein popped out on her temple.

So that's what an apoplexy looks like, Kerry had thought.

"Imran Patel? Imran Patel! Are you out of your tiny little fucking mind?" Gillian had shrieked.

"Gillian, please. Let's talk about this calmly," her husband had tried to soothe her, although his face too revealed his shock at his daughter's bombshell.

But Stephen had been somewhat less sanguine when Gillian had forced Kerry to concede that not only was Imran Patel an Indian, he was also a Muslim.

"Forget his race. Indians are good people, smart. Now, if he was Christian, or even Hindu ... but a Muslim! Kerry be sensible. You're Jewish. He's Muslim – this can't work," Stephen had pleaded with her.

"It will all end in tears – or worse. You mark my words," Gillian had said spitefully.

And now Hentie was forcing her to give voice to her mother's hateful prophecy.

"I ... I think ... Over the past few months, Imran has become more and more religious. More observant, you know? I mean, he wasn't religious at all when we first got together. Not even when we got married. But after Lily – well, he changed. He grew a beard and started praying and going to mosque all the time. Even during the lockdown when mosques and churches and shuls were supposed to be closed, he'd go. I think – perhaps there's something in Islam – something that says transplantation is wrong? Perhaps that's why?"

Hentie and Darryl shook their heads simultaneously.

"No, that can't be it," Darryl said. "That was one of the first things I thought of. I asked a couple of my Muslim colleagues and they all agreed. In Islam, transplantation is perfectly acceptable, even encouraged because – just as in Judaism – there is the belief that saving a life takes precedence over everything else. Again, just like in Judaism, there are some Islamic teachers who believe that organ donation is less acceptable. Which seems a little selfish to me – to say you can accept an organ but you can't donate your own. But that's not the issue here. The issue is that if Imran is following Islamic teachings – well, mainstream Islamic teachings – he wouldn't object to Lily having a transplant."

"Thank you to our religious scholar for those insights, but I think you're barking up the wrong tree," Hentie said. "There's nothing in Imran's application to suggest that it is being made on religious grounds. Having said that, his legal team is known to be associated with some of the more radical Islamic movements in South Africa. They've defended some people who were charged with terrorism for trying to join ISIS – and they did so pro bono apparently. Perhaps Imran has come under the influence of some fringe element of religious zealots, if you can call Muslims zealots, which, I think, was actually a Jewish thing. Whatever. So while there is nothing in the application to suggest that Imran's motion is grounded in mainstream Islamic teaching, the complaint that Lily is being subjected to 'cruel and unusual' treatment indicates that there is some kind of religious, or at least faith-based, reasoning involved in all this. But that still doesn't explain why he thinks she is being abused now."

"Do you think it might have anything to do with the therapy?" Kerry said. "Lily's been having intensive therapy – physio, OT and speech therapy twice a week. That's quite new. Dr Govender recommended it and it really seems to be working. The therapists have been coming to the house. Well, they've stopped now, of course. Because of the holidays – and the second wave. But I've been trying to continue with the sessions on my own."

Kerry swallowed, hesitated and then added: "Lily hates it."

"Hmm. You may be on to something. Go on. How do you know Lily hate it?" Hentie demanded.

"She – she cries right through the sessions. Actually, now I think of it, Imran can't handle it. He virtually runs away when it's therapy time."

"Uh huh," said Hentie.

"But it's doing her so much good – Imran can see that. I mean, before we started with the therapy, she wasn't able to move at all. She just sat there, getting frustrated and miserable. And now she is standing more or less on her own and trying to walk. She can actually cruise now, holding on to something. And she scoots around on her skateboard. She's loves being mobile. Her speech has improved too – Imran just loves it when she calls him 'Dada'."

"Right. Right. So, correct me if I'm wrong. She is doing well, right? She is making huge progress – correct?"

"Yes, that's what I said," Kerry said uncertainly, wondering why the advocate had suddenly become so aggressive again.

"Right. Hmm. I don't think it's the therapy itself that's the problem. I think it's the fact that the therapy is making such a positive difference. Not that that's a problem. The problem, as I see it, is this. Why on earth would you want to put her through the trauma – and the immense risk – of a heart transplant, or possibly even a heart-lung transplant when she is doing so well?" Hentie demanded triumphantly.

"Because she isn't. Not really. That's the problem! Don't you see? Nothing's really changed! Lily's heart – her heart – is not getting better," Kerry wailed.

"I'm confused," Hentie snapped. "I don't like being confused. You said she was doing well and was making such great progress. But now you say she is not getting better and nothing's changed. Which is it?"

Kerry bristled. "They're two totally different things. The therapy is helping Lily to catch up on her milestones – to help her do things like walk and talk like any other two-year-old. And that's fantastic progress – but it isn't making her better! It isn't changing the fact that her heart – her *heart* – is damaged and can't be fixed."

"Right. So you said. She was born with this defect – Tricuspid Atresia. I did a little research before this meeting after young Darryl here briefed me. From what I understand, Tricuspid Atresia is a relatively common congenital heart defect, as far as congenital heart defects go. And, from what I've read, most babies born with it live relatively normal lives without needing a heart transplant – a very dangerous, very risky procedure indeed. Right?"

Kerry nodded.

"Right. So Kerry, my question is – why do you want Lily to have a heart transplant that, let's be perfectly frank here – why do you want your child, your baby, to undergo a procedure that could kill her?"

Kerry flinched at Hentie's bluntness, but she shot back: "Because if she doesn't, she *will* die. Maybe not today, maybe not tomorrow – although we can't know that for sure. But she *will* die, and sooner rather than later. Now do you understand?"

"Not really. How can you be so sure? How can you know that without a transplant Lily will die soon?"

Kerry sighed. "I told you – Lily has cardiomyopathy. Her heart is failing. Failing!"

"I'm aware of that. But many people have this heart failure condition. They live with it for years. For most sufferers, a diagnosis of cardiomyopathy is a treatable, manageable condition."

"Not for Lily," Kerry said flatly. "For Lily, it is a death sentence."

"That's what your cardiologist told you?"

"Not in so many words, but yes," Kerry said. She suddenly felt cold – but for the first time since the ordeal with Hentie began, she felt calm, in control. "Dr Govender made it pretty clear. He said she has *intractable* heart failure. He said we should start thinking about a heart transplant because her heart is extremely enlarged and it's not responding to medication. As a result, the heart muscles are very, very weak and are getting weaker. There's no way of knowing how much longer her heart will be able to keep pumping blood around her body before it gives out completely."

"But it seems to me that you are doing more than just thinking about the possibility of a transplant, aren't you? Seems to me you have made up your mind to give her a transplant, haven't you?"

"Whose side are you on?" Kerry exploded. "You sound like Imran."

"I thought Imran wasn't talking to you about this?"

"He isn't. But I know him. I'm sure that's what he's thinking."

"Do you think that's why he is objecting to taking steps towards Lily having a transplant? Why he's refusing to sign the consent forms for a – what did you call it? A *cath* procedure he has consented to in the past? Because he doesn't want to feel pressured to put her on the transplant list?"

"I don't know. No. Yes. I suppose so. But putting Lily on the list isn't the same as her actually having a transplant. Once she is on the list, we still have to wait for a heart to become available. That could take years."

"Or a heart could become available tomorrow – or next week. Think of all the kids who might die in the next few weeks in our annual Christmas road accident carnage," Hentie said.

"That's horrible," Kerry said. "But okay, I suppose it's possible. The point really is that Lily needs a new heart – so the sooner she goes on the list, the better."

"Your husband clearly disagrees. So I have to ask you this – what if she is put on the list and, miracle of miracles, a heart becomes available tomorrow? What would you do? No, don't interrupt," she said as Kerry opened her mouth to answer.

"Think about it, my dear. Lily is doing well – you said so. She is making great progress. Are you willing to submit your child, your happy little girl who is learning to walk and talk so nicely – are you prepared to have her undergo a dangerous, risky procedure that, excuse me for being blunt – that she might not survive?"

"Yes, of course I am. I have no choice – there is no choice," Kerry whispered.

"Really? As things now stand, there is a likelihood of Lily having some good years ahead. There is a chance, possibly a good chance, that you will get to spend quality time with your little girl even with her weak and enlarged heart. Right?"

Kerry nodded.

"So," Hentie continued relentlessly, "are you prepared to risk her life – to have her possibly die today, right now – in the hope that a transplant would be successful? It's a gamble. On the one hand, she might live a good, long life with a transplanted heart; on the other, the transplant itself could kill her. Even if she survives the surgery, she might reject the heart – and she can't live without a heart. There's no Plan B for a rejected heart like there is for a failed kidney transplant. So, yes or no, Kerry? Are you prepared to gamble with your child's life?"

Kerry stared at the advocate's unflinching, square face in horror. "I ... I don't know. I don't want to think of it like that."

"You have to think like that. Because I'm pretty sure that's exactly what Imran is thinking. I strongly suspect that his application is based largely on the fact that *he* is not willing to gamble with your child's life, not when she is doing so well. The 'cruel and usual' complaint indicates that. So, if you want to fight him, and retain some control over your child's life, you are going to have to be absolutely certain that if a heart were to become available for Lily tomorrow, you would be willing to risk her dying right now, and potentially end up blaming yourself for the rest of your life for forcing her to have surgery that she didn't need – yet. So, I'll ask you again: are you willing to take that chance?"

"I ... I ..." Kerry sucked in a deep breath. And suddenly it was clear. So clear.

"Yes," she said. "Yes! Lily is a fighter. She has fought for her life from the day she was born. I am her mother. I can't give up on her and let her just fade away. Because that's what will happen if she doesn't have the transplant. I can't just hope and pray that it will all come right on its own. Imran believes in the power of prayer. I don't. I believe god – if there is a god – helps those who help themselves. This isn't a Hallmark movie where a heart will miraculously become available at the last minute, when the patient is on her deathbed. This is real and I can't just wait and wait until it is too late, like it was for Anesta. I have to fight for my baby's life right now – as hard as I can, no matter what!"

"Right," Hentie said, her thin lips stretching into a beaming smile. "*Now* we can prepare our response to your husband's interdict. Now we can start fighting for your little girl's future."

Chapter 37

Kerry paced – from the lounge to the bedroom, to the kitchen and back to the lounge, nibbling at a loose cuticle. She hadn't bitten her nails for years, not since those snotty bitches Rachel and Bridget – the two most popular girls in Grade seven – had gleefully explained that they couldn't invite her to their birthday party because it was a mani – and pedi – party (Rachel's older sister had recently qualified as a beautician) and they didn't want Kerry to be embarrassed.

Now, worrying about unkempt fingernails was the least of Kerry's concerns. Fortunately, the children seemed to sense that something big, something important was happening today and that Mom was uptight and distracted. Leo played quietly in the corner with his blocks and cars and hadn't nagged her once. Lily was napping in her camp cot. She'd barely cried all morning. She'd even managed to keep her peg feed down – mostly. She'd be waking up soon and there was no telling what her mood would be like then, but for now the house was quiet. Imran had thankfully disappeared early, just as the sun started peeping through the curtains in the bedroom she shared with her daughter. He had probably gone to the mosque, to pray for success. And then he must have gone to his lawyers' offices to listen to his high-priced advocate telling the judge what a bad, cruel, dreadful mother she was.

Darryl had suggested that she follow the Zoom proceedings from Hentie's offices, but she'd had to decline. Who was going to take care of Lily and Leo while the legal battle took place? Not Imran, that was for sure. He wanted all of the control without any of the responsibility. Jason had offered to come over and watch with her, but she'd declined that too. She didn't want to watch, she couldn't. Anyway, she couldn't risk Leo hearing what was going on – not that he would understand, but you never knew. And she couldn't risk Leo telling his father that Jason had actually come inside the house.

Hentie had assured her that the whole process probably wouldn't take very long and they could expect the judge to rule by the end of the day or by the next day at the latest, given the urgency of the application. All the motions and supporting affidavits had been submitted. All that was required now was for the lawyers – Hentie and Imran's team – to make oral arguments in support of their case.

"So I won't have to give evidence or be cross-examined?" Kerry had asked, somewhat relieved that she was to be spared that ordeal, but also peeved that she wouldn't be allowed to plead for her daughter as she would have liked. As she should. It would have been scary, but no one else could plead for Lily's life as well, as passionately, as her mother. Despite Darryl's assurances that Hentie was 'the best', Kerry was sceptical how much sympathy for Lily's plight the brusque, unattractive women would elicit from the court.

"Hentie doesn't have to charm a jury. You watch too many American courtroom dramas. The judge will weigh up the legal merits of the case, without emotion," Darryl had reassured her.

"Even a judge is human. Do we know yet who the judge will be? I hope it's a woman, and a mother. No mother could deny another the right to do whatever is necessary to save her baby."

"Don't be so sure. Some of those women judges are tough – they've had to be to get to where they are. They don't want to be accused of being 'emotional' or soft – so some of them go to the opposite extreme. It's almost as if they want to prove that they are as tough as a man. On the other hand, some of the men judges are real softies – and when a child is involved, they often bend over backwards to ensure that the child's best interests are at front and centre of the case. But, unfortunately, a lot of the male judges are also closet chauvinists, if not exactly misogynists – although some are. They may object to a wife trying to 'disobey' her husband. If we get one of those, Hentie will have her work cut out to ensure he understands that this is not a fight between a husband and his unreasonable wife, but about what's best for the child. But we've got strong affidavits from Lily's doctors supporting your position."

Kerry's heart sank. "Imran also has medical opinion that says the exact opposite. How will the judge decide which doctors to believe?"

"I think it's likely the judge will be more inclined to accept the opinions of the doctors who know Lily and have been treating her since she was born."

"I hope so, I really do. But what if we end up with a judge who might not like the fact that a wife is going against her husband? If that happens, the fact that I'm being represented by a woman could count against me too, couldn't it?"

"Oh I wouldn't worry too much about that. Hentie can be extremely persuasive – and legally, she is as sharp as they come. The judges respect that. She'll make him – or her – see that all we want is what's best for Lily and that it's Imran who is being unreasonable."

When Darryl called to say they'd been assigned a woman judge, Kerry's relief had been palpable. But not for long. Their judge – actually an acting judge without much experience on the Supreme Court bench – was unmarried and childless.

"The court is still in recess over the holiday season so only a few judges are available for urgent applications. This will be her first. She'll be afraid of making a mistake, or of being perceived to have made a mistake. It'll be interesting to see what line she takes, whether she questions Hentie and Imran's counsel. They are both far more experienced legally than she is. My guess is that she'll just let them make their presentations and deliver her ruling based on the written documents," he said.

"Then why have the hearing at all? Isn't it just a waste of time?"

"In some respects it could be – but she might require clarification about some of the points made, particularly the medical submissions," Darryl said.

"Will Hentie be able to answer her?"

Darryl laughed. "We're talking about Hentie here. She probably knows as much of every detail about Lily's condition, and every piece of current research around it, as your doctors do. And she's also as clued up on Imran's doctors' arguments. I told you, don't worry. She has this."

When Kerry's phone rang at 3.47 pm, she was surprised to see that it wasn't Jason, who had called her virtually every hour on the hour to keep her updated about the remote proceedings from the Johannesburg High Court. Nor was it Darryl, who had also called several times, mainly to reassure her that things were going well, that the judge didn't seem to want to ask questions, and that she seemed to be paying careful attention to what Hentie – and Imran's advocate – was saying. Kerry debated whether to accept the call – it was probably a wrong number, or someone hoping to sell her something she didn't need.

"Hello?" she said impatiently, her finger hovering over the red 'end call' button.

"I'm so sorry," a gruff voice said. "But it's not the end of the world."

"Who ... What are you talking about?"

"Oh sorry, yes. Hentie here. I'm sorry. Hasn't Darryl called you yet?"

"No! I was waiting for his call."

"Oh dear. Silly boy. Anyway no harm done. I wanted to speak to you about it myself so ... look, we were all taken by surprise and ..."

Kerry's heart stopped. "What? Did we lose? Did Imran win? Is he – does he ..."

"No, no, no Kerry. Nothing like that. We didn't lose – and Imran didn't win."

"So what happened?"

"Well, the judge refused Imran's petition for sole guardianship of the children."

"Great! Yesss." Relief surged through her – and irritation. If Imran's application for guardianship had failed, why wasn't Hentie celebrating?

"That's good, isn't it?" she demanded.

"Right. So it's good – and not so good. Her ladyship ruled that guardianship of the children would be joint," Hentie said.

"I don't get it. Hasn't it always been joint?"

"Well technically not really. As the law currently stands, when neither parent has sole custody or guardianship of a minor child – for example when parents are still legally married or when there hasn't been a custody settlement in a divorce case – then either parent can approve medical treatment or a medical procedure for that child. That has been the situation with you and Imran to date. That is what Imran is trying to change."

"So you're saying that I don't need Imran to sign the consent forms for Lily's cath and for putting her on the transplant list?"

"You didn't. But, unfortunately, you do now. Her ladyship, in her infinite wisdom, ruled that it is in the best interests of the children – Lily specifically – that the parents agree on everything relating to the children. You can't make a decision without having Imran's consent. She ruled that if the two of you can't come to an agreement on your own within twenty-eight days – so around mid-January – the court will appoint an independent guardian to make the decision for you."

"What?" Kerry shrieked. Lily, who had been sitting quietly on the floor watching television since waking up after an unusually lengthy nap, jumped and started wailing. Leo rushed over and flung his arms around her legs.

"Are you saying that the court will appoint some stranger to decide what is best for my kids?"

"I'm afraid so. But only if you and Imran can't agree."

"But … but that's crazy!"

"Perhaps. But her ladyship stated that as Lily didn't appear to be in imminent danger there was still a possibility that you and Imran could sort out your differences. In effect, her ruling is really an instruction to do so – in Lily's best interests – and to do so within the next month, which is fair enough given it's the holiday season and nothing much happens over the holiday season. I'm pretty sure Imran will be appealing this decision as soon as possible, probably early in the new year. We could too, if you want – but in the meantime, that's where we stand."

"But … but Imran won't give in. And I can't wait – Lily can't wait – for some stranger to come in and decide what's best for my child. I know what's best. She has to have the cath procedure. We need to get her on the transplant list as soon as possible. I thought you understood that."

"I do, Kerry. Believe me when I tell you that I do. But, in some respects, her ladyship has done us a favour."

"What do you mean?"

"I mean having an independent, court-appointed guardian might not be the worst thing in the world. No, don't interrupt. A qualified professional – probably a social worker – is highly unlikely to go against the recommendations of a child's dedicated, respected medical team."

"But it could happen," Kerry insisted bitterly.

"It could," Hentie agreed reluctantly.

Chapter 38

The tension in the house and Kerry's own mood – a tepid soup of anger, frustration, depression and despair – seemed to have affected the children. Although Covid-19 infection numbers were starting to decline after the record highs over the summer holiday season, Kerry was still terrified to leave the house, not even to buy groceries. And Imran seemed to have decided his role was to monitor her every move, openly yet surreptitiously – letting her know he was watching her yet simultaneously pretending to ignore her. And doing anything and everything to annoy her, like praying in the lounge, which he had never done before.

"Come Leo," he said, switching off the television despite the fact that Kerry and Leo were watching. If Lily had been in the lounge, she'd have screamed blue murder at having her beloved Barney switched off while she was watching, but she was napping in the bedroom she and Kerry shared alone. "Come Leo, come pray with Daddy."

"Don't you think he's a little young for this?" Kerry asked quietly.

"Here's your own little prayer mat I got for you," Imran said.

Leo looked uncertainly at his mother, torn. He wanted to please his father, but he didn't want to upset his mother. Kerry nodded at him and walked out the room. She wasn't going to allow Imran to use their son to get at her. But he knew how she felt about this. It was just another way he was showing her that he was the boss, that these were *his* children and her wishes counted for nothing. That she was nothing more than a glorified nanny and housekeeper.

She walked into the kitchen, fuming. It was nearly lunchtime. Lily would wake soon, but feeding her would be easy. One bottle of Frebini into her peg tube – simple. Leo and Imran on the other hand ... she opened the fridge. It was virtually empty, apart from Lily's medicines and a dish of left-over macaroni cheese, some wilted lettuce and a tomato. She hoped Checkers would deliver her online grocery order soon. Frowning, she took the mac and cheese out the fridge and stared at it. Probably enough for Leo and Imran, but there wouldn't be much for her as well. She popped it into the microwave, hit the three-minute timer button and waited for it to warm.

The microwave pinged. Kerry carefully removed the hot dish and placed it on the kitchen counter. She dished a portion onto Leo's blue plastic plate and scooped the rest onto a white dinner plate. She carried the two plates of food into the lounge. Imran and Leo had just finished their prayers – or Imran had. He was rolling up his prayer mat. Leo was flat on his back, playing with his fingers.

Kerry placed Leo's dish on the plastic table before his little red chair. She put the other plate in front of the blue chair the speech therapist always used and sat down.

"Lunchtime Leo," she said. "Come and eat before it gets cold."

Leo scampered over. "Oooh yum," he said, sliding onto his chair. "Maccie cheese!"

From the corner of her eye Kerry watched Imran. He put his prayer mat down carefully next to the couch, sat down and put the tray he'd taken to eating off on his lap. And waited.

"Where's my ..." he started.

Kerry delicately lifted a forkful of mac and cheese to her mouth. "It is yum, isn't it?" she smiled at Leo.

"I don't know how much longer I can go on like this," Kerry whispered. "It's not fair on the kids."

She'd closed the front door behind her when she'd hurried

outside to take Jason's call, but she wouldn't have been surprised if Imran was standing on the other side trying to eavesdrop on her conversation. He certainly didn't care about her hearing his conversations with his lawyers. In fact, he made a point of putting them on speaker so that she could hear exactly what they were planning. It was as if he was daring her to say something – or perhaps he was just trying to intimidate her. But Kerry didn't want to do the same to him. Her conversations with Darryl, and especially with Jason, were private.

She'd stopped telling Imran who was phoning her. Before, whenever Jason had called, she'd muttered: "It's Jason – about work. It's urgent," although it wasn't urgent at all. But now she didn't bother. It was none of his business – although it was thanks to Jason and the work he sent her that she was able to put food on the table, pay the rent and put petrol in the car that Imran used to drive to mosque.

"Leo's become really tearful and clingy," Kerry told Jason sadly. "He won't even let me go to the toilet without following me. And Lily – well, she's become really subdued. I miss her laugh and her big, booming voice. She hardly plays any more and she hasn't ridden on her skateboard for days. I put her on it this morning and she barely scooted around; she pushed for a bit and then just stopped and sat there, staring into space."

"Is she okay? I mean, she's not getting sick again is she?" Jason asked.

Kerry drew in a deep breath. The thought had been niggling at the back of her mind, but she hadn't had the courage to actually frame the question.

"I don't think so. She isn't feverish, she isn't coughing. She just seems to have so little energy. She spends more and more time lying, rather than sitting, on her little makeshift bed on the lounge floor in front of the TV. It's been ages – well at least a couple of days – since she's practised her walking. Honestly Jason, I think she's probably just being affected by the awful atmosphere in the house – Leo too. It's horrible."

She blinked furiously. She didn't want to start crying again.

That's all she seemed to do whenever she spoke to Jason. If she kept this up, she'd drive him away too. And Imran would see that she'd been crying – and she wasn't going to give him that satisfaction.

The front door opened. Leo, who was still too small to open it on his own, stood there.

"Mommy. Lily's vomited. Daddy said I must tell you to come inside and take care of her."

∽ ✑

When her alarm went off at 6am Kerry just let it ring. She hoped it would be loud enough to wake Imran who was snoring away on the couch in the lounge. Unlikely though. He hadn't stirred at all throughout the night. She, on the other hand, had hardly slept. Lily had had a bad night, more restless than she usually was. But usually when Lily couldn't sleep, she'd want to play. Not last night. She'd just lain in her cot, staring at the dark ceiling, whimpering occasionally.

There was something wrong; Kerry knew it. She'd checked Lily's temperature repeatedly throughout the night, but it had remained 'normal'. So was Lily's breathing – at least, it was as 'normal' as it always was. But something was different. Something wasn't right.

Kerry hit the snooze button on the alarm and carried it into the lounge. She set it down on the ottoman and waited. It rang. Imran opened his eyes, glared at her, and turned over.

"Lily's not well. We need to take her to the hospital – just to get her checked out," Kerry said.

Imran sat up and swung his legs off the couch. His hair, desperately in need of a cut, stood up in spikes; there was some drool in his beard next to his mouth.

"No," he said.

"I'm telling you, something is wrong with her."

"No."

Kerry glared at him, daring him to ignore her.

"Forget it," he said. "You're just making an excuse to get her to the hospital so she can have the cath and you can get her on the transplant list. I won't let you."

"You're crazy – you're paranoid. I wouldn't do that. I can't do that – you've made damn sure of that, you and your fancy lawyers. Who is paying for them, by the way?"

"Who is paying for yours?" Imran shot back.

Kerry shook her head. "Imran, I'm sorry. Please, let's not go down that path. Not when Lily isn't well."

"Lily's fine!"

"She isn't. Something is wrong with her."

"Rubbish! What's her temperature?"

"I ... I'm not sure. The last time I checked it was normal. But ..."

"Her breathing?" Imran interrupted. "Is she gasping for air? Have you checked her saturation?"

"Yes, of course I have. It all seems okay but I know Lily. She isn't right. Please Imran, let's take her to Sunninghill. Let's just get her checked out."

"No. Not a chance."

"Well, I'll just take her on my own then," Kerry said, looking at the hook next to the front door where they kept the car and front door keys. There was nothing there.

"Looking for these?" Imran said, digging under his pillow and holding up the keys in triumph. "You don't think I'd be stupid enough to leave them lying around, do you? Imam Omar in his wisdom told me to hide them from you. I said it wasn't necessary but he was right. He's always right. You're not to be trusted. No woman is, especially a woman like you. A kafirah. A non-believer."

Kerry gaped at the stranger she was married to. Hateful, spiteful words spilled incoherently from his lips.

"It's you. You're the reason Lily is sick. You're why she isn't getting better. No matter how hard I pray, no matter how devout I am, you – your arrogance, your disbelief – you cancel it all out. Lily won't get better, not while you continue to place your shallow, misguided faith in doctors, western doctors, puppets in the pay of the greedy profit-driven pharmaceutical companies and the exploitative medical aids. It's your fault Lily is sick. She wouldn't have been born with a damaged heart if you had been a better mother, a devout, pure woman. Instead you insisted on working for those Jews, flirting with that Jew – and you still flirt with him – and maybe more than flirt, you have no shame. And you want to remove Lily's heart, when you know taking out her heart is the surest way to kill her. Not even prayer will save a child without a heart. You are cruel, you are crazy, you are not a mother. You are a monster. You are to blame. You ... you ..."

His tirade faltered and he collapsed back onto couch like a deflated balloon. He put his head in his hands and wept.

"Mommy? Daddy?" Leo had wandered unnoticed into the lounge and was staring bewildered from his sobbing father to his white-faced, trembling mother.

"Oh Leo!" Kerry bent and gathered her shaking son into her arms. "It's okay Leo, it's okay. Daddy's just a little sad. That's all."

She carried Leo back to her bedroom, remembering to grab her cellphone as she passed the ottoman.

She WhatsApped Jason: **"Please come get me and the kids. Now!"**

Chapter 39

"Of course I'll watch Leo," Gillian Aarons said, lifting her crying grandson out of the car. "But what's going on? What's happened?"

"Not now Mom – just watch him. Don't let him play outside alone. Don't let him out of your sight. I'm taking Lily to Sunninghill – I'll phone you from the hospital. Leo," she called to her son, "I'll see you later. I love you. Have fun with granny and grandpa."

She watched briefly as her mother carried Leo towards the house and turned away. This was worse than she could ever have imagined. She looked down at Lily lying limply in her arms. She wasn't over-reacting was she? It wasn't just her imagination – Lily's breathing did seem a little more laboured. And she was a little warm, wasn't she?

"Drive – just drive," she said to Jason. "We have to get there before Imran."

Jason put his foot down and his big BMW surged forward. He must have broken every speed limit getting to her house. She'd barely had time to get dressed and throw some things in an overnight bag for the children and herself, before Jason messaged to say he was waiting outside and did she want him to come in.

"On my way," she'd messaged back, grabbing her handbag, Lily, the portable oxygen concentrator, and the bag of spare medicines and bottles of Frebini she kept in the fridge, ready for emergency trips to the hospital. "Leo come," she whispered, walking as quickly and quietly as possible under her load to the front door. She fumbled in her handbag for her spare set of front door keys, and managed to unlock the door without dropping anything.

Imran, still sitting on the couch with his head in his hands, looked up. "What are you doing? Where are you going?" he demanded.

"Out," Kerry had said.

Fortunately there was little traffic on the M1 motorway as Jason's car ate up the kilometres between Norwood and Sunninghill. Still, with the detour to her parents' house to drop off Leo, it would be a miracle if they got there before Imran. Although ... Kerry felt in her handbag for her purse. She quickly checked – and grinned. All the cash she had withdrawn from the ATM two weeks ago, and her credit card, was still there. Imran's credit card, she knew, was maxed out. And he'd mentioned a couple of weeks ago that the car was on empty and he'd need money to fill it. He'd driven to the mosque since then, but he hadn't asked her for money. Nor, it seemed, had he taken any from her bag without her knowledge. So, he might not have enough petrol to get to Sunninghill. That should hopefully delay him long enough for her to get Lily admitted. She *had* to get her admitted before Imran – or his lawyers – arrive to object.

"You do realise you'll be in contempt of court if you admit Lily to hospital without Imran's consent," Darryl had said when Jason insisted on calling him as they'd sped away from the Kempton Park house. Kerry had looked back, almost expecting to see him running down the road after them, but there was nothing.

"So I'll be in contempt. What will they do? Arrest me?"

"Actually, yes. You could be arrested. Kerry, this is serious," Darryl said.

"Well, that's too bad. At least Lily will receive the treatment she needs."

"And what about Jason? He could be arrested as an accomplice."

Kerry had gasped, but Jason grinned. "That's okay," he'd said. "Lily is more important."

Jason screeched to a halt right at the entrance to Sunninghill Emergency department. Kerry, remembering to put on her mask, jumped out and ran with Lily and the portable oxygen concentrator, through the doors. There was no sign of Imran, his lawyers, or the police.

"You can't come in here," said a security man. "Patients only. Covid regulations."

Kerry ignored him and rushed to the counter. "Call Dr Govender and Dr Sinclair," she told the receptionist. "There's something badly wrong with my daughter and I'm not leaving until they've seen her. Please."

She sat down heavily in the nearest chair, Lily on her lap. The portable oxygen concentrator hummed. Kerry felt Lily's forehead – she was definitely developing a fever.

"Hold on," the receptionist said. "I think Dr Govender is around somewhere. I saw him when I came on duty. I'll page him."

Kerry waited, keeping one anxious eye on the door, almost expecting to see Imran rushing in to claim his daughter.

Dr Govender came bustling across the emergency room towards her. He looked at Lily critically, put a hand on her forehead and barked at the receptionist: "Get a nurse over here. Now! Take this child to the resus room. Get a reading on her sats. Now! Mrs Patel, I'm sorry, you can't come with – damn Covid – I'll let you know what's going on as soon as I can."

Lily objected loudly as a nurse put her on a stretcher. The sound was music to Kerry's ears – Lily still had some fight in her. That was good. She could hear Lily screaming as she was wheeled away through the emergency room doors and breathed a sigh of relief. Lily was going to get help – and there was nothing Imran could do about it now. There was no way a court would order a child to be removed from the hospital against doctor's orders – would it?

"Please fill out these forms, and then I'm afraid you are going to have to wait outside. Or go home," the receptionist said.

Kerry smiled grimly behind her mask: one of the forms was a consent form, just like the one Imran had refused to sign. She signed it with a flourish.

Dr Govender came bustling back through the doors. "Her sats are low – even for Lily. And she is spiking a bit of a fever. She also seems to be battling to breathe. We need to nip this in the bud. I'm admitting her to the ICU. Fortunately, we've a bed available – last week, it was a different story. We were having to transfer patients all over the country to find them ICU beds. Mrs Patel I have to ask – this couldn't be Covid, could it? It doesn't look like it but you never know. We've tested, of course, but it will be a while ..."

"No," Kerry said. "It can't be Covid. Lily hasn't been out of the house for weeks – neither have I. And we haven't had any visitors. We've been very careful, all of us."

Except Imran, Kerry thought. He had insisted on going to that damn mosque. What if he had infected Lily? If he had, she'd kill him – she really would!

Kerry's phone buzzed. She glanced down. A new WhatsApp message. From Imran. Another one. **"Where are you?"**

"Imran again?" Jason asked. They were sitting on a bench outside the hospital. Jason had flatly refused to leave Kerry there, despite her assurances that she'd be just fine on her own while she waited for news.

"You're busy – you have work to do and I don't think your assistant is going to be much help to you for the next couple of days. Honestly Jason, go! I really appreciate your help but I'll be fine," Kerry said.

"I'm sure you will. But work can wait for a while. Don't you think you should at least tell Imran what's going on?"

"Why? After what he said to me ... no way. Anyway, if I tell him, he'll have me arrested – and try to have Lily removed from the hospital. No. Let him stew."

"I'm going to find us some coffee. And something to eat. I don't suppose you've eaten anything today, have you?"

Kerry shook her head.

"Okay, I'll be back soon."

"No – I don't want anything. Please Jason, go. I feel bad enough dragging you into all this. The last thing I want is for you to get into trouble. And Imran is going to figure out where I am soon enough. If he finds you here with me, it will just make it worse."

"Will you be alright? He won't hurt you, will he?"

"No – he's not violent."

"How will you get home? Do you plan to wait here all day?"

"I don't know. I'll call you, or my dad, to fetch me later."

"Are you're sure?"

"I'm sure."

Kerry watched Jason walk away. She'd never felt so alone in her life. But she shouldn't have called him this morning. It wasn't fair. To him. Especially as she wasn't really sure how she felt about him, about anything. But she couldn't think about that now, not with Lily sick again. She'd think things through when Lily was better. She and Imran couldn't keep going the way they had been. Imran. She wasn't sure how she felt about him either. His outburst had shocked her to the core. And terrified her. Did he really hate her so much?

"Kerry!"

She looked up. Imran was striding towards her. Kerry's heart jumped into her throat. He looked different. She couldn't put her finger on it – and then it hit her. His beard was gone.

"What's going on? Where's Lily? What have you done with Leo?"

Before she could answer, her phone rang.

Chapter 40

"What?" Imran demanded as Kerry ended the call.

Kerry hesitated. She wanted to tell him – he deserved to know – but she also wanted to punish him. She wanted him to suffer for what he had done, for what he was doing, to her, to the children.

"Kerry, for god's sake, tell me. What is going on. Where is Lily?"

"If I tell you, will you have me arrested? You could, you know. I'm sure your fancy lawyers have already told you that."

"What are you talking about? Why would I have you arrested? Where is Lily?"

Kerry looked up at him in surprise. He was shaking. Under his mask, his face was ashen.

"Lily's in ICU," she said. "That was Dr Sinclair – her paediatrician. They've had to put her on to high flow oxygen."

"Why? She was fine this morning!"

Kerry exploded. "She wasn't fine. I told you she wasn't but you ... look, I'm not going to fight with you, not now. Lily has pneumonia."

Imran sat down heavily in the spot recently vacated by Jason. Kerry shifted away slightly.

"Is it Covid? How did she get Covid?" he asked.

"It's not Covid. It's an adenovirus again. Like she had before. It's the bad one – the really bad one."

"And her heart?"

"They're running more tests now. Dr Sinclair said it looks like her heart has enlarged even more since her last cath – but, of course, she hasn't had another cath recently, so we don't know how long it has been more enlarged, do we? If she'd had the cath procedure, if you had let her have the tests when Dr Govender wanted to do them – in November, remember? Well, then we'd know, wouldn't we? And maybe we'd have been able to treat it – but you knew better, didn't you? You and your ... your effing Imam and your fancy lawyers. Now look where we are!"

Kerry couldn't go on. She wanted to pummel Imran to a pulp with her fists. She wanted to scream. She wanted the huge rock crushing her chest to go away. The world darkened and receded. She was alone with her anguish. She doubled over and moaned at the pain of her breaking heart. Someone was wailing, a dreadful keening noise that grated her raw nerves. She realised it was her but she couldn't stop. And then she became aware of someone holding her, rocking her; she could hear a soothing voice in her ear. She pushed Imran away.

"Kerry, I'm sorry. I'm so sorry," he said, tears streaming un-checked down his face.

She looked away. She didn't want to see his pain. If she did, she'd have to forgive him and she couldn't. She wouldn't. Not after everything he'd done. Everything he'd said.

"Kerry? Please. I'm sorry. I should never have behaved like that. I was crazy. I realise it now. Muhammed said so too."

"Your brother? What has he got to do with this?"

"After you left, I called him. I wanted to chase after you only I had no petrol. He came – and he was so angry."

"Yeah, I can imagine," Kerry muttered.

"No, no, he wasn't angry with you. He was angry with me. He said I was crazy, that I'd been acting crazy for months. And he was right. This morning, even when I was saying all those terrible things to you, I realised just how nuts it sounded. It was crazy, stupid. I was just repeating what Imam Omar had been saying – all those months he'd been on and on at me about you, about Lily. Muhammed had tried to make me see that he was wrong but I wouldn't listen to him. He stopped coming to the mosque with me – I hadn't seen him for ages before today. But Imam Omar – he made sense to me – I mean, I felt like he was giving me some power again. No, not power. Some explanation for the mess my life had become. I was so useless, so helpless – and you were so capable and holding everything together. I hated feeling like that. But I'm not making excuses, Kerry. Nothing can excuse what I've done, how I've behaved. I don't know why ... I can't believe I let myself believe the crap I spewed at you ... But when I saw your face this morning. When you took the kids and walked out ... It was like a curtain lifted. I didn't know where you'd gone and it terrified me. It terrified me to think I'd driven you away – that I'd lost you, like Muhammed said I would. But I didn't blame you – I don't blame you for going. I don't blame you for anything. I'm so sorry. Please believe me. I'm sorry. I love you."

Kerry took off her mask and blew her nose. She shook her head. She didn't want to hear any more. It was all too much. She looked at her watch. She'd been sitting on the bench outside the hospital for nearly four hours. She put her mask on again and stood up.

"I'm going to stretch my legs. No, don't come with me," she said as Imran made to follow her.

Kerry tossed and turned in her childhood bed. Leo slept peacefully on the mattress on the floor alongside her. He'd refused to sleep in his uncle Eliot's old room. He'd stared at his father through the window of his grandfather's car when they'd gone to pick Kerry up at the hospital in the late afternoon, but he hadn't waved, or smiled. He'd insisted that Kerry sit in the back of the car with him on the ride to his grandparents' house. And he hadn't left her side since. Kerry's heart ached for him. He was old enough to understand that something was very wrong, but too young to understand what. He knew that Lily was back in hospital. That always upset him, but not to the extent that it had now. Kerry had explained that she was staying with granny and grandpa because it was closer to the hospital – and he was staying there too so they could take care of him when she went to the hospital to visit Lily.

She'd said much the same to her parents. Gillian had raised a disbelieving eyebrow but a warning grunt from her husband had served its purpose. She hadn't raised the subject again although Kerry was sure she was dying to ask why Jason had brought her to the house, and where Imran was.

"Why can't I come to the hospital too," Leo had grizzled. "I'll stay in the waiting room like before. I did that when I was a baby – I'm grown up now. I can do that again," he'd said.

"I'm sorry Leo. It's because of Covid – they are not allowing anyone into the hospital," she'd explained.

"But they let you in!"

Kerry hadn't answered. She was desperate to see Lily. Dr Govender, when he had finally called her in the evening, said he and Dr Sinclair were trying to arrange for her to be allowed in for a short visit in the morning. They might be able to persuade the hospital authorities to make an exception for her, and Imran, provided they wore full PPE – personal protective equipment.

As for Lily's condition – well, it was too soon to say.

Kerry picked up her cellphone to check the time. The room was starting to lighten. It was only just after five. Too early to get up. Too early for any updates from Dr Govender or Dr Sinclair.

There was a message from Imran: **"Any news?"**

She wanted to ignore it, but she couldn't. **"No,"** she messaged back.

He responded: **"Are you okay?"**

"No," she messaged again – then sent another: **"You?"**

"Not really. So sorry. How's Leo?"

"Sleeping."

"That's good."

Kerry switched off her phone and watched the shadows fading on the ceiling. She couldn't just lie in bed any longer. She got up and padded to the kitchen. She put the kettle on and made a cup of coffee.

"You're up early," Gillian said, wandering into the kitchen in a flowing purple dressing gown.

"So are you. Want some coffee? The water's just boiled."

"Thanks – I just drink boiling water in the morning. It's

supposed to be good for the skin, not that you could tell looking at me without my face on."

Kerry smiled politely. She knew her mother was trying hard to reach out to her. But she couldn't bring herself to respond. She knew if she gave her mother an inch, she'd have to tell her everything – and she wasn't ready to do that. Not yet. Not until she'd had time to process everything herself.

"I need to check my phone, Mom. To see if there's a message or anything from the hospital."

"Why don't you phone them?"

"If there's no message, I'll call later. I don't want to disturb them when they're getting ready to change shift."

She went back to the room and quietly switched on her phone again. There was a message from the ICU sister. Lily hadn't been managing well on the high flow oxygen. The doctor on duty had ordered her to be put on the CPAP machine. Kerry groaned quietly: this was bad. Although it was non-invasive, the CPAP was really just one step away from a ventilator. Lily had been on CPAP before. It hadn't prevented her needing a ventilator then. She hoped it would do the trick now.

Her phoned buzzed again. A WhatsApp from Jason.

"You awake? How's Lily?"

"Hi. Not good. They put her on CPAP."

"What's that?"

"Mini-ventilator."

"Oh no! Are you going to the hospital? Do you need a lift?"

"Waiting to hear from doctor. My dad will take me. Thanks anyway."

"Okay. Let me know if I can do anything."

"Thanks. Will do. Bye."

She clicked off her phone. Hesitated, then opened it again. She WhatsApped Imran: *"Hospital messaged. Lily on CPAP. Waiting to hear from Dr G or Dr S. Will let you know when I do."*

Then she switched her phone off again.

Chapter 41

Dr Govender was waiting for her on the stairs in front of the hospital. Imran was already there.

"Come," Dr Govender said. After sanitising their hands, having their temperatures checked and signing a register with their names, ID and contact telephone numbers, he led them down the corridors towards the ICU. The route was so familiar to Kerry, it felt a little like coming home.

Just before the double doors leading into the ICU, Dr Govender stopped. "Wait here."

They waited, not speaking. Kerry kept her eyes fixed on the doors. She could sense Imran standing next to her and moved away.

A nurse in full PPE came through the doors and handed them each a pile of garments. She pointed towards the toilets. "You can get changed in there. I suggest you take off your own clothes, rather than put the PPE over them. It gets really hot. Leave your stuff at the nurses' station. You can't take it into Lily's ward. Wait here when you're done. I'll be out to fetch you soon."

In the Ladies, Kerry struggled into a blue, long-sleeved disposable gown. Over that she put a yellow plastic apron. She put a white, cone-shaped mask over her nose and mouth, and immediately felt stifled. It was far harder to breathe with it than with the triple-layered cloth mask she had been wearing. She folded her clothes into a neat pile with her mask on top and went out to join Imran. He looked almost unrecognisable in his PPE. They waited in silence.

The nurse reappeared. "Please sanitise your hands and then

put on your gloves before entering Lily's room," she said and led them into the ICU.

A figure dressed from top to toe in PPE, who had been sitting at Lily's bedside, stood up as Kerry and Imran entered the glass enclosed cubicle.

"Hello Kerry, Imran," Dr Sinclair said.

Kerry looked at her in surprise. Her eyes were moist, red-rimmed. Had she been crying?

On the little cot, Lily lay naked. She was motionless except for her battle-scarred chest which was rising and falling rapidly. She had a catheter so she didn't need a nappy and there was an intravenous drip feeding saline and some medications into a vein in her neck.

"I'm so sorry," Dr Sinclair said. "I've been watching her and I think – I think we're going to have to intubate her. To fully ventilate her. We haven't been able to break her fever despite the antibiotics we're pushing into her, and her sats are still dropping."

Kerry's legs turned to jelly. Imran caught her and helped her to a chair.

"What are you saying?" Imran asked slowly.

"I'm telling you that your little girl is very, very sick. But – hey, this is Lily we're talking about, right? She's a little Tiger, right? She's come through this before. We're doing everything we can to help her get through it again."

Kerry nodded. She couldn't speak. Was it only yesterday that she'd brought Lily to the hospital? Was it only yesterday that she'd wondered if she was over-reacting? Deep down, she'd wondered if she was only really doing it to spite Imran. She'd just thought Lily hadn't been herself. But not this. Nothing like this. How had things got so bad so quickly.

"Should ..., would it have ... should we have brought her in sooner?" Imran asked the question that Kerry hadn't dared to.

"Perhaps. No, probably not," Dr Sinclair said hastily. "Don't blame yourselves. This is a very aggressive infection. And Lily's heart – well, you know how susceptible she is to infections and pneumonia."

"What about a transplant? Would that help?" Kerry asked softly.

"A transplant? Now? No, even if a heart were to become available now, even if Lily were on the transplant list, it wouldn't make a difference. Lily's too sick to survive a transplant. If she pulls through this – and she might, she's fought off bad infections before – we could look at transplant again. But for now, I'm afraid all we can do is help her to breathe and fight the infection."

They had been banished from the ICU while Lily was being sedated before being ventilated. Dr Sinclair and Dr Govender had called for a full resuscitation team to be on standby. Dr Govender had explained that the ventilation procedure itself was dangerous, that Lily's heart could stop while they were doing it and they needed to have everything and everyone in place to resuscitate her if it did.

Imran reached for Kerry's hand. Kerry started to pull her hand away, and then relented. It felt good to have someone to hold on to, even if their plastic gloves made the contact somewhat sweaty and uncomfortable.

After hours, days – or perhaps it was only a few minutes – a nurse came through the ICU doors. "You can come back now," she said.

Kerry heaved a sigh of relief. Lily – Tiger Lily – had come through again.

They sat, side by side, watching over their daughter. Her entire faced was covered in white plasters and tape holding in place the thick pipes that had been shoved into her little nose and mouth. Her eyes were puffy yet slightly open. Her little hands were bandaged and tied to the cot sides, a precaution, Kerry knew, to prevent her trying to pull her tubes out if she should somehow wake up.

Kerry swallowed a protesting cry. This wasn't right. Lily had been through so much. She'd fought this battle before. It just wasn't fair that she had to do it all over again.

The nurse entered and gently put drops in her eyes, to prevent them from drying out. Kerry nodded. She knew the drill. Only this time, if felt different.

Imran and Kerry watched, not speaking, not looking at each other. Kerry looked up at the monitors that showed, oh so graphically, that Lily's sats were low. Too low. Her heart rate remained high – too high. The nurse came in and checked Lily's catheter, scribbled something on the big chart and underlined it. Kerry got up to look at the chart, then she looked at the catheter bag. It was empty.

Kerry gently rubbed Lily's feet – they were freezing cold.

"Shouldn't we put a blanket on her?" Kerry asked the nurse when she came in to check Lily's drip again.

"Not a good idea with her fever so high," the nurse said.

"But she's freezing! Feel her feet – and her hands."

The nurse reached for Kerry's hand and gently placed it on Lily's chest. It was burning hot. "She's using all her energy to fight the infection where it counts – her heart, her lungs. That's why her extremities are so cold," she explained.

Lily's sternum moved up and moved down. Perhaps she was imagining it, but Kerry was convinced she could see Lily's oversized, enlarged heart beating slowly, so slowly, in her emaciated chest. The monitors flashed and flickered.

"I can't do this anymore. I can't breathe in this mask. I'm going crazy," Kerry said.

"Let's wait outside," Imran said.

"I'd rather go home – Leo needs me. And I need to see him. I'm sure they'll call me – us – if anything changes."

"I'll take you. I brought the car today. I want to see Leo too."

"No ... no, My dad will fetch me."

They changed back into their clothes and discarded their PPE in the bins provided – all except their masks. Once outside the hospital, Kerry ripped the cone-shaped mask off and drew in a deep breath of clean, fresh air.

She starting sending a WhatsApp to her father when Imran stopped her.

"Kerry, we need to talk," he said.

"Not now. Let's just get through this – we can talk when Lily is well again."

The unspoken question – *what if she doesn't get well* – hung unspoken between them.

Kerry woke with a start. She shivered. She checked the time on her cellphone. Quarter to five. She pulled the duvet up around her shoulders. A cool, early morning breeze drifted through the curtains. It was always coolest before the sun came up. She checked her WhatsApp messages. Nothing.

She threw the duvet off. It was too hot to lie under it. Leo had kicked off his duvet too, lying uncovered on his mattress. Kerry reached down and felt the back of his neck. He was comfortably warm. She pulled the duvet over him, but left his arms uncovered. She shivered again. And waited.

Her cellphone pinged. A message. From Dr Sinclair.

"Come to the hospital as soon as you can."

Fully kitted up again in the stifling PPE, Kerry and Imran sat side by side and watched their baby fade away.

"We had to resuscitate her earlier this morning – just before five," Dr Sinclair had told them when she'd met them on the steps of the hospital to ensure they gained admittance despite the Covid protocol that banned visitors.

"Normally, I wouldn't have tried to resus a child in her condition. We knew her organs were shutting down – her kidneys, her liver, her heart, of course. But I was hoping she'd hang on until you could get here. I thought you'd want to be here when she goes – and I thought she'd want her mommy and daddy to be with her too. To say goodbye."

Kerry burst into tears. So did Dr Sinclair. They held each other and cried together.

"I'm sorry," Dr Sinclair said when they'd both calmed down. "That was totally unprofessional of me, but well – every now and then, you get a little patient who is very special. Lily is one of those. A very special little girl indeed. Come now, let's get you PPE'd up and to your baby."

She led the way to the ICU, waited while they changed, and then escorted them to Lily's bedside.

"How long?" Imran asked.

"Not long now," Dr Sinclair said.

"Is she in any pain?" Kerry asked.

Dr Sinclair shook her head. "No. We've given her a little morphine to take the edge off."

They waited. And watched. Even on the ventilator, Lily's entire body had a deep bluish tinge. Even on the ventilator, it was obvious that she was struggling to breathe. Her heart was beating so hard, it seemed it might push itself right out of her chest.

Kerry pulled off her plastic glove and held her daughter's hand. Imran did the same.

"It's okay Tiger. You can go now," she whispered.

Next to her, Imran sobbed.

Almost imperceptibly Lily's breathing slowed, became shallower. Her heart slowed too. Kerry looked at the monitors over the cot. The nurse had turned the monitors away from them, but Kerry had turned them back. She needed to see the numbers dropping – it was the physical proof that made the situation real. Her daughter was fading away. The countdown proceeded remorselessly – her sats, her blood pressure, her heart rate ...

And then – nothing.

"She's gone," the nurse said quietly, switching off the ventilator and the monitors.

Dr Sinclair gently removed the tubes from Lily's nose and mouth.

"Stay with her as long as you like," she said, giving Kerry's shoulder a squeeze.

For the first time since Lilly had been admitted to the ICU, she could see her daughter's full face, unhindered by tubes and pipes and sticking plaster.

Kerry blinked.

"Imran look! Look at her. She looks so well. I can't believe it. She's always had that blue tinge around her mouth – and her nails were always so dark. But look at her. She looks healthy!"

Imran stared at Lily in amazement.

"She's beautiful, so beautiful," he muttered.

They sat, shoulder to shoulder, revelling in their daughter's transformation. After nearly three years, Tiger Lily's battle to live was over and she looked better than she ever had. She was at peace, sleeping like the baby she had never had the chance to be. Kerry drank in the sight, savouring it – this was how she wanted to remember Lily. Forever.

For the first time in nearly three years, Kerry felt – she didn't know how she felt. Sad of course, immeasurably sad. But seeing Lily looking so healthy and serene took the edge off her pain.

Imran stood up.

"Come," he said.

He held out a gloveless hand. Kerry took it in hers. A vision of Jason flashed through her mind. She pushed it away. Right now being with Imran was right. So natural. Like coming home. With hands clasped, they walked out of the ICU, out of the hospital, side-by-side into the summer sunshine.